QUEEN OF DREAMS
THE
HUNTING
OF THE
PRINCES

Peter F. Hamilton was born in Rutland in 1960 and still lives in that county. He began writing adult science fiction and fantasy in 1987 and since then has sold over two million books in the UK alone and is the UK's bestselling science-fiction author. He has two young children who inspired him to write for a younger audience. *The Hunting of the Princes* is the second book in the fantastic The Queen of Dreams children's fantasy trilogy.

D1022932

CALGARY PUBLIC LIBRARY

SEP   2016

Also by Peter F. Hamilton

The Secret Throne

THE QUEEN OF DREAMS

THE HUNTING OF THE PRINCES

PETER F. HAMILTON

ILLUSTRATED BY ROHAN EASON

MACMILLAN CHILDREN'S BOOKS

First published 2016 by Macmillan Children's Books
an imprint of Pan Macmillan
20 New Wharf Road, London N1 9RR
Associated companies throughout the world
www.panmacmillan.com

ISBN 978-1-4472-9114-5

Text copyright © Rutland Horizon Ltd 2016
Illustrations copyright © Rohan Eason 2016

The right of Peter F. Hamilton and Rohan Eason to be identified as
the author and illustrator of this work has been asserted by them in
accordance with the Copyright, Designs and Patents Act 1988.

All rights reserved. No part of this publication may be reproduced,
stored in a retrieval system, or transmitted, in any form or by any means
(electronic, mechanical, photocopying, recording or otherwise),
without the prior written permission of the publisher.

1 3 5 7 9 8 6 4 2

A CIP catalogue record for this book is available from
the British Library.

Printed and bound by CPI Group (UK) Ltd, Croydon CR0 4YY

This book is sold subject to the condition that it shall not,
by way of trade or otherwise, be lent, resold, hired out,
or otherwise circulated without the publisher's prior consent
in any form of binding or cover other than that in which
it is published and without a similar condition including this
condition being imposed on the subsequent purchaser.

This one is for Dylan and Matilda Lewis.
The finest test readers in the whole Outer Realm.

CONTENTS

1

A QUIET RIDE HOME

Taggie Paganuzzi was cycling home when her mobile rang. It was a four-mile ride from Stamford back to her mum's house. The tiny country road just outside the lovely old market town cut a winding route past fields guarded by ancient stone walls. Nobody else was using it.

Today was a warm sunny day, and now Taggie was thirteen her mum was quite relaxed about her being out on her own. It probably helped that Mum was a Third Realm sorceress and Taggie had inherited that side of the family's magical strength. So while a lot of parents these days were fussy about allowing their daughters out by themselves, getting permission to go swimming at the municipal pool with her school friends was no problem for Taggie.

The mobile kept on ringing with the annoying tune she'd deliberately chosen for her younger sister Jemima. It was the only sound she could hear. Taggie squeezed the brake and came to a halt beside one of the big oak trees lining the narrow road.

There was the faint noise of an engine in the distance as Taggie took her backpack off and started rummaging through it for the mobile. Her charmsward bracelet caught on the bag's big zipper. The charmsward was made up of several slim bands of brass and wood that were twined together. They were engraved with symbols which, even after a year of wearing it, Taggie wasn't completely familiar with. But it was what the charmsward contained that was truly important, the memories of all Taggie's First Realm ancestors who'd sat on the shell throne. It was like having a dictionary of spells permanently in her head. A useful thing to own for a Queen who only last year had no idea she was the rightful heir to the throne of the First Realm.

Finally she pulled her mobile out of the bag, disentangling it from the wet towel. The sound of the engine was growing louder now. Taggie looked over her shoulder to catch a glimpse of a huge black motorbike slicing along the road towards her. The small rider was dressed in black leather with a matching shiny black helmet.

She tapped the 'accept call' icon.

'Death spell!' Jemima's voice yelled out of the mobile. 'Duck!'

Taggie looked up, her mouth opening to grunt 'Uh?' The motorbike was twenty metres away, rushing headlong at her with incredible speed, its rider sitting up in the saddle, an arm raised high with deadly blue magical light flaring around each finger.

Taggie instinctively shoved her own arm out towards the black rider. The charmsward bands spun smoothly, their slender engravings shining violet as the wave symbol lined up with the moonstar and a shield. *'Elakus!'*

Taggie bellowed, and felt the shielding enchantment coil protectively round her.

A vivid-blue death spell flashed out from the rider's hand like a hostile comet. It hit Taggie's enchantment shield. The impact was like being struck by the boulder at the front of an avalanche. Taggie was knocked off the bike's saddle to flail about in mid-air before crashing painfully on the shaggy grass verge. But the shield enchantment held and the death spell sizzled down into the ground, killing the grass as it went.

Taggie was badly frightened and in a lot of pain. Overriding that, however, was anger that someone should just come along and try to murder her like this. Even before she hit the verge the charmsward bands were sliding round again, aligning rock with wind. She landed on her side, skidding along through grass, nettles, and brambles. Her hand pointed a rigid forefinger at the back of the rider who had zipped past. '*Israth hyburon*,' she growled furiously, and her arm lit up like a neon orange sign. The hot summer air in front of her warped as if she was looking through a giant magnifying glass. It became a big translucent fist that surged forward. The motorbike was punched up into the air, its engine shrieking wildly, wheels spinning. And the rider went flying over the drystone wall, legs and arms waving frantically.

The motorbike thumped down, banging and scraping along the tarmac until it finally came to a halt and its noisy engine stalled. Silence reclaimed the country lane.

Taggie staggered to her feet, wincing at the sharp pain in her bleeding knee. Now the shock was fading she realized how strong that death spell had been; even Jothran, the Karrak Lord who had tried to steal the shell throne from her last year, hadn't been this powerful. 'So who in all the Heavens is the rider?' she asked herself with growing worry. Her instinct was to get back on her bicycle and get away as fast as she could, as the idea of fighting some crazed killer was terrifying. But she suspected attempting to flee wouldn't be any use. This threat had to be faced down.

She was shaking in fright as she refreshed her shield enchantment. Then it was a slow limp towards the moss-covered wall where the rider had gone over. By the time Taggie reached it, she was in no mood to waste time clambering over.

'*Droiak*.'

A wide section of wall exploded as her destruction spell hit it, sending smoking chunks of stone shooting up into the air. Mum and Dad were always telling her not to use magic here in the Outer Realm, but right now she decided normal rules didn't apply. Besides, technically, she was a Queen so she could do whatever she liked – although that never seemed to count for as much as you'd think with either parent.

Taggie stepped through the gap, and looked round for her assailant. But there was no sign of the black-clad rider. The meadow spread out ahead of her, with a flock of very startled sheep staring at her. There was nowhere for anyone to hide. 'What? How . . .'

Another death spell came streaking down out of the sky, hitting Taggie's shield right in front of her face with a fizzing burst of brilliant blue light. Again she went tumbling backwards, smacking into the remnants of the wall. 'Oww!' she cried. Her hand automatically went to her stinging nose. When she took it away there was blood on her fingers. The sheep were running away as fast as their spindly legs could manage.

Above her, a huge black eagle swooped round in a fast curve.

A shapeshifter! Taggie realized in alarm. This was an incredibly complex magic that she'd never even tried to master. Anger finally overcame her fear. She stood up and snarled as she faced the eagle which was soaring round to line up on her.

'OK then,' Taggie snapped. 'If that's the way you want it.' She hadn't asked for this battle, but if someone was stupid enough to try and kill a Paganuzzi with an unprovoked attack, they were going to have to learn the hard way what a seriously bad idea that was. Taggie licked her lips in determination as the charmsward's bands slid round obediently.

The eagle began its dive. Magic crackled round its talons.

'*Ti-Hath*,' Taggie chanted. Halfway between her and the eagle, a wide circle of air turned rock hard.

The eagle smacked right into the patch of enchanted

air at considerable speed. Its head crunched to one side, the rest of its body and wings followed, whacking into the solid sheet of air with equal force.

'Urrgh!' a girl's voice exclaimed. And for an instant, the eagle was spread out wide in mid-air.

The dark bird slid vertically down the invisible barrier to the ground, and flopped about on the meadow grass. A couple of feathers drifted down gently above it.

Taggie pointed her finger at the befuddled bird. '*Quillazen.*' A general counter-charm, that really ought to work on a shapeshift spell . . .

It did. The eagle shimmered, turning to a ball of seething black mist. And for a moment Taggie thought she was going to see a Karrak Lord emerge; the effect was so similar to the smoke cloaks they always wore to protect themselves from any kind of light.

Instead, a girl of about seventeen was revealed, wearing the black biker leathers. She was short and slender, with skin a shade darker than Taggie's, but with hair exactly the same rich chestnut. The nose was slightly flattened, and the lips were thin. But it was the intense brown eyes that startled Taggie. It was like looking into a mirror.

The girl wiped a hand across her mouth, staring harshly at Taggie. 'You stupid little brat, you're ruining my reputation,' she said haughtily.

'Reputation?' Taggie's hand was still pointing warily at the girl, charmsward bands locked for another destruction spell. Taggie had never actually used a death spell but she was starting to think today might just be the day.

'I always kill quickly and cleanly, and leave no sign of my presence.' The girl gestured angrily at the smoking stone wall. 'Now look!'

'Yeah, I'm really sorry about that.' Taggie said sarcastically.

The girl took a step closer, her back arching as if she was about to crouch, then pounce. Taggie wished she'd just try it. Two years of martial arts lessons with Mr Koimosi, her sensei, had taught her a lot about physical combat. Especially when it came to brash arrogant people who thought they were superior because of their size and strength.

'Who are you?' she asked.

'The last person you'll ever see.'

'Oh dear. Did it take you a long time to come up with that? Or was it out of a Christmas cracker?' Taggie retorted.

The girl snarled. She clicked her fingers, and another death spell came flashing out of her hand. It broke apart on Taggie's shield. Taggie flung her destruction spell, which the girl parried. Magical light flared and danced through the air between them. As it cleared, Taggie screamed. A massive snake was hurtling towards her. Taggie hated snakes. She stumbled backwards, squealing in fright, but the snake just kept coming. Its head was as big as hers, while the sinuous body with its black and livid-green scales was thicker than her leg. Jaws parted wide to reveal fangs as long as fingers, while a nasty forked tongue flicked out amid a piercing hiss.

The snake lunged forward. Taggie jumped back, and collided with the big oak tree on the side of the road. Before she realized what was happening, the snake coiled round her and the oak trunk, binding her to the tree, pinning her arms at her side. Her enchantment shielding prevented the snake's scales from actually touching her, but the thick coil contracted, squeezing tight. Little purple cracks spread across the shielding. Taggie groaned at the pressure. She could barely breathe.

The snake looped a second coil of itself round her and the tree. Another patch of her enchantment shielding creaked as the purple stress-lines multiplied. Now most of Taggie's chest was a mass of slender glowing purple streaks.

Slowly the snake's head rose up in front of Taggie. The horrible tongue vibrated out between the fangs, which dripped gooey venom from their tips.

'They warned me you were strong,' the girl's

voice said. 'But even so, you're hardly a match for someone with my superior skill.'

Taggie didn't dare try to channel any magic into an aggressive spell. It was taking all her strength to keep her enchantment shielding in place. And that was gradually failing under the terrible pressure the snake was applying. She looked round desperately for something that could help.

The snake's head lunged forward, trying to close its jaws round Taggie's neck. It was only just repelled by her shield. Purple light rained all across Taggie's face.

Taggie caught sight of something moving across the meadow. It gave her an idea. One which was stupid, a completely mad idea. But she hadn't got anything else. '*Cozal-wo.*' She sent out a tiny courage enchantment that needed hardly any magic to make it work.

The snake's head withdrew, its red and green eyes studying her in puzzlement. 'So, you need bravery to face your doom?' the girl's voice sneered. 'Fancy having to use magic to give that to yourself.'

Taggie sucked down a breath. 'Yes. I don't suppose you need anything to reinforce your cowardice.' She was looking behind the snake's head, across the meadow where the ram from the flock of sheep began to run towards them. It was a big animal, with dirty-yellow horns curling up from its head.

The snake hissed angrily, and its head snapped forward again. Taggie thought her shield would fail this time, but it held against the hammer blow. Just. Only a couple more strikes like that would break it now.

'I am no coward,' the girl claimed. 'My profession is amongst the most noble in all the Realms.'

Taggie just managed to gasp out: 'What Realm calls "thug" a profession?'

As she expected, her provocation made the snake pull its head back, ready to strike again. Its jaws opened wide and the enraged hiss began – then abruptly changed to an astounded wail of surprise and pain. The snake's huge head twisted round, and Taggie felt its body turn rigid with shock. The ram's horns had jabbed forcefully into the snake, and Taggie was abruptly surrounded by writhing black mist again. Then she found herself face to face with the girl who was hugging her and the tree. She had an expression of wide-eyed suffering. The ram backed away, withdrawing his curving horns from the girl's bottom.

Taggie didn't waste time forming a spell. She headbutted the girl. *Hard*. Never mind how un-regal that was.

Her assailant tottered back, letting out another anguished wail. Taggie held her arm out. It was tempting, but today wasn't going to be the day for a death spell after all. '*Israth hyburon.*'

Magical orange light flared once again. The air warped as it smashed forward, and the girl went somersaulting backwards to thud down on the road.

'Who are you?' Taggie demanded, closing in on the prone figure in black leathers. 'Who sent you?'

The girl growled wordlessly at her. Then with an impressively fast motion she sprang back to her feet like a gymnast coming out of a difficult manoeuvre. She looked over Taggie's shoulder and pressed her lips together in annoyance. 'Still need Mummy's help, do we? What a Queen you make.'

'I . . . what?'

The girl's hand made an impatient gesture, and the big black motorbike lifted itself upright. The engine burst into life, and she leaped on to its saddle.

'Hey!' Taggie yelled. Some part of her was desperate to know who she was dealing with, but an altogether more sensible part was extremely glad the terrible girl was leaving.

'Don't worry, I'll see you soon enough, Queen of Dreams,' the girl sneered, and twisted the throttle.

'Not if I see you first,' Taggie shouted in a shaky voice. It was a good comeback, but she didn't think the girl would hear her above the engine roar. And anyway she was already riding off, speeding away down the lane.

Taggie watched her go, and suddenly she was aware of her injured knee. And the mass of scratches and torn clothes from the brambles. And the patches of skin that were hot from nettle stings. And her ribs hurt where the snake-illusion had squeezed. She dabbed at her face to find her nose had thankfully stopped bleeding. But it was very sore.

It was hard not to start crying. There was nothing she

could do about her trembling legs and arms.

Her mother's big grey Range Rover came tearing round the corner. Tyres squealed, and smoke actually squirted out of the wheel wells just like it did in action films as the car performed an impressive handbrake skid-turn-stop. Taggie had no idea her mum could drive like that. But then until last year she hadn't known Mum was a Third Realm sorceress, either.

Doors slammed open, and Mum was running across the road. 'My darling, are you all right?' she demanded, looking up and down at Taggie's ruined clothes and battered skin.

'Yes, Mum. I think so.'

'That's my girl.' Mum hugged her tight, which made everything a whole lot better. Taggie hugged her back, grateful for the contact.

'Who was that?' Mum asked in a cold, angry voice.

'Don't know. I've never seen her before.'

'Her?'

'Yes. She tried to kill me! And she could shapeshift.'

Mum stiffened. 'Oh could she now?'

'Yes. And, Mum, she looked familiar somehow.'

'Really?' Mum looked worried.

'A Third Realm sorceress, then,' Felix announced. 'And academy tutored, too, if she could shapeshift.'

Taggie saw the big white squirrel had jumped on to the Range Rover's bonnet, to gaze down the lane after the motorbike. Felix was a special agent of the First Realm's Palace Guard, assigned as Jem's bodyguard. A job he took very seriously indeed, as indicated by the tip of his fluffy tail flicking from side to side in agitation.

'I can still see her aurora,' he continued. His glasses with their purple lenses were designed to reveal magical energy from the Realms.

Jemima came racing round the back of the Range Rover. She was in her best party dress ready for her friend Sienna's birthday. 'I called you as soon as I saw the vision,' she said breathlessly. 'You took so long to answer. I was really scared for you.'

Taggie put her arms out to her sister and they hugged for a long moment. 'Thank you, Jem. I think you saved my life.' Her little sister might be irritating at times but she was shaping up to be a very accomplished seer.

'I just saw this crazy black shape flinging a death spell at you. I knew it was about to happen.'

'You saw perfectly, Jem. And crazy is the right description of her.'

Jemima smiled delightedly.

Something horribly wet and warm nuzzled the back of Taggie's knee. There was an affectionate bleating sound behind her.

'Taggie?' Jemima asked. 'Why is that sheep licking you?'

'Long story.'

2

RUNNING FOR COVER

'Stop squirming!' Mum instructed, for what must have been the tenth time.

'Oww,' Taggie replied.

Mum was smoothing some weird-smelling ointment over the bruise on Taggie's elbow. Taggie hadn't even known she had a bruise on her elbow, there were so many other aches and pains to endure. She'd been lying on the leather settee in the lounge for half an hour now, while Mum used gentle enchantments and smelly herb potions to heal all the cuts, scrapes and bruises. Mum was superb at the healing art, but clearly believed that medicine wasn't any good unless it stung/ponged/tasted awful.

'Do you think Sienna's mum will hang on to my party bag for me?' Jemima wondered. She was sitting on the floor, holding Taggie's ankle in her hands. As well as being the Blossom Princess, Jemima also had a healer's talent. Taggie could feel the ache of the sprain subsiding beneath her sister's cool fingers.

'Jemima, you're twelve,' Mum said shortly. 'You don't get party bags any more, especially not for a trip to the cinema.'

Jemima screwed her face up into a well-practised pout. 'But I'm not going to get to the cinema now, am I?'

Taggie ignored her.

Felix scampered in through the open patio door and hopped up on to the grand piano that took up a quarter of the lounge's floor space. The purple-lens glasses were still balanced on his head, but he'd shrunk back down to normal squirrel size again.

Taggie never could work out what made him constantly change size; she presumed it was part of the curse placed on him and his family. But Felix never gave details, and she wasn't about to ask. 'I've taken a good look round from the roof,' he said. 'I can see no trace of magic from any other Realm close by. But I took the precaution of renewing the alarm charms around the garden.'

'And I can't see anybody threatening us,' Jemima said primly.

'Thank you, Jem,' Mum said. She gave Taggie a last examination. 'I think that's all of them, darling.'

'Thanks, Mum.' Taggie pulled her dressing gown on and stood up cautiously.

'You're healing up,' Mum warned. 'But every injury will be tender for a few days, so just take it easy.'

'Yes, Mum.' She put some weight tentatively on the ankle Jemima had healed, and gave her sister a thumbs-up.

Mum started bundling up Taggie's torn and dirty clothes. 'These will have to go. Don't worry, you and I will go on a shopping trip to get you some new clothes.'

Taggie smiled in delight at the prospect, and went upstairs to her room. Mum's house was ultra-modern, complete with just about every domestic gadget ever invented. But she had been allowed to decorate her own room as she wanted. So it had a blue ceiling with white clouds painted on, and furniture that was now possibly a little too pink and girly for a thirteen-year-old.

After a nice long soothing shower, Taggie opened her chest of drawers and took out a pair of clean jeans just as her mobile started playing the national anthem. It made her grin, even though she knew she really ought to change it.

'Hello, Harry,' she said as she wiggled into the jeans, frowning at how faded they were at the knee.

'Taggie.' Prince Harry's voice boomed out of the mobile. 'Are you all right? My cousin said she sighted a bit of trouble up your way this afternoon.'

'Tell Beatrice she's got good sight. But don't worry, nothing I couldn't handle.'

'Thank heavens for that. Was it the Karrak Lords?'

'No. It was a sorceress girl I've never seen before. She wore black biker leathers. Do you know if she came through a Great Gateway recently? She certainly wasn't Outer Realm.'

'I'll check with MI1 for you.'

'Thanks, Harry.' MI1, or to give the department

its proper name, Mage Intelligence 1, operated out of Buckingham Palace, keeping a quiet watch on all things magical occurring in the UK. Thankfully, outbreaks were minimal these days. The Royal Family, themselves descended from mages of the First Times, just like Taggie was, were responsible for keeping magical incursions to a minimum across the UK.

'No problem,' Harry said. 'Look, I can assign you a few Knights if you need some help. They're good, you know. I've served with them myself on a few hairy missions.'

'I'll be fine,' she assured him. Besides, good though the Knights of the Black Garter were, she knew that the mad shapeshifter girl would have torn them apart like a soggy pizza.

'OK, Taggie, but we're here if you need us. And by the way, Grandma sends her love.'

'Thank you, Harry, I'll call if anything changes. And please let me know if you hear anything.' She ended the call, still grinning.

As she came downstairs, she heard the unmistakable sound of a certain ancient Land Rover turning into the drive. Sure enough, its gears grated in a noise that set her teeth on edge. She flew down the rest of the stairs and flung the front door open.

Dad was climbing out of the battered green Land Rover. She ran over and flung her arms round him.

'Hey,' he said gently. 'You look OK. You did well against her.'

'How did you know?'

'Felix sent word. I came straight away.'

Taggie felt her lips tremble as her eyes watered. 'She tried to kill me, Daddy!'

For a long moment he stroked the back of Taggie's head. 'Yes, well, I'm going to make sure that doesn't happen again.'

She looked up at him through moist eyes. Dad never changed, that was one of the reasons she loved him so much. His thin hair that was about to turn grey, glasses that always sat at a slight slant, wide mouth that was normally half smiling, crooked nose – that was him, always there and reliable, making the world a better place. Even last year when he'd been kidnapped by Lord Golzoth, getting him back was all she'd thought about.

She caught sight of the exquisite pearl-white tunic he was wearing as its gold braid caught the bright evening sunlight. The old oilskin coat he'd pulled on to try and cover it up was a half-hearted camouflage. 'You really did come straight away, didn't you?' she said in admiration.

'Of course I did, my darling.'

They went inside, and Jemima received her share of kisses and hugs. It had been a month since either of the sisters had seen Dad. These days he lived in the First Realm, sitting on the shell throne as regent governor while Taggie and Jemima went to school and lived a normal life in the Outer Realm. The plan was that Taggie would sit on the throne permanently once she was eighteen.

'You need to come to the First Realm,' Dad told her when they were all settled in the lounge. 'You'll be a lot safer in the palace.'

'No!' Taggie exclaimed. 'I'm halfway through my exams. Mum?' It was a cheap trick, but she was desperate. Mum and Dad had been separated for years, and sometimes they could be played off to her advantage.

'The sorceress who attacked Taggie could shapeshift,' Mum said, mainly to Dad.

'That settles it,' Dad said. 'You're coming back with me, this evening.'

Taggie glanced from one to the other, and tried not to sigh. She wasn't going to be able to manoeuvre them, not when they were both in this mood. They didn't agree often, but when they did . . . 'What's going on? I saw that look.'

Dad shrugged at Mum, who simply shrugged back.

'We need to find out why someone was sent here to kill you,' Mum said. 'From the sound of it, the assassin was from the Invisible Lodge.'

'What's that?'

'Bad news,' Felix said solemnly. 'Very bad. The Invisible Lodge is an ancient guild of assassins based in the Third Realm.'

'She was a professional assassin?' Taggie blurted.

'Cool,' Jemima murmured.

'No, it is not cool,' Mum snapped. 'The Invisible Lodge should never have accepted a contract for Taggie, and

19

they know it. That's why I came to this Realm, so such nonsense would be over for good.'

'The Third Realm is always trouble,' Dad said in a very disapproving voice.

'Those days are over,' Mum said sharply.

Dad closed his mouth quickly.

'What days?' Jemima asked.

'There used to be conflict between the great sorceress houses,' Mum said. 'Sometimes silly little wars would break out. It's all in the past now, the Third Realm is unified under the Queen, and has been for centuries. Simply because we sorceresses are more powerful than mages from the other Realms, our reputation suffered.' Mum looked sternly from Taggie to Jemima. 'Nothing for you two to worry about. Now go and pack your bags. You're going with your father.'

'Mum!'

'And I'll be coming with you.'

Dad's eyebrows shot up. 'You will?'

'Until we know more about what's going on I need to be close by. That Invisible Lodge assassin might manage to get close to Taggie again. But she'll never get past me.'

Mum drove Felix and the sisters up to Orchard Cottage, with Dad following in his Land Rover. She parked at the side of the ancient ramshackle building where Dad had lived during his self-imposed exile. A pair of retired palace guards were tending it now, keeping an eye out for questionable travellers coming through the Great Gateway from the First Realm.

Dad led the group across the unkempt orchard at the back. At the far end was a roundadown, which looked like the top of a stone-lined well. As the five of them stood round it, the hole looked unnaturally dark, with no bottom in sight.

Until last year Taggie had always been slightly uneasy about the deep shaft into the ground. The roundadown was where her adventures had begun. This was where she'd first seen a Karrak Lord, and *that* image was still fresh in her mind: of Lord Golzoth pulling Dad down into the darkness at the centre of the roundadown. It had been a momentous day when she not only discovered who she really was, but also that the Realms existed. Such magical things held no fear for her now, and she couldn't wait to walk down to the Great Gateway at the bottom.

'Let me do it,' Jemima pleaded. 'Please, please.'

'Go on then,' Dad said.

A smiling Jemima picked one of the tiny periwinkle flowers that grew abundantly around the top. She dropped it into the dark hole and chanted: '*Zarek fol.*'

Just below the rim of the well, a stone slid out with a loud rumbling sound. Another started to come out just below it, then a third, a fourth . . . After a minute, they were looking at a spiral staircase winding down into the impenetrable shade.

Taggie took out her hand-pumped torch, and started

down. As always, it seemed to take an age, but eventually she reached the bottom to stand on a spongy floor of dry leaves. Set into the wall in front of her was a single iron-bound wooden door which had no handle.

After Mum, Dad and Jemima, Felix was the last down. As he reached the floor, the stones all retracted back into the wall with loud grumblings.

Taggie shone her torch on the doorway. 'Arasath, I am Taggie Paganuzzi, Queen of Dreams, and I wish to return to the First Realm.'

'Welcome home, Queen of Dreams,' Arasath's solemn voice said from somewhere behind her. The wooden door swung open. 'And you too, Blossom Princess,' the Great Gateway added. 'You have grown since last you came this way.'

Jemima grinned at the door. 'Thank you.'

There was a long curving passageway of brick on the other side. Taggie walked along it, her smile growing broader with every step. She'd spent her first twelve years living in the Outer Realm, knowing nothing of her birthright. Yet after just a year of too-few visits, she knew beyond any doubt this was her true home.

There was another door at the far end of the passage, which swung open as she approached. Taggie walked out into the First Realm.

'Oh my,' Mum murmured as she looked round. 'I never knew it was so beautiful.'

Ahead of them, an emerald quilt of fields, meadows and

forests curved up as if they were facing a gigantic valley wall. Yet no matter how far they tipped their heads back, that green countryside just kept curving up and up. They were standing on the inside of a sphere that contained an entire world with all its fabulous mountain ranges and glittering seas. Clouds like puffy white marshmallows were scattered everywhere, drifting along slowly. Right at the centre of the First Realm, thousands of miles above their heads, a tiny sun burned brightly, wrapped within the tattered webbing of its moonclouds, those dense coloured streamers that cast vast shadows across the ground, bringing night to whole sections of the landscape. Towns and cities within the nightshadows glittered brightly with magical luminescence.

'Your Majesty.'

The respectful voice made Taggie pull her gaze away from the bizarre and wondrous inside-out world. Two ranks of the palace guard were lined up outside the doorway. The men were all Holvans, a race with two arms sprouting from each shoulder. They wore the glamorous white-and-silver armour of the palace, with an ice-blue shell crest on the helmet. Swords, shields, bows and fireangs (like boomerangs but enchanted) flashed in the sunlight as the Holvans performed a complex salute no one with a mere two arms could manage.

Taggie bowed formally to them. The palace guard had suffered heavily at the hands of the Karrak Lords, but were now almost back to full strength again, with a lot of new recruits eager to serve their Queen.

Standing in front of them was Mr Anatole, equerry to the Queen of Dreams. The tall old Shadarain had skin the ruddy-red colour of baked clay. He wore the grandiose robes of his office, a tunic of scarlet, indigo and emerald, complemented by a broad cloak woven with gold thread. He looked impressive and solemn, every inch the royal adviser – right up until he broke into a huge smile. Jemima ran over and hugged him tight.

'It is so good to see you again, Majesties,' he said.

'It's good to be back,' Taggie said earnestly.

She, of course, couldn't be as free and exuberant as Jemima, not here. In the First Realm she was the Queen of Dreams, and as she'd learned last year, she had to behave appropriately. She set about it as if she was playing the part in a school play, acting out the regal royal role. It was hard to stay in character at times.

She offered the dear old equerry her hand, and he bowed down to kiss her knuckles.

'Majesty,' he murmured, but she saw the happiness in his eyes. 'I'm so glad you're all right.'

'Thank you.'

While she greeted him, the wildflowers in the grass behind the palace guard were welcoming Jemima's arrival. Flutterseed buds opened up, flapping their colourful petals and breaking free of their stems to swarm up into the clear sky. Roses and honeysuckle flowers bloomed wide, thickening the air with their scent. Even the serious palace guards smiled at that. Jemima, the Blossom Princess, always had that effect on plants wherever she went in the First Realm.

Taggie and her party walked down the path to the Gateway station, escorted by the palace guards. The station sat all by itself in the middle of the countryside. There was only one platform, which had an overhanging canopy roof that ran alongside a broad canal. Five turtles were already waiting for Taggie. They were huge, the size of an Outer Realm lorry, with shells that shone a dull brass colour under the sun. Traditional wooden benches were fixed on top of the shell, painted in jolly colours. Taggie climbed the wooden steps that curved up the side of the shell. Three palace guards sat behind her, looking round alertly. Dad and Mr Anatole sat with her, while Jemima, Mum and Felix took the second turtle with their guards. The rest of the palace guards climbed aboard the remaining turtles.

'All aboard,' the turtle hummed soothingly, and started paddling along the canal.

'I'm afraid seers have been gossiping, Majesty,' Mr Anatole said. 'The city of Lorothain is expecting you.'

'Oh.' Taggie couldn't really sound disappointed. Having huge crowds cheering you wherever you went wasn't exactly bad for her self-esteem and confidence. It had certainly helped cure any lingering shyness. Much to the dismay of the palace guards, she always tried to say hello to as many people in the crowds as she could; they all seemed to have such fascinating lives.

'People will want to see you are all right,' Mr Anatole continued. There are already rumours about the assassination attempt.'

The canal took them through several towns, where the banks were lined with cheering folk who waved eagerly at her. Once again, Taggie was amazed and pleased by how many different kinds of people could all live together.

'How do your studies go, Majesty?' Mr Anatole asked.

'I've read up on all the Realms now,' she assured him. 'I want to visit them all, especially the Fifth.' Which was disgraceful flattery: the Fifth Realm was the original home of the tall and graceful Shadarain.

'I would be delighted to arrange a royal procession for you there, Majesty,' Mr Anatole said, looking content.

Taggie was pleased she stayed in character, never dropping the small smile. In truth, while she'd been reading up on the Realms, the Fifth had sounded a bit mundane compared to some – just an ordinary land with different folk living in it. The Sixth, now, with its huge seas and multitude of archipelagos where monsoon rains fell almost every day, that would be a wonderful trip, especially with all the elves living there. There was also the Seventh Realm, the original home of the Holvans, although after the Great Gateways opened they became renowned travellers, settling in every Realm – again a bit average. Then there was the Eighth Realm, with its rugged mountains and yawning valleys enjoyed by the trolls who mined and dug through the rock to find precious metals and jewels which they traded enthusiastically; visiting that would definitely qualify as a duty. Giants strode across the Ninth Realm, perfectly suited to a land whose mountains were twice the size of those in any other Realm, and the oceans deeper and wider. That might be interesting. But most of all she wanted to visit the Realm of Air where the skyfolk dwelled.

She'd heard that a lot of young royals went travelling incognito, so they might enjoy the Realms as they were meant to experienced, rather than under the constraint of an official tour.

'Oh, hello,' Dad said, smiling, as they cleared Blogalham town. 'Here she comes.'

Taggie didn't have to ask. She searched keenly through the air above, and saw something producing a thin red contrail that streaked towards them at an astounding rate. Seconds later the twinkling contrail's tip was overhead, and Taggie half expected to hear a sonic boom. But the contrail curved round, and its energetic tip finally slowed down. Taggie stood up and waved frantically.

Sophie the skymaid dropped out of the sky to hover directly in front of Taggie. She was the same age as Taggie, but Sophie's hair was a vivid red, with its long strands waving round her head in languid motions. She wore a grey-and-green tunic with turquoise stars embroidered round the short skirt. Her big translucent wings shimmered behind her. 'Taggie!' she exclaimed breathlessly.

'Sophie!' Taggie squealed and held her arms out. The two embraced happily. They'd met last year, and Sophie had played a vital part in rescuing Dad from the Karrak Lords and restoring Taggie to the throne.

Mr Anatole and Dad shuffled along the bench so Sophie could sit beside Taggie. Her feathery triangular feet folded up neatly as she landed, and the girls nestled up close.

Sophie grinned at her friend. 'I've missed you loads,' she said. 'It's no fun around here while you're away.'

Taggie sighed wistfully. 'I missed you too, but I could really do without any more excitement right now.'

'I know! I heard. So go on then, tell me all about the assassination attempt.'

The palace of the Queen of Dreams stood just outside the city of Lorothain. It was a huge building of high stone walls and courtyards and towers that was practically a town in itself. Surrounded by gardens and extensive parkland the palace was visible from a long way off.

As the turtles paddled along the river Trambor, Taggie saw the palace rise out of the summer haze; it was a comforting sight. The heart of the palace was an old castle, with sturdy fortifications and deep protective enchantments. Dad was quite right to say she'd be safe inside. She hadn't realized how tense and nervous she was until she saw it.

There was a huge crowd clustered round the royal wharf, comprised of a huge variety of folk. Taggie got to shake a few hands and say hello to some overexcited children as the palace guard hurried her to a covered coach. Then it was a swift five-minute drive to the palace along the mighty greensward lined by oaks and cedar trees.

Work on repairing the palace after the Karrak Lords had tainted it with their own alterations was nearly complete. Dad spent a couple of hours before supper, proudly showing them the restorations he'd supervised. At least the Queen's private wing was now finished, which gave Taggie a huge suite of rooms all to herself. Here the furniture and decor was elaborate and formal, like some kind of five-star hotel. The luxurious four-poster bed was practically the same size as her entire bedroom back in Mum's house. Then there was a lounge, a day room, a dressing room, a study . . . The walk-in wardrobe was packed with clothes, both formal and normal – so many vintage dresses from princesses down the ages, all hers now! And the adjoining marble bathroom was just plain decadent. She loved it. Plus, here she got a personal maid from the palace staff.

She'd lost track of what time it was when she finally had a quick supper with Mum and Dad and Jemima. But her body knew it was very late, and Jemima was practically asleep in her food. Mum left as soon as they'd finished eating, to inspect the protective enchantments. Taggie didn't mind. She was too tired. As the nightshadow swept across Lorothain, she crept into her huge bed. Sleep came almost at once.

And as always when she was in the First Realm, Taggie dreamed.

In her dream she sat on the shell throne in the palace's huge throne room with its crystal dome roof and three tall arching doors. The line of anxious visitors waiting to see her wound along the corridor outside into an unknown hazy distance.

The first person to stand before her was a young boy of perhaps seven years. He smiled up expectantly at Taggie, though she could see he'd been crying.

'What's the matter?' she asked.

'I have trouble with my letters, Your Majesty. I try hard at school, I really do. I want to read, but . . .' He shrugged.

'Don't worry about it,' she told him. 'I know how overwhelming classes can be sometimes. I'm still at school, too, you know. There's so much teachers want to make us learn, and it always seems difficult.'

'I know,' the boy said miserably. 'But my teacher Mrs Pengath is impatient with me. She shouts at me all the time. It's scary.' He glanced fearfully over his shoulder. 'Now she's followed me here. She always follows me. Every night. I can never get away.' His shoulders started shaking in misery.

Taggie looked to see a grotesque woman standing behind the boy on the throne-room floor. Almost as tall as a giant, she wore a grey cardigan and skirt made of some thick wool that clinked like chain mail. She stood hunched over, with her hands trailing along the ground. Her mouth had jagged yellow fangs sticking out as she jeered at the poor boy, and her fingernails were made of chalk. When she scraped them on the throne room's tiled floor they made the most appalling screeching sound.

Taggie felt so desperately sorry for the boy who conjured up this nightmare figure every time he slept. 'You,' she said firmly to the caricature of Mrs Pengath. 'Go back to your classroom.'

The nightmare Mrs Pengath let out an annoyed grunt, but she turned and started to shamble out.

'That is where you are to stay,' Taggie ordered. 'Do not venture out after dark again. I, the Queen of Dreams, command it.'

Mrs Pengath passed through one of the throne room's big doors and into nothingness.

'There,' Taggie told the boy. 'She's gone. And look,' she said with her arm round his shoulder. 'Here are your friends, waiting for you to play.'

Sure enough, one of the other doors now opened on to a meadow where a dozen children were running round, laughing happily. 'Off you go,' Taggie told him. She watched for a long moment as the boy joined his friends, and together they all raced off into the warm summer's day.

When she turned back, a young woman was standing in the middle of the throne room.

'What's the matter?' Taggie asked.

'It's my husband, ma'am,' the woman said. 'We've only

been married these past four months, and now he's left to go to sea. He's a fisherman, you see. I miss him so. I know that's stupid.'

'I don't think it's stupid at all,' Taggie assured her. She beckoned. The woman's husband strode through one of the doors. 'See, here he is.' And Taggie smiled as the two embraced.

The next person was one of the spherical people who lived in the First Realm, all anxious and swaying about.

'How can I help?' Taggie asked.

Taggie woke with a big smile lifting her mouth. As always when she'd spent her own dreams helping the people of the First Realm get through their troubled nights, she felt as if she'd been asleep for days, and was refreshed and completely content. Back when she was in the Outer Realm she often felt a pang of guilt that she wasn't here to use her magical talent. Mr Anatole had informed her that not even her grandmother, the last Queen of Dreams, had dreamed every night, which made her feel better – and anyway she visited every school holiday.

3

PRACTICE REALLY SHOULD MAKE PERFECT

'Come on,' Mum said. 'Try again now.'

Taggie wanted to slump her shoulders and stomp away in a sulk. It was a lovely day. She was in the palace grounds, in a garden surrounded by high beech hedges so no one could see. And Sophie was somewhere close by along with her older cousins, Tilly and Elsie, who'd flown in specially to have some fun. Taggie could hear them all laughing with Jemima.

As Mum held Taggie's wrists, she could feel a weird tingle of magic seeping into her flesh, magic that was different from any enchantment stored in the charmsward.

'It feels odd,' she said, fighting the impulse to squirm.

'This is the kind of magic practised in the Third Realm,' Mum said. 'It is stronger than anything you've been used to. So treat it carefully. But you have nothing to fear. Any daughter of mine is perfectly capable of handling so much power.'

'Why is magic more powerful in the Third Realm?'

'We were brought to the Third Realm by archangels rather than the ordinary angels who delivered the people of the other Realms from the heavens at the start of the

First Times. Naturally that makes us considerably more robust.'

'Is that why the Third Realm wars were so much worse?'

'Great ability always makes people more demanding, less tolerant. A culture like that, backed up with power . . . It wasn't good. Millennia of politics in a Realm where the slightest sign of weakness can prove instantly lethal tends to sharpen your own survival skill to the highest level.' She gave Taggie a lofty smile. 'And you're the end product of that evolution – even though you haven't learned how to apply it yet.'

'All right. I'd like to learn.'

'Good. Now feel the shape I have placed in the magic,' Mum said hypnotically. 'That is the spellform we call *Adrap*. Hold it in your head.'

Taggie closed her eyes, and tried to keep hold of the spellform's complicated shape – difficult, so difficult.

Mum let go. 'That's good. Now search your memory for the dog.'

Taggie remembered Jaspar, the neighbours' chocolate Labrador. Bounding about the kitchen, happy and excited, tail wagging, beautiful slick dark-ginger coat. She murmured '*Adrap*', and clicked her fingers, which was the normal trigger for Third Realm magic. The spellform closed about the memory of Jaspar, and the two merged. Taggie could feel a tingle as the magic began to expand, sliding along her skin, tickling . . .

She grinned, which made the spellform waver. When

34

she opened her eyes she saw her arms had become dog forelegs covered in brown fur.

'Yes!'

The spellform broke. Magic burst away from her in random spurts. The collapsing enchantment was like an electric shock zipping through her fingers.

'Oww!' Taggie yelped, and flapped her hands frantically.

'That's because you didn't concentrate,' Mum snapped.

Taggie hung her head. 'Sorry.'

'All right,' Mum said, taking a breath. 'Practice is the key here. We'll start again after lunch. You must keep that spellform together in your mind. That's the key to this.'

'I know. It's just that the charmsward normally does it.'

'Hmm.' Mum raised an eyebrow in disapproval. 'When I was training to be a sorceress, we weren't allowed any artificial help. We had to memorize every spellform, and woe betide us if we didn't.'

'Really?' Taggie was fascinated. Mum rarely spoke about the Third Realm.

'Yes, really. But the old sorceress mistresses who taught us were complete terrors. It's just as well you don't attend their academies, they're very strict. And Jemima would be zapped to a cinder thirty seconds after she walked through the front gate – the mistresses wouldn't put up with her cheek.' Mum looked up at the top of the palace's Layawhan Tower, the tallest structure in the whole First Realm. 'Sometimes I think I made a mistake leaving.'

'I'm glad you left,' Taggie said. 'I'm glad you met Dad.'

'Oh, sweetheart, pay no attention to me. I couldn't be prouder of you.'

'So how long were you at the academy?' Now Mum was talking about the Third Realm, Taggie suddenly felt bold enough to ask for more detail.

'Twelve years.'

'No wonder you're so good at magic.'

'Sweetheart, you only found magic existed last year. I think you're doing quite brilliantly despite your lack of formal training. At the academy, they wouldn't even begin teaching you shapeshifting until year ten. Shapeshifting is one of the most demanding enchantments there is.'

'What are the other tough ones?' Taggie asked immediately.

Mum laughed. 'Oh, you really are my daughter, aren't you? Alchemy is supposed to be the most difficult of all, turning ordinary metals into gold. Personally I believe it's levitation, lifting yourself off the ground and flying like one of the skyfolk.'

'Really?' Taggie asked breathlessly. 'There are enchantments for those things?' She couldn't find them in the charmsward.

'Oh my, what have I done?' Mum laughed.

'Do you know them? Can you teach them to me? Pleeease!'

'Yes I know them, but I'm not even going to start teaching you things like that until you've mastered how to shapeshift. Prove you can do that, that you have the discipline, and I'll think about the others.'

'I will, I promise, Mum, I'll do it.'

'Well, we'll see, won't we?'

'Mum, what about curses? Can you lift those?' Taggie asked eagerly.

'You mean the one affecting Felix, don't you?'

'Well, yes, I suppose . . .'

'The Karrak Lords brought that vile discipline with them through Mirlyn's Gate. I know the Third Realm's senior sorceresses had been studying these Dark Universe curses for an age without much success in devising counters. I would say that it probably cannot be lifted because the enchantment is now a part of him, what he is. Remember it has been passed down his family for generations, it runs through the Weldowens as brown eyes run through our family line.'

'Oh.'

'Don't worry. He seems able to live with it, and all such curses have to have an end clause woven into their structure in order for them to begin. Not even a Karrak Lord can bind magic for eternity. So there is always hope.'

'And the Great Gateway? Do you know the spellform to forge a Great Gateway? Oh, and what about walking on water? That would be so cool. And—'

'Enough! It's lunchtime.'

The palace's banqueting hall was huge, with a vaulted ceiling supported by great carved timbers arching overhead. Big colourful paintings of merry scenes hung on the walls below the high circular windows that sent sunlight streaming down on to the marble floor. It was all very elegant, and Taggie couldn't wait for the first state banquet to be thrown. But that was still a while off; a third of the hall remained covered in scaffolding so artisans could remove the runes and crude carvings left behind by the Karrak Lords and Ladies during their brief occupancy.

But the ash table long enough to seat a hundred and fifty people was unscathed. It was quite fun to have just ten people using it. Taggie sat at the end, flanked by her friends as the kitchen staff brought in quiches and salads and sausage rolls and Scotch eggs and new potatoes (the palace cook had never quite mastered chips). Felix got a big bowl of seeds and nuts. Taggie found it odd to have both Mum and Dad sitting with them. Odd but nice.

Mr Anatole arrived barely a minute after they'd all started tucking in. 'Majesty?' He bowed.

'What is it?' Taggie asked.

'There is an envoy from King Manokol outside, a Lady Jessicara DiStantona. She urgently wishes to speak with the Queen of Dreams.'

'Then show her in,' Taggie said.

Lady Jessicara DiStantona was a young woman dressed in an extravagant purple velvet tunic. Her glossy blonde hair was woven into long braids which then blended together into a wide scarlet cloak. With Mr Anatole escorting her, she strutted into the banqueting hall, gazing round as if she

found it unsatisfactory.
Taggie waited until
Lady Jessicara stopped
at the table in front of
Mum. She swept the
oversized beret
with five huge
fluffy emerald
feathers from
her head in
an extravagant
gesture, and bowed low. 'Majesty.'

From the corner of her
eye Taggie could see Jemima
starting to giggle. She scowled
a warning at her sister.

'Welcome to the First Realm, Lady Jessicara,' Taggie
said gracefully from the other side of the table, and stood
up.

The envoy gave her a surprised look. '*You* are the fabled
Queen of Dreams?'

Taggie was suddenly conscious of her jeans and scruffy
T-shirt.

But Mum rose to her feet, suddenly clad in the full
lustrous pearl-and-gold robes of a Third Realm sorceress,
implausibly tall and intimidating. Her transformation was
wonderfully impressive.

'Have a care, madam. You address Usrith's heir, The

Queen of Dreams herself. Protector of the First Realm. Conqueror of the King of Night's army. General of the Palace Guard. Knight Commander of the Dolvoki Rangers. And *my* daughter!' she said in a regal voice.

Lady Jessicara gulped, and bowed even lower in Taggie's direction. 'Majesty. I meant no disrespect.'

'Please,' Taggie said, slightly overwhelmed herself. 'None was taken. Now do join us, you must be hungry after your travels.'

Sophie moved along a seat so the envoy could have the chair next to Taggie – though the skymaid made sure she took the Outer Realm ketchup bottle with her. As Lady Jessicara sat, her peculiar hair cloak slowly drifted down out of the air.

'I'm afraid I bring unwelcome news, Majesty,' the envoy began, as the kitchen staff brought her a plate of food. 'Prince Rogreth, King Manokol's first son and heir is dead. We believe he was murdered.'

Taggie's hand flew to her mouth. 'No!'

'What happened?' Mum asked.

'The prince was leading a hunting party,' Lady Jessicara said. 'He was trying to bring down a tothgat. They are vermin in our Realm, flying predators which almost rival a rathwai for their size and bad temper. This particular one had been causing trouble for some hill farmers, carrying away livestock, damaging barns and fences. The prince and his friends undertook to bring it down for them. Unfortunately, it takes a great many crossbow bolts to dispatch one of the wretched things. One struck the prince.'

'Didn't he wear armour?' Taggie asked.

'Of course. But he was riding his pegasi at the time, a winged horse favoured in our Realm for hunting. He was a thousand feet in the air when the assassin's bolt struck.'

'Assassin?' Taggie said in shock. All she could think of was the girl in black biking leathers.

'We believe so, yes. But there is more bad news. Just as Prince Rogreth's body was brought home, we heard from the Sixth Realm. Prince Fasla, the heir to the throne there, was also murdered by an unknown person who escaped.'

The hall fell silent, with everyone staring at Lady Jessicara in dismay.

'Have you heard from any other Realms?' Mum asked.

'Several,' Lady Jessicara said. 'So far, the remaining heirs appear to be safe. But two have been killed, and you yourself, Queen of Dreams, only just escaped assassination. It is becoming clear to us that the Karrak Lords and Ladies are hunting down the princes in every Realm, knowing the young royals with their openness and freedoms are more vulnerable than the kings and queens themselves who are surrounded by the trappings of state. What they can never take by force, they attempt to steal by treachery.'

'Well they won't succeed here,' Mum said resolutely.

'King Manokol was gladdened to hear your assassin was thwarted,' Lady Jessicara said. 'As were all of us in the Second Realm. Since last year, you have become a source of courage and resolution to all people within the Realms, Queen of Dreams. By your example of reclaiming the shell throne you have shown all of us that the Karraks will never triumph.'

'Thank you,' Taggie murmured, somewhat abashed. 'But it's not like I did it alone.'

Lady Jessicara appeared not to hear that last part. 'I am here to extend an invitation from King Manokol to attend a Gathering of Kings in our capital, Shatha'hal. The leader of every Realm will join in conclave to decide how to meet this dire threat to our sovereignty.'

Taggie shot a glance at Mr Anatole, then Dad. Both of them inclined their heads.

'I thank King Manokol,' Taggie said formally. 'And I will attend the Gathering of Kings.' She paused. 'And Queens.'

The envoy never blinked. 'We thank you for your support, Queen of Dreams. Your presence will undoubtedly make the Gathering a success.'

4

THE JEWEL OF THE REALMS

The royal yacht was nearly thirty metres long, with two imperial purple sails rolled up tight on their cross masts. The golden figurehead was some kind of fish with wings, twice the size of a man. There was a cabin at the back – not that Taggie and her party used it. Twenty trolls sat in the midsection, rowing with huge oars.

They cast off from the royal wharf at dawn the following day, keeping the sails furled so the trolls rowed them steadily down the river Trambor. By mid-morning they'd reached the coast at Shieldport. An island made up from two tall mountains was just visible ahead, where the sea began to curve upward, both peaks hazed in white mist.

'That's the Great Gateway, Harrolas,' Mr Anatole said. He was standing on the decking up at the prow, next to Taggie and Sophie. She couldn't help noticing now they were on the sea itself how he kept a white-knuckle grip on the gunwale. His red skin was turning a strange purple shade as cold sweat prickled his brow. 'It connects to the Second Realm.'

'It's on the island?' she asked.

'Not quite. Excuse me, Majesty.' He hurried along the deck to the aft cabin.

Taggie watched Felix scamper up the rigging to the top of the mast, and sit down comfortably on the furled sail, his fluffy white tail curling round the canvas. Behind her, the trolls began to row faster, propelling the yacht quickly across the sea.

'Thanks for including me,' Sophie said.

Taggie smiled back at her friend as the sound of poor Mr Anatole being ill could be heard. 'I have to have someone I can talk to,' she told her friend, giving Lady Jessicara's back a guilty glance.

The rest of the royal party consisted of Jem, of course; a detachment of the palace guard; and Mum. There had been quite an argument, but in the end Dad conceded that he should stay behind and carry on the duty of regent governor. After all, if the assassin made another attempt on Taggie, she would be up against Mum's magical strength as well.

Jemima had her arm round one of the figurehead's odd wings, leaning forward into the spray with growing excitement as they neared the island with its twin peaks. She didn't even look round when Felix scampered up to the top of the figurehead, and held on to its neck with a forepaw.

'Where's the Great Gateway?' Jemima asked.

'Just up ahead,' Felix said. 'Between the two headlands,

there.' A forepaw pointed, a small claw extending. Jemima could just make out the tall cliffs on either side of a narrow inlet. It was directly below the valley formed by the two mountains. When she closed her eyes and concentrated in that specific odd way she'd come to learn, her sight showed her a tremendous waterfall at the end of the inlet. 'Cool,' she crooned. 'Is this the one you've been through?'

'Yes. It is widely used by trading ships. Those whose captains have courage, anyway.'

'I wish I could go to other Realms like you did,' Jemima said wistfully. 'It's so exciting.'

'Apart from the Outer Realm, of course, I've only been to the Second and Fifth Realms,' Felix said. 'And both times it was a duty. I have never been a tourist anywhere.'

'Can't you take time off? It's not like you haven't earned it.'

'I'm not sure I'd trust anyone else to look after you. And there are assassins around right now.'

'I'm a seer. I can *see* any trouble coming a mile off,' Jemima said proudly.

'Except your own death,' Felix reminded her. 'Seers can never see that. And you can't see *everything* that happens . . .'

'Oh, thanks a bunch, Felix. I needed to hear that today!'

'This crisis will pass, never fear.'

'I know. And when it does, I'm going to visit all the Realms,' Jemima announced. 'And you'll have to come too, because it's your duty to accompany me. So!'

The squirrel's teeth chattered for a moment. 'Some duties you just have to accept without complaint.'

Jemima grinned at him, before turning back to the headlands.

The trolls rowed onward, never slowing. Rock rose up on either side of the yacht until the rugged cliffs towered high above them, blotting out most of the light. That was when they heard the roar of the waterfall swelling out. It was half obscured by mist, but soon they could see the massive curtain of water falling over two hundred metres, filling the chasm between the cliffs.

Lady Jessicara came up to stand beside Jemima, her blonde hair and airborne cloak billowing dramatically behind her. By then the roar of the waterfall was so loud that Jemima could barely hear anything.

'By order of His Fabulous Majesty, King Manokol, Absolute Ruler of the Second Realm,' Lady Jessicara shouted into the waterfall's driving spray, 'I command you to give me safe passage home.' She threw a few small copper coins into the sea.

Jemima thought the envoy could perhaps be a little less cheap when it came to asking a Great Gateway to open. So she added, 'Please, Harrolas,' even though nobody could hear her.

The prow of the yacht was barely twenty metres from the falling water, and still surging forward when a gap appeared in the colossal downpour. It widened as the gold figurehead reached it, parting just enough to take the width of the royal yacht. Jemima gasped; she could see nothing but absolute blackness beyond, as if there truly was a wall of solid rock. Which if they hit at this speed . . .

Then amid the darkness she saw a tiny twinkle of blue light, like a star winking. It was directed at her alone – she knew. 'Thank you,' she mouthed to the Great Gateway.

The yacht passed into the impenetrable shadows. Then almost immediately the prow was again surging through a wide breach in a waterfall. They rowed out into a long fjord, whose rocky sides were almost as tall as the ones they'd just left behind in the First Realm.

Here in the Second Realm the sun burned with a blue-white brilliance that Jemima had to shield her eyes from.

And the land didn't curve up into a sphere as it did in the First Realm. The royal yacht left the fjord behind and rowed along the coast for several miles until it reached a vast estuary, over four miles wide. There were towns on both sides, with dozens of quays lining the banks. Buildings were made from a yellow stone, without any sharp edges; even the roofs were domes or arches.

'These are fishing towns,' Felix told Jemima as the yacht began to sail upstream, moving amid flotillas of smaller boats. 'And this is the river Zhila. It will take us directly to the capital.'

'Shatha'hal itself,' Lady Jessicara said proudly. 'Blossom Princess, you are soon to see the jewel of all Realms.'

The land on either side of the Zhila flattened out. Tall palm trees lined straight roads. Groves of trees separated by long irrigation canals stretched away into the distance.

The sun was so fierce that Jemima had to put on a floppy wide-brimmed straw hat. White canvas awnings were unfolded over the trolls to protect them from the heat as they continued their smooth strokes.

After an hour, mountains were rising out of the ochre landscape on either side of the Zhila. The farms gave way to raw desert, and still the royal yacht rowed on. They weren't the only boat on the river. Skiffs full of fruit were sailing along with them, fishing dinghies bobbed about. There were also sleek four-masted pleasure yachts slicing cleanly through the sparkling water, whose owners were clearly very rich. There were other craft, too: odd metal cylinders without sails that churned up a furious wake as they zipped about.

'How do they work?' Jemima asked. 'I thought it was only the Outer Realm that had engines.'

'Anamage contrivances,' Felix said, studying the metal boats with something approaching envy. 'They'll have artificial tails or some such under the water. I've seen them in the harbour.'

Jemima watched them keenly; it was the first display of anamage magic she'd seen. It seemed such a wonderful ability, the power to make inanimate objects move as you wanted.

On either side of the Zhila the mountains grew taller. Then Jemima noticed dark shapes up ahead wobbling in the heat-haze that covered the sand. She frowned, her sight revealing glimpses of the city hidden by the boiling air.

'That can't be right,' she murmured.

But it was. The trolls rowed them into a curving network of canals that flowered out from the main river. Around the ribbons of still water the elusive shapes of the city of Shatha'hal grew solid as they approached. Shatha'hal comprised seven gigantic buildings spread out across a stretch of irrigated desert. The two structures at the perimeter of the canal network were stone cubes a mile high with twisted edges as if they had slowly wound up out of the desert bedrock. Twenty colossal archways were cut into each side, stacked one above the other, granting glimpses of vast internal caverns. Then there was the tower, a white-marble cylinder ringed by a thousand garden balconies, that flared out to an elaborate onion-shape spire at the summit. In front of it were three spheres, measuring a good half-mile in diameter, arranged in a triangular formation. Their smooth surfaces were bejewelled with a million windows, while each had five river-sized waterfalls gushing from their equators, to cascade into lakes on the ground below. But most amazing of all was the building at the centre of the spheres. The heart of Shatha'hal was a colossal pyramid. But this pyramid sat upside down so its tip was the part that rested on the ground, presenting a massive square roof to the bright sky. Jemima's sight showed her the upper surface was covered in lush parkland vegetation, complete with deep pools, meandering streams, and pretty pavilions.

'Oh wow,' Jemima gasped. 'Why doesn't it fall over?'

'Because we built it not to, of course,' Lady Jessicara announced smugly.

'I had forgotten how extraordinary this city is,' Mum said in a subdued voice.

'You've been here before?' a dazed Taggie asked. She was so awed by the city she even forgot Lady Jessicara's pompous attitude for a moment.

Mum nodded. 'A long, long time ago. The Regent House Academy of Sorceresses ran an exchange scheme with the Royal Society of Anamages.'

The canal ran right to the bottom of the pyramid. As

they passed into the vast shadow cast by the pyramid above them, Jemima realized the water was now being carried by an aqueduct, which curved gently up on its supporting arches until it was rising vertically into a gaping maw in the side of the pyramid a hundred metres above the ground. Oddly the water didn't seem to be gushing down, it was as calm as the rest of the canal. Jemima saw some boats sliding casually along it – or rather up it – seemingly with no trouble. 'Oh, triple wow,' she gulped.

Sure enough, the trolls rowed the yacht along the aqueduct's upward curve as if it was the universe's slowest ever rollercoaster track. But for Jemima and everyone in it, the yacht still felt as if it was perfectly horizontal. Within a minute they were sliding up the vertical canal, and into the pyramid.

Inside, the pyramid was divided into eight levels, with amphitheatre walls of houses and shops and studios and public halls overlooking the main plaza floor that surrounded the massive central sunlight well. Every terrace's road thronged with people.

There were four aqueducts rising up through the interior around the edge of the sunlight shaft. Boats followed the yacht upward, and several slid down the other way. The yacht rowed up to the eighth level and turned on to a small aqueduct that twisted round to take them into the harbour pool of the pyramid's topmost and largest amphitheatre. The circumference was a wall of grandiose mansions and palaces, with the royal palace directly in front of the harbour pool.

'Uh-oh.' Jemima nudged Taggie. 'You're on.'

The largest mooring pier in the harbour pool was packed with solemn dignitaries. Behind them, gathered around the edge of the pool, a crowd of many thousands had gathered to see the famous Queen of Dreams, the terrifying warrior girl who had defeated the Karrak Lords.

Taggie stepped forward as the yacht pulled alongside the pier. She had changed into her arrival costume: a desert-style robe of bright white-and-blue cloth, one of a dozen that they'd hurriedly commissioned from Lorothain dressmakers. Finally she was dressed as smartly as Lady Jessicara.

King Manokol was at the head of the reception line. Taggie thought he looked terribly sad: a big man with a flowing beard, but who lacked any kind of joy. His wife, Queen Danise, was by his side, clad in mourning black. They were holding hands, drawing comfort from each other, but there was no hiding their sorrow.

As Taggie stepped on to the pier, a huge cheer went up. The crowd began waving, and colourful magic stars zipped through the air; some strange-sounding horns were blown loudly, adding to the din. She noticed a flock of odd little birds whizzing about above her. Except they weren't birds, she realized, not real ones. They were wonderfully made models, with slender bodies crafted from brass wire and sprouting colourful paper wings.

'Careful,' Felix warned. 'What the seespy birds see, so do their owners. And they're all looking at you.'

Taggie immediately straightened her back, becoming very self-conscious.

King Manokol gathered himself with an effort. 'Welcome, most sweetest Queen of Dreams,' he said.

'Thank you, my most gracious host, King Manokol,' she replied formally, as Mr Anatole had tutored her. 'I am honoured to finally be here in Shatha'hal, truly the jewel of all the Realms.'

At that the crowd gave another huge cheer. Taggie couldn't help waving at them despite the solemnity of the occasion. The cheer became even louder. Behind the King, his courtiers maintained their fixed smiles; none of them, it seemed, had anticipated how popular the Queen of Dreams would prove.

'Your pardon if I do not attend to you personally during your stay,' the King said. 'I have many guests, and I still mourn my beautiful son.'

'I understand,' Taggie said. She took his trembling hand, worried that he was about to start crying at the mention of Rogreth. 'If I could dream for you and ease your suffering, I would. Perhaps, sometime, you would care to visit the First Realm where I have that power.'

'You are most kind, my dear.' His voice became stern. 'But I will never lessen the pain, nor with it the memory. I will not lose purpose, for that is the hole they plot and scheme for me to fall into. You too, if you are not on your guard.'

'I will watch for the Karraks, fear not,' she said, feeling that this was what he needed to hear.

'You beat them once,' the King said. 'How the Realms rejoiced with that news. And now you are become our hope and inspiration, Queen of Dreams. How we pray a thousand – ten thousand – Karraks will soon burn in the same hellish light you unleashed upon them in the First Realm'

'Of course,' Taggie said uncomfortably.

The King gave her a sad smile. 'I have charged my second son, the Prince Lantic, to attend to your needs before the Gathering of Kings.'

'And Queens,' Taggie said levelly.

'And Queens,' he agreed. Then he frowned and looked round. 'Lantic? Confound it, boy, where are you?'

'Here, Father,' a wheezing voice said. The courtiers parted to allow a gangling boy through. At his appearance, the noise from the crowd finally started to ebb away.

Taggie guessed he was no more than a year or two older than her. His dark hair was stringy, and hadn't been cut for a while so it flopped over his eyes. The black tunic he wore obviously belonged to someone else, someone taller and broader; it would have been smart if it had been new, or even fitted. From the way he refused to look up and meet Taggie's gaze, it was clear he wanted to be anywhere else but here. She felt a burst of sympathy for him.

'Pleased to meet you,' Taggie said and held out her hand.

'Go on, boy,' the King growled.

'You are most welcome, Queen of Dreams,' Prince Lantic said. 'And we hope your laugh will fill our Realm.'

'Light,' the King snapped. 'Hope your *light* will fill our Realm. Stars preserve us, can you get nothing right?'

Prince Lantic hung his head, his cheeks flushing scarlet. 'Sorry, dear Queen,' he stammered.

'That's all right,' she said with a sympathetic smile. 'You can call me Taggie.'

Prince Lantic turned his head, as if to seek his parents' approval or guidance. He stopped, and looked directly at Taggie, making an effort to gather his courage. 'That's, ah, kind of you. I'd like that. Oh, er, and I'm just Lantic. To you! Obviously.'

'She knows that, boy,' King Manokol said, shaking his head in dismay. 'She was being polite to you. Heavens alone know why.'

Queen Danise put her hand on the King's shoulder. 'It's all right, my dearest.' She smiled at Taggie. 'My apologies. You do not find us at our best today.'

Taggie glanced at Lantic, who had turned bright red, and hung his head so he didn't have to meet her gaze. All the courtiers were now giving him disapproving looks. Had there not been so many people watching she would have given him a big hug there and then, and never mind royal protocol. 'I appreciate what you are going through,' she said. 'On behalf of the First Realm, I will do what I can to help.'

The King gestured to the cliff of fabulous mansions behind him. 'Let me walk you to your apartments, Your Majesty. You must be tired after your trip. And fear not, Lady Jessicara will also be part of your official escort here in Shatha'hal. You won't have to rely entirely on Lantic.'

'Your Majesty is most kind,' Taggie said, and tried not to groan at the prospect of being in Lady Jessicara's company for the rest of her visit.

5

FAMILY MATTERS

It was Prince Lantic who escorted Taggie and her entourage to the opening session of the Gathering of Kings (and Queens) later that afternoon. Mr Anatole and Lady Jessicara led the procession across the eighth level's grand plaza to the Hall of Council, which was a quarter of a mile from the mansion Taggie was staying in. The Hall's splendid central dome rose high above the other structures, almost reaching the curving ceiling above. Taggie and Prince Lantic were second in the line. Mum, Sophie and Jemima followed, with a squad of the King's Blue Feather regiment bringing up the rear.

Once again Shatha'hal's citizens were out in force to watch the foreign royals. Taggie could see several other similar processions marching across the giant plaza, all heading for the Hall of Council. To one side of her the water in the four aqueducts formed shimmering ribbons around the sunlight well, with boats sliding up towards roof level nearly quarter of a mile above – and other craft making their way down to the Zhila far below. She didn't think she'd ever get used to the way they defied gravity.

'It must have been amazing growing up here,' Taggie

said to the prince. 'There are almost as many anamage contraptions here as there are machines in the Outer Realm. Oh, is that the right word? "Contraptions"? I don't want to offend anyone.'

'It is,' Prince Lantic replied. '"Apparatus" is also acceptable; as is "contrivance" or "mechanism",' he added, growing bold. 'But you should never call what anamages produce a "gadget".'

Taggie gave him an encouraging smile. 'I'll try and remember that.'

'That's reserved for Outer Realm things.'

'And anamages look down on them?'

Lantic glanced round. 'In envy half the time,' he confided.

Taggie laughed.

'What's so funny?' he asked.

'Nothing. It's just that mages seem to be terribly conservative folk, no matter which Realm they're in.'

'I've never been to another Realm,' Lantic said. He shook his head, flicking his hair to one side so he could look at her. 'I'd so like to see the Outer Realm – and the First, too,' he said hurriedly. 'My brother used to tell me stories of the amazing machinery they have in the Outer Realm. He travelled to just about every Realm, apart from the Fourth, of course.'

'You miss him, don't you?' Taggie said kindly.

'Everybody misses him. He was the greatest prince ever. Soldiers fought to serve in his guard. Maidens fought over him, too, the daughters of the grand city barons were desperate to be seen on his arm at parties. The city nobility and the country gentry held him in the highest regard and sought his counsel on all matters. Everyone was delighted he was to be our King after Father.'

'And now that's you,' Taggie said encouragingly.

'Yes, which just adds to Father's despair.'

'I don't see why.'

'Ha!' he snarled bitterly. 'Do you know what they call me? "The ana-nerd prince".'

'Why?'

'I am good at our Realm's animation magic, Taggie, really I am. But nothing else. You need to know a lot more than how to rouse objects with magic to be King. People have to look at you and have confidence, and respect. That's not something I possess. I doubt even the Karrak Lords will bother to send their assassins to murder me.'

'Don't talk like that,' she said. 'You never know what you will become. I didn't even know the Realms existed until last year. Now look at me.'

'Yes, Queen of Dreams. Look at you. So many people do. You are adored wherever you go. I just get sneered at – that's if anyone can even be bothered to do that.'

'You don't have to be mean about it,' she said irritably. 'I just did my best. That's all anyone can do.'

'I apologize,' he said immediately. 'I meant no offence. Least of all to you.'

'It's all right. I'm just nervous about this Gathering, that's all.'

'Don't be.' He actually managed a sly smile. 'The royals in the hall are under your enchantment, not the other way round, I promise you.'

That was the first time Taggie had seen any kind of smile on his face. It was rather nice, she thought.

The Hall of Council had a grand cathedral-like outer chamber where all the royal parties were to be formally introduced to each other before the first session was called. Lady Jessicara announced she would perform the introductions as protocol required.

'How long before we meet the Highlord of Air?' Sophie asked eagerly, peering over the heads of the crowd. 'I've heard about his fledgling. He's supposed to be really handsome.'

'The Highlord and his party will be the sixth to be introduced to the Queen of Dreams,' Lady Jessicara sniffed. 'After the Fourth Realm's King in Exile.'

Taggie was taking a good look round the crowd herself. The costumes and gems on show were astonishing, as if every royal party was trying to prove its worth by its wealth. Stupid, of course, but she was relieved to be in a formal blue-and-white silk gown, which was weighed down by various pieces from the palace's royal jewellery collection, with an uncomfortably heavy tiara glittering on her head.

Over in the distance she saw a group of elves from the

Sixth Realm, which cheered her up. She caught sight of Earl Maril'bo among them, and waved eagerly until she saw Lady Jessicara staring. Earl Maril'bo winked.

Prince Andrew from the Outer Realm was there, representing the Queen. He gave Taggie a quick thumbs-up.

King Xalwen of the Ninth Realm loomed over everyone on the other side of the hall. He was a giant with lustrous green hair flowing down his back, taller even than the elves.

Lady Jessicara cleared her throat. 'Queen of Dreams, may I present Queen Judith of the Third Realm?'

Taggie stepped forward to face the sorceress queen. According to Mr Anatole, they were both supposed to bow to each other in unison, thus acknowledging they were of equal rank. Taggie bowed. However, the tall figure in opulent cream-and-gold robes facing her did not: she was staring directly over Taggie's shoulder. And when Taggie looked at her she was startled by just how similar that face was to . . .

'Sister,' the sorceress Queen said in a voice so cold it could have been mountain air. 'How delightful to see you again after all these years of your ignoble exile.'

'Sister,' Mum said in an equally vicious tone. 'The care of the throne weighs heavy on your shoulders, allowing you to mature so handsomely since we parted.'

Taggie's mouth dropped open. 'Sisters?' she gulped. 'You're kidding.'

'Oh, wow,' Jemima muttered, a wicked grin spreading over her face.

Queen Judith looked at Taggie for the first time. 'And this is your daughter, the famous Queen of Dreams. My niece, no less. What a lovely little thing you are, Agatha. Your mother must be very proud.'

Taggie bristled at the use of her correct name. There was something about Queen Judith that Taggie instinctively didn't like. The face might resemble Mum's, but that was where any closeness stopped. 'Nobody told me you were a Queen, Aunt Judith. In fact, nobody even told me I had an aunt.' And for the very first time in her life, Taggie had the courage to glare at her mother.

'The throne of the Third Realm is passed in strict rotation among the great houses of sorcery,' Mum said. 'My darling younger sister cannot pass the title on. Her good fortune is down to the luck of timing, not hereditary greatness.'

'What a joyous reunion this is,' a dismayed Lady Jessicara said. 'How lovely for all of you. Now, Queen of Dreams, the King of the Seventh Realm is awaiting your—'

'Hang on,' Jemima piped up in a voice that silenced Lady Jessicara and made everyone else look round. 'If you're the younger sister, how come you get to be Third Realm Queen? Shouldn't that have been Mum?'

Queen Judith apparently didn't hear. She and Mum were still locked in a combative stare.

'There is a limited time only until the opening session begins,' Lady Jessicara said desperately.

'When she was on her deathbed, our gracious mother named me as the true heir to our house,' Queen Judith said eventually.

'Indeed she did,' Mum replied levelly. 'So you see, Jemima, that's why I stood aside and retired to the Outer Realm.' She held up a finger, as if an afterthought of no importance had just come to her. 'Oh yes. Sadly no one other than your aunt actually heard your grandmother's dying nomination. I was abroad when it happened.'

Lady Jessicara's shrill nervous laugh filled the silence that was spreading out across the huge chamber. 'Please, Majesty, the King of the Seventh Realm . . .'

'I can wait,' a voice called out.

Queen Judith finally deigned to glance down at Jemima. Her expression indicated she might be looking at a cockroach in her soup. 'I've heard of you, too, Blossom Princess. The impetuous one. The seer. Did you see me coming, sweetie?'

Jemima's answer was a dark glower.

'Did you not train either of your daughters in the ways of our Realm, sister?' Queen Judith asked lightly.

'Not in your ways, sister.'

'Touché,' Queen Judith said. 'But the best news is that this happy family reunion is not yet over. Agatha, Jemima, may I present my daughter, Katrabeth?'

A girl in a splendid white satin dress stepped up beside

Queen Judith. A pretty face set with brown eyes produced a lopsided smile that was all mockery.

'Hello, cousin,' Katrabeth said sweetly.

'You!' Taggie yelled. It was the assassin.

6

EASILY EXPLAINED

'This is all very unfortunate,' King Manokol said.

'Unfortunate?' Taggie spluttered. 'She tried to kill me! She's part of this conspiracy.'

They had been taken to the King's private office in the Hall of Council, Taggie and her family squaring up to Queen Judith and Katrabeth. King Manokol and Prince Lantic stood between them.

'It is all a tragic misunderstanding,' Queen Judith said smoothly. 'That's all.'

'Rubbish,' Taggie spat.

'Let's all just sit down, shall we?' King Manokol said. 'Lantic, have some tea brought in. I'm sure we can clear this up.'

Taggie was about to shout that she wasn't going to sit down, or have tea, that she was jolly well going to have her say, and that Katrabeth should be flung in jail, and . . . and other things, too, when Mum's hand came down on her shoulder. It wasn't a heavy hand, but it seemed to drain the fight out of Taggie. With an exasperated grimace, she sat down on a long red velvet settee.

Queen Judith sat down opposite her, looking irritatingly serene.

'Would you like a cushion?' Jemima asked Katrabeth innocently.

'A cushion?'

'I thought you might still be sore,' Jemima continued earnestly.

'Sore?'

'Baaah!'

Katrabeth gave Jemima an evil glare.

'So exactly what misunderstanding allowed a sister of the Invisible Lodge, the greatest group of professional assassins in the known Realms, to try and murder Taggie?' Mum asked with icy fury. 'I'm most curious.'

'An unknown woman placed the contract,' Queen Judith said. 'She paid a huge amount of money to have my dear niece eliminated. Obviously, the Invisible Lodge didn't know she was an agent of the Karrak Lords. The Lodge Mistress assumed that there was some petty family squabble for the shell throne of the First Realm, and the Invisible Lodge had been brought in by a disaffected relative who sought to inherit. It's hardly the first time the Lodge has been involved in the royal succession in other Realms.'

'Not in the First Realm,' Mum said. 'And Taggie is your niece. How could you allow this?'

'Surely you remember your time before exile, sister? Sentiment is a particular weakness the Third Realm has long since expelled. Certainly it can play no part in the affairs of the Invisible Lodge. Once accepted a contract must be carried out.'

Taggie gave Katrabeth an incredulous look. 'You're a member of this awful Lodge?'

'I am a sister of the Invisible Lodge, yes,' Katrabeth said. Her aloof expression hadn't faltered the whole time in the lounge. It was as if she barely belonged to the crisis, rather than being the cause of it. 'As I am not to be Queen after my dear mother, I needed to find a suitable position in the Third Realm. The Invisible Lodge is most prestigious, and commands huge respect. It is also incredibly difficult to join.'

'What?' Taggie said in derision. 'You have to kill one of the existing sisters to get in?'

'Oh, you are familiar with our rules, after all.'

'Uh!' Taggie's jaw dropped open.

'Anyway, it is in the past now,' Queen Judith said. 'And no lasting damage is done.'

'Well that's a relief,' King Manokol said.

'Was it the Invisible Lodge who sent assassins after Prince Rogreth and Prince Fasla?' Jemima asked hotly.

'No,' Queen Judith said. 'The Invisible Lodge was only employed to eliminate Taggie. In a way it's a compliment, my dear. You were obviously the one the Karrak Lords considered most dangerous.'

'One small point,' Mum said. 'As I'm sure you recall, dear sister, once a contract has been accepted by the

Invisible Lodge, by their own rules it can only be revoked by the person who originally placed it. Has this mysterious agent of the Karraks done that?'

'No,' Katrabeth said in her sweetest voice. 'She has not.'

Taggie wanted to punch her.

'Then we have a very big problem,' Mum murmured.

'Not at all,' Queen Judith said. 'A royal decree can override even the rules of the Invisible Lodge; after all, it operates within the royal prerogative.'

'And you have issued such a decree?'

'When we discovered that the other royal heirs were also being murdered, it was obvious the woman who placed Taggie's contract must be an agent of the Grand Lord. I immediately revoked the contract. Happily so. After all, you are my sister – my blood – and she is my beloved niece. If only you had written to me and told me you now had children, all this unpleasantness could have been avoided.'

'Dearest cousin,' Katrabeth said, her hand going dramatically to her breast. 'I realized we must be related right after our encounter. It was such a terrible shock to me. Those fiends tricked us all. I hope you can find it in your heart to forgive me. I throw myself on your mercy.'

Liar! Taggie thought as she stared at her cousin's crestfallen expression with those treacherous trembling lips and wide eyes on the verge of fake tears. *Liar. Liar. Liar. Well, two can play that game.* She held out her hands in a pantomime of friendship and forgiveness to Katrabeth, who immediately took hold. 'Oh, you poor thing,' Taggie said magnanimously. 'To think I could have so easily killed you at your unsuccessful ambush.' Katrabeth's grip started to tighten. Taggie squeezed back just as hard. 'Now I know who you truly are, I'm so glad I spared you.'

Katrabeth was now going for a knuckle-crush, while Taggie was jabbing her thumbnails up into the girl's palms. Their linked hands began to fizz with faint blue light as their antagonism built.

Prince Lantic moved over to them, standing so his father couldn't see the gripping hands with their little bursts of hostile magic. 'Both of you are the reason why the Dark Lords and Ladies fear us so much,' he stammered. 'You embody the virtues that every Realm should dedicate themselves to.'

'Well said, boy,' King Manokol said in surprise.

'Let us not keep the other Kings waiting any longer,' Lantic said, and put his hand out, keeping his face expressionless as he held Taggie's gaze.

'Of course,' Taggie said, and stood up, letting go of Katrabeth to accept his proffered hand. 'And Queens.'

'And Queens,' Lantic confirmed.

A relieved King Manokol hurriedly offered Queen Judith his arm, and they led the way out of the study. Katrabeth followed dutifully one pace behind.

'Baa,' Jemima muttered.

Katrabeth's back stiffened, but she kept walking.

Taggie winced and shook the pain from her aching hands. 'Thank you,' she said to Lantic.

He shrugged his bony shoulders. 'We really do have to sort out the threat from the Karrak Lords and Ladies first.'

'Yes,' Taggie conceded. 'But when this is over, I swear I'm going to slap that smug, arrogant smirk right off my cousin's cutesy, conceited face, and hopefully all of her teeth with it. As the Heavens are my witness. Forgiveness indeed!'

Mum chuckled softly. 'So are you still cross with me for not ever taking you to visit my family before?' she asked.

Taggie let out a long sigh, wishing she didn't feel like a five-year-old again. 'Why didn't you?' she asked, trying not to let it sound too sulky.

'I didn't want to involve you in the whole dynasty fight, it's too vicious and lethal. Judith stole the throne a long time ago. I no longer care. And as I can't ever go back to the Third Realm without starting it all up again, I chose not to tell you and Jemima or teach you any Third Realm magic. Your father and I agreed the First Realm would be your destiny. Besides –' her face took on a puzzled expression – 'I never expected you'd ever encounter your aunt. I'm actually amazed Judith came here in person; her position has never been that secure. She knows a lot of the Third Realm houses question her ascension to the throne.'

'You mean there'll be a revolution while she's away?' Jemima asked in wonder.

'No,' Mum said. 'Not a revolution. The Third Realm doesn't work like that. If she shows any sign of weakness, a whole new batch of contracts will be placed with the

Invisible Lodge as the houses squabble for status and influence – and a squabble among Third Realm houses is a terrible thing. So her confidence must have grown since we parted. I wonder why . . .'

The Hall of Council's representation chamber was found beyond the huge reception chamber, below the massive dome itself. Broad oak desks were arranged in circles around the raised dais in the middle where King Manokol sat. Above his head, playing across the black shell of the dome, stars and comets and moons glowed as they moved around the vast hemisphere, reflecting what was happening in the skies above the Third Realm.

The Kings (and Queens) settled behind their desks, with their respective advisers sitting behind them.

'My fellow Kings,' Manokol began, his gaze flicking to Taggie, sitting directly in front of him, before he inclined his head at Queen Judith. 'And Queens. I bid you welcome to this esteemed Gathering. I only wish it could have been under different circumstances. But these are dark and terrible times. I myself have suffered enormous personal tragedy . . .'

Taggie stretched her feet out under the desk and did her best not to sigh. Mr Anatole had explained that the opening session was little more than a chance for each King or Queen to make a speech introducing themselves to the Gathering, and boast about how excellent their reign was. Only in tomorrow's session would they start to debate the new threat from the Karraks and what they were going to do about it. But first there was the formal banquet to be thrown by King Manokol tonight.

It was going to be a long day.

7

JEMIMA'S BIG DAY OUT

Sheer belligerent persistence on Jemima's part finally paid off. A whole afternoon and evening devoted to nagging, wheedling and pleading, all directed at Mum, finally resulted in her snapping, 'Yes, for heaven's sake, you can go out tomorrow. And don't blame me if an entire army of Invisible Lodge sisters come after you!' That was at eleven o'clock at night, after they arrived back at their mansion following the formal banquet. Mum had stomped off to bed, leaving Jemima smiling smugly.

So the next morning, when Mum and Taggie left for the Gathering, Jemima finished her breakfast by herself, then headed for the front door. Once again she tried to get her iPod to play, but it still wasn't working. Lady Jessicara had told her that the sheer quantity of magic pulsing through Shatha'hal always interfered with electrical items from the Outer Realm. Jemima missed hearing decent music.

'Where's Felix?' she asked Mr Anatole.

The old equerry gave her a weary smile. 'Felix has been granted a day off by your sister.'

'He has?' Jemima said in perplexity. She hadn't known that. Felix was somebody her sight could never quite grasp properly. She suspected it was a side effect from his curse; it took an exceptional wardveil to stop her from seeing someone.

'Yes, Princess. I believe it is his birthday today.'

'Oh!' Jemima pressed her lips together in annoyance. 'He never said.' Which was unusual: although he was a squirrel, and duty-bound to accompany her everywhere, she liked to think they were good friends.

'Did you need him?' Mr Anatole asked.

Jemima realized this was a perfect chance to be alone, and do whatever she wanted, for a change. How delightful. 'No, that's OK.' She smiled brightly at Mr Anatole, and opened the door. 'See you later.'

The plaza on the eighth level was broad and impressive, with lots of fountains and trees rising out of its marble floor. But not very exciting. Jemima wandered around for a while, watching the boats on the vertical canals – she still couldn't get used to that.

After half an hour of being on her best behaviour and nodding politely to people, she felt the urge to venture into the lower levels. She got down to level seven via a huge spiral ramp on the corner of the plaza – one of twelve such spirals, Lady Jessicara had told her when they'd arrived.

The seventh level's plaza was slightly smaller, although still over a mile across, but here the surrounding amphitheatre of buildings had some stores and cafes and arcades with market stalls. There were more people walking about, and children playing. Some of the open arches showed her glimpses of older children sitting in lessons. So school seemed to be the same no matter which Realm you lived in: a thought that depressed her.

She made her way down the wide stairs between terrace rings and on to the plaza floor itself. The gaping sunwell in the middle glared brightly, filled with dust and pollen and insects and birds; even some anamage bird contraptions flittered about. It illuminated the seventh level as if it was open to the sky, although the air was very dry and hot.

Jemima made straight for the next set of spirals. It was something she had to do: she just knew the lower levels were more appealing. She'd long ago learned to follow her instinct in such matters as it invariably came from her sight. As she went she kept looking round, a feeling of unease making her arms prickle. She stopped for a moment and shook her runes. The little black stones had been in Dad's family for generations, passed down between those who had the seeing talent. She examined how the stones had finished up in her palm, reading the symbols.

The story they told was of people following her: Lady Jessicara DiStantona, pretending to be shopping as she wore glasses enchanted to a small bejewelled seespy bird that circled high above Jemima; and hanging back some distance behind her was a squad of soldiers belonging to King Manokol.

Jemima pressed her lips together in annoyance. She supposed some kind of bodyguard was inevitable, given

the reason for the Gathering. At least they weren't trying to stop her going anywhere.

As she started down the next spiral she caught a glimpse of a boy, maybe fifteen years old, standing in a shop entrance fifty metres away. He was dressed in the usual long robes of all Shatha'hal residents, but what made him stand out was his long mane of white hair. That and the way he kept glancing in her direction.

Jemima stopped and looked back. The shop doorway was empty. She shrugged and kept going. The sight wasn't always accurate.

It was the fourth level where Jemima spent the most of her time. Here there seemed to be more shops and arcade markets than there were homes. It was also on the fourth level that she saw a gol for the first time. It was pulling a handcart full of heavy cloth rolls, looking like a suit of armour made from clay baked to a dull rust-red colour. Except she immediately knew there was no one inside; besides there were no eye slits in the bulbous head. Its limb joints were lined in brass that was tarnished from age. One of its knee joints squeaked softly.

'A stone robot,' she gasped in delight, as the thing clumped past her.

'It's called a "gol",' the owner of a small dress shop told her as she stood outside, watching the handcart go past.

'Oh. What are they?' Jemima asked.

'The anamages craft them. They do most of the heavy work here in the Second Realm. I have a couple myself to shift my biggest crates.'

'And they do whatever you tell them?'

'More or less. Each has its own command enchantment, so they only follow the orders of their owner. Instructing them is quite a skill – they can't think for themselves. And they don't move quickly, at least general labour ones don't; soldier gols are a lot faster.'

'Could they – oh, I don't know – tidy up my room?' The amount of times Mum shouted at her to clear up back home, a gol would be very handy indeed.

'That would require very detailed instruction. You'd have to be quite proficient with gol handling.'

'Shame,' Jemima sighed.

'You're the Blossom Princess, aren't you? I was there in the crowd when King Manokol greeted the Queen of Dreams.'

'Yes, that's me. The Queen of Dream's sister.' There wasn't too much bitterness in her voice, she thought.

'Can I interest you in some of my dresses? It would be a privilege to have you wear one. I'd be happy to offer a huge discount.'

'Really?'

As it turned out, the fourth level had a lot of small dressmaker shops, all of them filled with swish, colourful garments. Jemima spent a long time going between them. She wound up with several skirts, some blouses, a beautiful pair of glittering boots that were amazingly soft. Then she discovered the terrace of anamage houses. Each one had a grand master presiding over a hierarchy of masters, journeymen and apprentices. They laboured away in workshops at the back of the building, while their showroom was given pride of place at the front.

They were as fascinated to meet the Blossom Princess as she was to see their magical wares. Most of them had pot plants of fig trees, vines or cacti which she coaxed into full bloom for them. In return they offered her amazing deals, claiming they were losing money by selling to her at such a low price.

She watched a demonstration of a little wheeled insect which ate up dust and small bits of rubbish. Two of those went into her already heavy bag – if she couldn't get away with having her own gol, these would come in useful for her room back home. Then the next anamage house showed her seespy birds. She wore some glasses as the little contraption zoomed out over the plaza, and she could see everything from its viewpoint.

'Brilliant!' she applauded. That went in the bag. No hesitation there.

She went on to check out revealor glasses, like the ones

Felix had, that showed magical auroras. Staring out across the level she saw a remarkable number of people who glowed with power. 'Yep.' And how fun it would be when she spotted an approaching mage before Felix!

She blushed when the anamage also offered her a pair of glasses which he claimed would show if a boy was in love with her. But she handed over her coins and quickly stuffed them down to the bottom of her bulging bag. Then came butterfly hair clips that would carry braids aloft; and cloth that floated in air the way cork floated on water . . .

The next terrace down housed anamages who specialized in weapons. She didn't buy anything there, but she couldn't resist admiring the shining swords that could cut through enchantment shields; shields that could ward off any attack spells; throwing-knives that always hit the target; crossbows with a huge range, and repeat-fire bolt magazines; incredibly expensive armour, with tiny threads of *athrodene* woven in strategically to reinforce it (she wondered what that house would say about her own armour, which was completely made of *athrodene*). Halfway along the terrace she spotted Sophie, who was trying out crossbows that had clever, half magic, half mechanical devices to automatically reload bolts. The skymaid was quite a demanding customer, judging from the disgruntled face of the battlemage master. Jemima dodged away: she liked Sophie, but this was her day alone.

Eventually she wound up outside an anamage house that was showing off a dolphinous, which was like a personal swimming contraption that could speed you through the water. By then she didn't have enough money left for anything that expensive, though she was sorely tempted by the same house's skates that they claimed would work on any surface.

The next terrace down was mostly potion-maker stalls, which she rather fancied sampling. But when she reluctantly turned away from the skates, something like a cold flame lit inside her, making her shiver despite the desert city's warmth. Jemima instinctively knew she had to go further down Shatha'hal. She was getting a lot better at recognizing the guidance that came from her talent now, the difference between knowing things and mere impulse.

Just to make sure, she took out the runes and shook them in her hand. When she looked at the symbols and how they were arranged, there was no doubt. There was something odd on the lowest level of the city.

'Down I go then,' she muttered, as she tucked the runes back away into their little purse.

The lowest level of the upside-down pyramid was the smallest. But sunlight still shone brightly down the central well, illuminating the vines and creepers which scrambled over the stonework, bringing the level a lushness that was lacking in those above. Markets sprawling along the terraces favoured food, with chickens and sheep and pigs and geese, in cages and pens, squeaking and squawking away. The air was laced with exotic spicy scents and the smell of ripe animals.

Jemima stepped down on to the plaza floor. It was narrow, no more than a couple of hundred metres between the bottom terrace of buildings and the edge of the sunwell. A lot of that space was taken up with the canals that branched off the main aqueducts, leading to harbour pools.

Boats laden with crates and foodsuffs glided about sedately on the dark water. Jemima stood at the side of a canal, her head swivelling about as people jostled along behind her, paying her no heed. After a moment she set off without hesitation along the canal.

The harbour pool it emptied into went right up to the wall of the first tier of buildings. Big dark archways opened into warehouses, where cargo was constantly loaded and unloaded by dock workers and the gols they commanded. Normal boats and barges were tied up at the stumpy little quays, along with several of the unusual metal-cylinder craft. Jemima saw one at the back of the pool that was almost hidden in shadow, right beside a warehouse archway. Its hull was a dark shade of grey, and it thrummed quietly. There were three hatchways open along its upper deck, although nothing was to be seen inside, the holds were so dark. Not even Jemima's sight could show her what it was carrying.

Shadecast! she realized. That was what had drawn her down to this level: the boat was carrying something wrong. Something bad. Jemima knew she had to see what was inside, but the loading was nearly finished.

She was just about to take the seespy bird from her bag, and send it over the odd craft, when she saw two gols pick up crates from a pile just inside the warehouse and carry them to the metal vessel. There were only a couple of crates left.

'Curse it,' she grunted, and hurried forward.

For all her sight, it took her a while to notice that the looks of admiration and welcome she'd been given on the upper levels were absent now. Dock workers and ship crews directed sullen suspicious glances at her.

As she approached the metal craft, one of the crew supervising the gols caught sight of her. Jemima almost faltered then – the hostility coming from him was so great. Determination kept her going, because she knew neither Taggie nor Mum would ever stop and turn tail.

'What you want here?' a dock worker asked gruffly.

'Just looking,' Jemima replied airily, and scuttled past him.

Two more crew had appeared out of the craft's open hatches; heavy men with scowling faces. Finally their malice succeeded in putting her off. She'd almost reached the gangway up to the craft, but instead of going up she hurried along the quay to the warehouse archway. One of the gols was lumbering out of it, carrying the last crate. She sniffed the air, which had a smell that was almost familiar.

'Hey,' the dock worker shouted behind her. 'You! Girl. You not belong here.'

Jemima was right in front of the gol's ruddy clay body, and just knew it wasn't going to stop for her. She pressed back against the stone archway to let it clump past. As it did so, she put her hand on the rough wood of the crate, and closed her eyes. Shadowy images appeared behind her eyelids. Unfortunately the contents of the crate made little sense to her.

'*Sathrata*,' someone shouted. '*Princess ak!*'

The gol stopped, and began to turn. Jemima didn't need her sight to understand that this was seriously bad news. She darted off along the quayside the way she'd come.

A piercing whistle sounded loud above the shouting dock workers. Lady Jessicara DiStantona was blowing it, drawing a heavily enchanted dagger as she frantically directed the bodyguard squad onward. Led by their captain, the soldiers were sprinting along the quay towards Jemima, waving their arms and shouting at people to get out of the way.

Another gol, carrying a crate of oranges along the quay, suddenly dropped its load as Jemima drew close. Its blank head turned towards her. Clay arms stretched out. Jemima backstepped quickly, yelping as she ducked down. A heavy clay hand swept through the air where her head had been a second before. She rolled forward past it. A clay foot kicked – too late. It hit the stone wall behind her, sending chunks of masonry flying. Jemima squealed in fright at the strength of the contraption, and scrambled to her feet. There was fighting right along the quay now, with dock hands defending their territory against what they thought was an invasion by the authorities. Punches were thrown on both sides. Lady Jessicara performed an impressive judo throw, sending a thuggish man flying through the air. He crashed into a pile of sacks and baskets, toppling them on to his mates. Chickens flapped out of broken wicker cages and squawked madly. Two wrestling men fell over the side of the quay and into the water with a huge splash. Jemima barely noticed the hostilities that had erupted: every gol in the harbour pool had abandoned cargo duties and was heading towards her.

Jemima ran along the quay, hoping speed alone would be enough to get her clear of the clumping gols. If she could just get out of the harbour she might manage to lose them amid the markets.

One of the soldiers drew his sword, and took a mighty swing at a gol. The blade, whose elegant hieroglyphs glowed with purple enchantments, simply bounced off the contraption's clay chest. It ignored the attack and carried on toward Jemima.

Worried shouts were rising above the sounds of the mass brawl as dock workers realized a powerful enchantment had taken control of their gols. Twenty metres ahead of Jemima, three gols were heading down the quayside towards her. They pushed past a soldier, smacking him into a barrel as if he was no more than a bundle of fluff. Two terrified dock workers scrambled out of their way.

Jemima looked round wildly. There were gols ahead and

behind now. The stone wall along the side of the harbour pool offered no way out. She dashed up a gangway to a moored cargo yacht. Only when she stumbled on to the wooden decking did she realize there was no escape: the yacht measured barely fifteen metres from prow to stern, and there was nowhere to hide.

The first gol reached the gangway and put its foot on the worn planking. Jemima screamed.

Someone landed on the quayside behind the gol. It was the boy with the white hair, who had somehow jumped down the wall. He stood up with a savage smile on his face, and drew a sword whose blade shone with a vibrant green light.

Jemima wanted to shout 'That's no use!' but she was so terrified she couldn't even move, let alone open her mouth.

The boy stood behind the gol as it stomped up the gangway. He brought the sword up, and swung it in an almighty arc, cutting through the gangway's tough planks in one powerful sweep. Gangway and gol plummeted down into the water.

Jemima gasped in surprise. Bubbles were roaring up from the gaps around the gol's brass joints as the water poured into its hollow body. Its legs fell off, then the arms. Its head was last, bobbing away from the torso and sinking without trace.

The boy winked at her, and took a sharp step back as the remaining gols arrived. They lined up along the side of the quay, facing the cargo yacht in silence. Jemima stared back at them, but they didn't move.

Then the dock hands arrived and began frantically counter-charming the gols, bringing their contraptions back under control. Lady Jessicara waited until it was safe, and the gols were marched away, before allowing Captain Feandez of the bodyguard squad to lower another gangway out to the yacht. She was first across, putting her arm round a shaking Jemima and helping her back ashore. When Jemima had recovered enough to look round, the boy with the white hair had long since vanished.

8

THE LAIR OF THE ANA-NERD PRINCE

'What were you thinking?' Taggie stormed.

Jemima scowled sullenly over her cup of tea. It was one of Mum's herbal infusions, supposed to calm her.

'Clearly she wasn't,' Mum said.

'But what an adventure, eh?' King Manokol said in an admiring tone. 'Just the kind of devilishly exciting scrape princes and princesses are supposed to have.' His gaze flicked dismissively over Prince Lantic, who stood at one end of the mansion's lounge, his slim shoulders all hunched up. 'Decent ones, anyway.'

'I'm so sorry about my sister,' Taggie said.

Jem huffed herself up, ready to deny all blame in her loudest possible voice – but Mum raised a warning finger.

'No real harm done,' the King said, stroking his beard. 'You did the right thing nipping on to that yacht to dodge the gols. Gols can't survive being dunked in water – they're not even happy in rain. Something about their animation enchantments breaking up . . . Ask Lantic here if you want the truly boring details.'

'Someone chopped the gangway apart for me,' Jemima

said quietly. 'I still can't sight who it was. I want to thank him.'

'Captain Feandez of the Blue Feather regiment is looking for him,' King Manokol said. 'Don't worry, he'll find the boy. After all, the fellow's a hero.' Again there was disappointment directed in Lantic's direction.

'Did the harbourmaster inspect the cargo?' Taggie asked.

'Sadly not,' the King said, pulling thoughtfully on his beard. 'By the time order was restored, the boat had sailed. It's most strange, nobody saw it on the Zhila afterwards.'

'I know they were using a shadecast in the cargo hold,' Jemima said. 'Maybe they expanded it to cover the whole craft.'

'Most likely,' the King said. 'But what with all the anamage contrivances we have to see through such enchantments these days, you'd think someone would have spotted the blighters. Apparently not. Which means the Blossom Princess was right to be curious. There was definitely some skulduggery involved, most likely contraband or unpaid fees. Some of those smaller boat captains are a troublesome lot, barely more than pirates.'

'Well, I thank you for your understanding,' Taggie said.

'Quite all right.' The King smiled at Jemima. 'Next time, give my officers some warning before you go gallivanting off after criminals, eh?'

'Yes, Your Majesty,' Jemima said in a respectful tone, which didn't fool Taggie for an instant.

King Manokol bowed courteously to Mum, who politely allowed him to take her arm. They swept out of the lounge together, with Lantic scuttling after them.

'Don't ever do anything like that again,' Taggie said to Jemima after the door had closed.

'Don't try and boss me about,' Jemima snapped back.

'Do you understand what you've done?'

Jemima held her head up defiantly. 'Uncovered a bunch of smugglers. The King was grateful.'

'No,' Taggie told her. 'You put us in the King's debt. Which he will no doubt remind me of if there's a vote in the Gathering for which he needs support.'

'Oh,' Jemima said, abashed. 'Sorry. I didn't think of that.'

There was a whole lot Taggie could have said on that subject, but nothing that hadn't been said a thousand times before. And it had never made any difference before.

'I had to go to that harbour pool, Taggie. I knew something bad was happening there. I just did.'

'I know.'

Jemima produced a sheet of paper. 'This is what I saw in the crates,' she said hopefully. 'Do you know what it is?'

Taggie took a look at the pencil sketch. It was typical Jemima: all quick and messy, with lines crossed out. She couldn't make much sense of it: a narrow cylinder with a ring at one end, and some kind of crude metal attachment at the other. 'I have no idea,' she said. 'It's got to be some kind of anamage contraption.'

'We have to find out,' Jemima implored. 'Please, Taggie, it's important, I know it is.'

Taggie sighed. There were times when Jemima was the ultimate annoying little sister, but . . . she couldn't stand the idea that one day the two of them would wind up like Mum and Aunt Judith. 'I suppose we could ask someone who knows all about the anamage art,' she said, with a slow smile spreading across her face.

Captain Feandez clearly didn't approve. That much was obvious from the way he walked, with a rigid back, and that he said nothing other than a curt 'Yes, Majesty' when Taggie asked him to take them to Prince Lantic. His face was also expressionless, which was strange, given that most of it was covered in tattoos of serpents and eagles that wriggled round each other.

He led them down a wide marbled cloister in the palace. One side had open window arches looking out across the river Zhila as it cut through the desert away to a shimmering horizon. When Taggie went over to one of the arches for a better look, there was nothing below her at all. It was a very long fall to the desert below. She felt the weird tingling of vertigo in her legs.

'Majesty, this is the prince's study.' Captain Feandez stood at a tall door inlaid with ceramic tiles depicting some kind of sea monster.

'Thank you,' Taggie said gracefully.

Captain Feandez knocked. There was no answer. He knocked harder.

'Come in.'

The captain opened the door, bowing. But not quickly enough to hide the flash of disapproval on his face. Taggie wondered who it was directed at.

Prince Lantic's study wasn't what she'd been expecting. Instead of some cosy bookshelf-lined room with a fireplace and leather wingback chairs, she found herself in a hemispherical stone chamber with several deep alcoves around the edges, one of which held a furnace. Overhead, five big window wells let in strong shafts of sunlight. There were several workbenches on the floor, along with other big wardrobes, chests and freestanding shelves that were scattered around at random. Every flat surface was occupied, mostly by a bewildering array of tools or glassware, some of which was bubbling or puffing out vapour. But there was also a disorganized clutter of anamage contraptions – little insect figures and clockwork devices, all in various stages of assembly (or disassembly). Crystal globes sparkled with odd colours, several of them floating just above a brass plinth, like a miniature solar system. Anamage birds, barely bigger than butterflies, skittered through the air, while things crawled, rolled and waddled across the floor. And the smell . . .

'Foo!' Jemima said, waving her hand in front of her face. 'What is that stink?'

Taggie's eyes were watering from the acrid smell.

'Hello?' She couldn't see Prince Lantic anywhere.

'Hello,' Lantic's voice called out.

'We need to ask you something.' Was he standing behind one of the cabinets?

'Um, Taggie . . .' Jemima said.

'Sure, no problem,' Lantic said.

Taggie prodded a brightly painted copper fish on one of the benches. It burped out a bubble, and wiggled through the air to cower behind a spherical aquarium. Taggie peered forward. There was an eyeball in the middle of the aquarium, staring back at her. She took a pace back. 'Wow! Do you craft all this stuff yourself?'

'Taggie!' Jemima's teeth were clenched together. She was looking up.

With her spine tingling, just like her legs had with the vertigo, Taggie tipped her own head back to stare at the curving roof of the chamber. Prince Lantic was riding a bike. It was something Taggie imagined an Edwardian gent would have – half elegantly carved wood, half crude iron struts. But the major difference was that it was scooting along upside down, directly above her. This didn't seem to bother Lantic at all. He waved down cheerfully. That was when Taggie realized his clothes weren't falling down – or should that be up?

'Hang on,' he said, and turned a sharp curve round one of the window wells to pedal down the side of the chamber.

Taggie gave him a sincere smile when he stopped in front of her. 'That's impressive,' she said.

'It's an olobike,' he said breathlessly. 'I just added a few ideas of my own, like the climbing enchantments.'

'Clever.'

He wheezed out a cough, and flicked his hair away from his eyes. 'Thank you. Would you like to try one? I've got another. I was experimenting.'

'I'd love to, but not right now.' She didn't know what it was about him, but he seemed so much more confident in here. No father constantly criticizing him, she supposed.

He grinned back at her.

'I need to know what this is,' Jemima announced.

Lantic jumped like he'd been jabbed by a pin. He blushed. 'What *what* is?'

Jemima found a relatively clear patch on a bench, and

unrolled her sketch. 'This is what I saw in the crates at the dock. Do you know what they are?'

Lantic put on some glasses and bent over the paper to examine it. 'How big was this thing?' he asked.

'That bit was about two feet long,' Jemima said, pointing to the cylinder.' And it was made from stone, or maybe china. Something like that.'

'Clay?'

'Could be. Yes.'

'What about this ring?' Lantic asked.

'Brass, I think,' Jemima said. 'Possibly copper. I can't be sure – I was seeing through the crate.'

'You were?' Lantic asked.

'Yes.'

'Your sight is a powerful one, Blossom Princess.'

'Thank you. This bit at the other end, that was iron, I think, definitely different from the ring.'

Lantic ran a hand over his brow, face all scrunched up as he stared at the sketch. 'This part –' he indicated the cylinder – 'I would have said is a gol forearm. But this, where the hand should be –' his finger tapped the iron attachment – 'I've no idea what that is, I've never seen anything like it. All I can think is it might be a part of some machinery such as you would build in the Outer Realm.'

Taggie gave the drawing an uneasy look. 'Outer Realm machinery never works too well in the other Realms, especially somewhere with as much magic as Shatha'hal.'

'Simple machines work here,' Lantic said. 'Mechanical

systems, things that don't require your electricity to power them. I know this. About a century ago, some farmers further up the Zhila used steam-powered traction engines to plough their fields. They were brought here from the Outer Realm.'

'What happened to them?' Taggie asked in fascination.

'They were expensive to use, compared to gols. We don't have your coal mines, so their coal had to be imported as well. Eventually they fell into disrepair. One of them now stands in the Hall of the Royal Society of Anamages. It is a required study for students. I remember being very impressed, for it is such a sturdy thing.' He took off his glasses to reveal a wistful expression. 'How I would love to see the machines the Outer Realm has these days. Rogreth told me that the traction engine is but a toy compared to their modern contrivances.'

'Your brother was right,' Taggie said. 'The Outer Realm has much better today. There are millions of cars, but they cause a lot of pollution, so scientists are developing hydrogen power and electric—'

Jemima suddenly clapped her hands together. 'Diesel,' she announced.

'What?' Taggie gave her an annoyed glance. Talking with Lantic had been easy; he was clearly growing used to her.

'You talking about cars reminded me,' Jemima said. 'I smelt diesel fumes coming from the smuggler's boat.'

'Are you sure?'

'Yes. It was vibrating and making a rumbling noise. That wasn't an anamage craft with a tail: it was using a diesel engine. A metal cylinder with a diesel engine. Taggie! It was from the Outer Realm. And that odd shape, Taggie, it was just like a submarine.'

'Impossible,' Taggie said immediately.

'Why?' Jemima demanded hotly. 'It makes perfect sense. Nobody saw it on the Zhila afterwards. Even the King admitted that was odd. But they wouldn't have seen it if it was underwater.'

'It can't have been from the Outer Realm,' Taggie insisted.

'Why not? Lantic just said they imported traction engines once upon a time.'

'But . . . what was it doing here?'

'Smuggling,' Jemima said with a huge smile. 'We know that.'

'But smuggling what?' Taggie looked at Lantic, who gave Jemima's sketch a further confused glance.

'I don't know,' he said. A smile to match Jemima's spread over his face. 'But we need to find out,' he said resolutely. 'I don't like the idea of Third Realm anamage contraptions being combined with Outer Realm machinery. To me that speaks of someone trying to gain a huge advantage over their rivals. Travel to the Outer Realm is strictly limited for a reason, and bringing back artefacts is even more difficult. It requires royal approval.'

'How many crates were on board?' Taggie asked.

'I'm not sure,' Jemima said. 'Dozens. '

'I can ask round the anamage colleges and houses,' Lantic said. 'See if anyone has been placing unusual orders for gol parts. And I will summon the city's harbourmasters, discover if craft like this one have berthed in Shatha'hal before.'

Taggie grinned at him. It was nice to see him so enthusiastic for once.

'I have a friend who is about the best art student in the city.' Lantic held up Jemima's sketch. 'Can you describe this in real detail to him? We need to get a better idea of what it can be used for.'

'Absolutely.'

'And I must consider incorporating seespy lenses into anamage fish. Craft that travel under the water – how wonderful.' Lantic seemed captivated by the idea.

'All right,' Taggie said, and held up both hands to try and calm things down. 'I have to go back to the Gathering for the afternoon session. Jemima, if you go out again, make sure you tell Captain Feandez, understood? He'll give you an escort.'

'Yes!' Jemima said petulantly.

Taggie wished Felix was back: the squirrel was the best person in all the Realms for keeping Jem out of trouble. But she could hardly begrudge him his birthday off.

9

THE SURPRISE PRISONER

By midday of the third day, the Gathering of Kings (and Queens) had accomplished very little, Taggie thought. They'd praised themselves a lot, and shouted angrily about the Karraks' attempts to hunt down and murder the princes and princesses (their children). Apart from that, nothing had been accomplished. It was the mood she worried about. Nobody seemed interested in why the Karrak Lords and Ladies would do such a thing, the only topic the Kings (and Queens) wanted to discuss was vengeance.

That bothered her a great deal; so much so, she asked King Manokol for the floor at the afternoon session. Public speaking wasn't her strong point – she hated the school debating club – but she felt she just couldn't say nothing while the others grumbled about war.

'We must be careful who we accuse,' she told the assembled dignitaries, trying not to shift about on her feet. Standing in front of King Manokol's dais, looking at the semi-circle of her fellow royals was an intimidating position. They didn't seem to be listening so much as judging. She clenched her hands behind her back to stop them trembling with nerves. 'It is easy to blame the Karraks for every misfortune we suffer. But they are not the only force of darkness at work in the Realms today.'

'Did anyone else usurp the First Realm last year?' King Iaswian of the Fifth Realm shouted; his naturally red face seemed even darker.

Taggie blushed. 'That is not the issue we are here for,' she countered in a shaky tone. 'There has been much talk of using armies and force. I have even heard the word "invasion" used.'

'And rightly so,' King Saraga said sharply. The King in Exile of the Fourth Realm was in his twenties, a big man who liked to tell anyone who listened about his prowess as a hunter and fighter. Taggie was worried by how aggressive he was the whole time. But then his family had been waiting for an opportunity like this for a very long time. 'We should not be afraid of using force. The Grand Lord certainly isn't.'

'But what actual proof do we have that the Karraks are behind these murders?' Taggie shot back.

'My son is dead,' the Queen of the Sixth Realm said in a shaken voice. 'Fasla was fourteen years old. Who else would do that to a child?'

'I don't know,' Taggie said meekly, unable to look at the Queen, who she knew was on the verge of tears. 'But I do know the assassin sent to kill me wasn't a Karrak Lady.'

Queen Judith rose from her seat. 'Just what are you suggesting?'

'You told me yourself,' Taggie said desperately. 'You didn't know who placed the assassination contract on me.' The rest of the Gathering all seemed to be glaring at her.

'I said we weren't aware at the time,' Queen Judith said.

'Do you know now?' Taggie asked. 'Did you find the woman?'

'No, she has vanished. No doubt back to the Fourth Realm from whence she came.'

'You don't *know* that,' Taggie continued, despite the tremble that had crept into her voice as she opposed the impassive sorceress Queen. 'None of this makes any sense,' she appealed to the circle of royals regarding her impassively from behind their broad oak desks. 'Why would the Karrak Lords and Ladies do this? How would they possibly benefit? All they are doing is stirring our anger. Is it not more likely to be driven by something else?'

'There is no other dark power at work in the Realms,' King Manokol said lightly. 'Dear Queen, perhaps you should take your seat again.'

'But you don't know there's nothing else at work here,' Taggie cried, hating the way her voice had risen, but she was cross now as well as angry. And these royals seemed to be able to argue much more convincingly than her. 'Please, we must have proof the Karraks are behind this before we do anything rash. We must examine the assassinations themselves and who really carried them out. We must find the reason behind them.'

'But we have none of the assassins,' King Saraga said.

'The cowards have vanished back into the darkness from which they came.'

'Actually, not all of them,' Queen Judith said levelly.

The representation chamber fell utterly silent.

Taggie turned round to face Queen Judith. 'What?'

Queen Judith ignored her. 'My dear friends, even my house was subject to this atrocity the Karraks are committing. In the hours before we departed for this esteemed Gathering, an attempt was made on my own precious daughter's life.'

A startled murmur swept round the hall. Taggie gave Queen Judith a suspicious glance.

'I am proud to say my Katrabeth thwarted the attempt.' Queen Judith gave Taggie a mirthless smile. 'I believe the Queen of Dreams wanted to talk to an assassin? Is that right, child?'

'I . . .' Taggie knew that somehow she'd been completely outsmarted. She wanted to run back to her desk, or preferably out of the chamber altogether. Bizarrely, all she could think of was Lord Golzoth turning away in the seconds before she'd unleashed the full power of the First Realm's sun to obliterate the Karrak Lords. He'd known he was about to lose, and he'd fled in time to save himself. Some small reserve of courage made her stand her ground.

Queen Judith bowed to King Manokol. 'I bring you a gift, my most gracious host.' She raised a hand and clicked her fingers in summons. The great doors to the representation chamber swung back. Like everyone else,

Taggie craned forward to see what was being brought in. Some kind of box, ten feet a side and draped with red silk, glided forward through the air. Katrabeth walked in front of it, dressed in the opulent robes of her family house, her face perfectly composed. Four older sorceresses walked alongside the box, each holding a black staff that crackled with magical energy. Taggie had to scuttle out of the way as the box slid to a halt in front of King Manokol.

'Behold,' Queen Judith proclaimed in a triumphant voice. 'Katrabeth's would-be assassin.'

Each of the sorceress guards turned to face the box, and held up their staffs. Katrabeth crooked one finger and beckoned. The red silk slithered to the ground, revealing a glass cage. Taggie, along with everyone else, gasped in shock at the figure hunched up inside. It was a Karrak Lady.

Nobody noticed Taggie slinking back to her chair. She hadn't wanted to see a Karrak again for as long as she lived, let alone be so close to one. This one wore the usual silver-hewed mist gown of the Dark Ladies, which swirled around her body, protecting it from the light. Her face had the whitest skin, stretched tight over her skull and around the thin nose with its single nostril. Unlike those Taggie had dealt with last year, she had no sunglasses. So for the first time Taggie could see the sunken eyes which seemed to be slits opening into a starless night sky.

'Why didn't she bring her out yesterday?' Taggie whispered to Mum.

'Timing is everything, especially in political strategy,' Mum answered. 'She was waiting for the best moment to strike, and you gave it to her.'

'But . . . this Gathering is supposed to bring everyone together, so we can help all our peoples as best we can,' Taggie protested.

Mum shook her head sadly. 'Oh my dear, thank the Heavens you were never born into the Third Realm. You wouldn't have lasted a week.'

Queen Judith took King Manokol's hand and led him gently towards the glass cage. 'You,' she said forcefully. 'Your name.'

The Karrak Lady stirred. Long bone fingers emerged from the sleeves of her mist gown to flex slowly. 'Lady Dirikal,' she hissed. 'Would you like me to bow as well, to complete your pitiful theatre?'

'Your kind will do more than bow to us before this is over,' Queen Judith said.

Lady Dirikal lunged forward, smashing into the side of the glass cage amid a blizzard of magical blue light unleashed from her fingertips. The sorceress guards were ready for her, thrusting their staffs forward. Emerald counter-spells streamed out and flared across the glass. The Karrak Lady staggered back, growling and snarling like an injured wolf.

Queen Judith hadn't even flinched. 'Tell us why you were in the Third Realm,' she commanded, as if nothing had happened.

Lady Dirikal slowly tilted her head to one side, regarding

Katrabeth contemptuously. Her dainty silver-tipped teeth grew into long fangs. 'To kill you. As we will kill all of your kind.'

Taggie gazed at her in amazement. She couldn't believe what she'd just said. The Karraks were the masters of treachery. They would never mount such a brazen attack. It was beyond stupid. And yet she'd just heard Lady Dirikal admit it.

'I believe,' Queen Judith said silkily, 'that settles any question of doubt.' She turned to give Taggie a victory smile that was mostly a sneer. 'Even for the most sceptical among us. My friends, you have heard the truth from this creature. But of course, you are free to ask it what questions you wish.'

Lady Dirikal had followed Queen Judith's gaze. She opened her mouth wide, a predatory hiss exhaling a long stream of grey icy breath as her empty eyes found Taggie. 'Ah, the Abomination herself,' she hissed. 'Ignore this Queen's foolish theatre, Abomination. It means nothing. You will die. You will all die. And all we will remember of you is your screams at the end.'

Taggie started to get up. She wanted to ask Dirikal a question. The most important question of all: *Why?*

Mum's hand came down on her knee. And Taggie couldn't move a single muscle.

'Not a word,' Mum whispered through unmoving lips. 'We are outmanoeuvred. For now. Do not weaken our position further.'

The King of the Fifth Realm stood to face the Gathering. 'Friends, only once before have the Realms been subject to such a perilous threat as we have been shown this day. Our revered ancestors faced the full might of the Dark Lords and Ladies before at the Battle of Rothgarnal when Mirlyn's Gate was bravely taken from them. I say we must respond to this new peril with the same absolute resolution of our ancestors. I nominate King Manokol as the War Emperor, that we may place the armies of every Realm under his command.'

Standing in front of the imprisoned Karrak Lady, King Manokol bowed in dignified gratitude to the King of the Fifth Realm.

King Saraga stood and punched the air vigorously. 'So say I!' he shouted eagerly.

'And I,' Queen Judith added serenely.

The call went round the chamber. Only Prince Andrew abstained, along with Taggie, while everyone else endorsed the proposition. Taggie was now free to move. But she sat motionless at her desk, saying nothing.

'I will not fail you, friends,' King Manokol said, with tears of pride and gratitude leaking down his cheeks. 'Together our armies will be unstoppable. We will storm the Fourth Realm, and finally throw the Karrak vermin into a darkness beyond even that which spawned them. A darkness from which no one returns. The King in Exile will be King again. This I swear to you.'

Taggie stared at the Karrak Lady. In turn, Dirikal hadn't

stopped looking at her – despite the anger raging around the chamber, despite the Kings and Queens promising to exterminate all her kind. Somehow Taggie knew the only victory in the chamber somehow belonged to Lady Dirikal. 'I will know the truth,' she told her foe soundlessly.

10

QUESTIONS ANSWERED

'There have been several sightings of the submersible craft,' an excited Prince Lantic said when Taggie arrived back at his hemispherical chamber. 'It's been visiting Shatha'hal for at least a couple of years, according to the harbourmasters. There might even be more than one of them.'

Jemima waved a big sheet of paper in front of Taggie. 'And this is a much better drawing of the gol arm.'

'Not that I understand the attachment yet,' Lantic said with a momentary flash of gloom. 'But once my friends from the anamage houses reply to my queries I might have a better idea of what it is they're all for.'

Taggie ignored their jabbering, and picked some books off a chair so she could sit down. 'Sorry,' she said. 'But we're facing something a lot more serious than some smuggling.'

Lantic nodded slowly once she'd finished explaining about the incredible prisoner and the last vote that had been taken at the Gathering. 'It's what my father wanted right from the start,' he said. 'That's the real reason he called the Gathering, in the hope he could somehow convince the other Realms to invade the Fourth Realm and take his war to the Karraks in their dark citadel. It's how he aims to avenge Rogreth's death.'

'And my aunt gave him the perfect excuse,' Taggie groaned.

'I think "excuse" might be the wrong word,' Lantic said meekly. 'The Karrak Lady was captured while trying to kill Katrabeth, after all.'

'Why her, though?' Jemima said.

'What do you mean?' Lantic asked.

'Katrabeth doesn't inherit the throne of the Third Realm. When Queen Judith dies, the crown of the Third Realm will pass to the next sorceress house on the list. In all the other Realms the Dark Lords have hunted down the princes, the heirs. Even Taggie was technically the heir, because Dad is the regent governor.'

'Oh,' Lantic said. 'Yes, I see what you mean. That is odd.'

'Queen Judith is up to something,' Taggie said through tight lips. 'I know she is. She and Katrabeth are in this together.'

'In what?' Lantic asked.

'I don't know.' Taggie turned to look at him. Lantic seemed to squirm on the spot, the way he did when his father stared at him. 'I need to talk to Lady Dirikal. There are things I have to ask her.'

'I . . . I'll talk to my father for you, of course,' the prince said. 'I'm sure he'll let you see him.'

'No,' Taggie said. 'I need to speak with Lady Dirikal

alone. I don't want anyone else there twisting things. There's been enough of that, enough politics, in the Gathering.'

'I don't think Father will agree to that.'

Taggie stood up and approached the prince, ignoring the panicked expression on his face as she stood directly in front of him. 'If Rogreth wanted to visit Lady Dirikal in private, how would he do that? Would he meekly ask the King's permission?'

'No. But . . . but . . .'

'You are his brother, you know. He'd be expecting you to do your duty. I'll bet he didn't treat you the way everyone else here seems to, did he?'

'No,' Lantic mumbled.

'And would he go marching off to a war where thousands of people are going to die, and not be certain about why it's being fought?'

'Well, obviously not,' Lantic said, refusing to meet her gaze.

'So. We have to do whatever we can to find out the truth. And if that means sneaking a visit to a Dark Lady . . .' The charmsward bands spun softly inside the folds of her sleeve. An enchantment to bestow courage was on the tip of her tongue.

'I'm not sure,' Lantic said miserably.

Taggie subtly let the enchantment slip through her fingers into Lantic, smiling reassurance as she did it – ignoring the startled look Jemima was giving her.

'Actually, yes,' Lantic announced with a sudden air of determination. 'You're right. This is exactly the kind of thing he used to do.'

'Right then,' Taggie said, as if she was impressed by his resolve. 'Now how would he go about getting in to see Dirikal?'

'One of his best friends, Bromani, is a lieutenant with the palace guard,' Lantic said boldly. 'He might help me.'

'Then please could you go and ask Lieutenant Bromani? We need to know this, Prince. We must uncover the truth.'

'Yes,' Lantic nodded. 'Yes, Queen of Dreams, I will do this, I will take you to the prisoner. I swear it.'

Three hours later, Taggie, Jemima, Sophie and Felix were following Lantic along the stone passages in the vaults below the palace. The courage enchantment was clearly still working: Lantic didn't hesitate as he led them through the maze of corridors until they were finally outside a pair of large metals doors, inset with runes that glowed with binding enchantments. Two tall gols stood guard outside, holding axes that looked like they could fell an oak tree with a single blow. Jemima flinched at the sight of them. Lieutenant Bromani was waiting beside the doorway – a handsome young man in the blue-and-green uniform of the palace guard. As he caught sight of them, he looked nervous, darting glances along the passageway.

'I thought you said just the Queen of Dreams,' he hissed

at Lantic. 'I can't allow all these children and a . . . *squirrel* in there as well!'

Felix's tail flicked in annoyance.

'I thank you for granting me a moment with the prisoner,' Taggie said in her 'royal' voice – which was basically as posh as she could manage without giggling. 'I will not endanger your favour by taking my friends inside. They can wait here and keep watch.'

Bromani didn't seem happy with the notion. The charmsward bands turned quietly around Taggie's wrist as she prepared an enchantment to make him more amenable.

'Taggie!' Jemima hissed in disapproval.

'Majesty,' Felix said more forcefully. 'I am responsible for your safety.'

'I believe I have shown I can take care of myself when it comes to the Karraks,' Taggie said firmly. She smiled politely at Bromani, and rested her hand on his arm. The obedience enchantment slithered into him. 'That will be satisfactory, surely? There will be no risk.'

He still didn't look happy, but came to a decision. 'Very well. You may have five minutes,' he said. 'No more.'

'Thank you.' Taggie avoided the suspicious stare Jemima was directing at her.

Bromani placed both hands on the doors, and chanted a long invocation. The glow changed to a flickering purple, and one of the doors swung back slightly. Taggie slipped through the gap. Lantic followed, with Bromani just behind him – Taggie didn't protest, even though she could have done without the guard officer present.

The vault was a simple circular space with stone walls, carved with runes similar to those on the door. They glowed with blue enchantments so intense it was almost violet. The glass cage sat in the middle, with worms of scarlet magic slithering with slow menace across the surface. Ten gols stood guard around it, holding enchanted swords and magical sceptres ready should the prisoner attempt to escape.

A lone window well in the roof shone a shaft of sunlight directly on the cage and its occupant who cowered within it. Her body was shifting constantly as she sought to avoid the light, but there was no escape. A relentless growl of suffering came from her throat.

Lady Dirikal's head snapped round as Taggie came into the vault. 'The Abomination,' she purred. 'I am honoured. Have you come to gloat?'

Taggie took a moment to gather some courage; for all her bravado in front of the others, the Karrak Lady still frightened her. 'I'm not a Karrak, so no,' she told Lady Dirikal, and lifted her hand, the charmsward bands sliding round. '*Hanyal.*' The bright sunbeam bent in mid-air, leaving the cage in gloom. Taggie made herself walk over to the glass, steeling her face so she showed no fright. 'Is that better?'

Lady Dirikal hissed softly as her body stilled. 'Do not think I will thank you, Abomination. I know what fate awaits me when the King comes next to visit. Though I expect there will be many such visits before he is done.'

'Is that fate worse than that which Lords Golzoth and Jothran planned for me and my family?' Taggie growled back.

Lady Dirikal tossed her head back. 'Grand Lord Amenamon was concerned at the rise of your power, Abomination. If I see him again, I will tell him not to worry, for you are as weak-minded as all humans. The power he fears is certainly less than that of your cursed aunt and her diabolical offspring.'

'Thanks to you, Katrabeth tried to murder me. Was that your idea, to award the Invisible Lodge that contract?'

Lady Dirikal turned back and opened her mouth so her silver-tipped teeth could grin mockingly. 'It amused us.'

'Why are you doing this? Why hunt down the heirs?'

'To weaken you. The royals of the Realms are the residue of the mages from the First Times, the true protectors of the Realms. Without you, the Realms will fall, and we will claim them for our own.'

Taggie shook her head slowly. 'I don't believe you.'

Lady Dirikal snarled, lungeing forward – but the glass cage held her easily. The soldier gols didn't even move.

Taggie was pleased with herself for not flinching. 'Oh, come off it,' she said. 'Upstairs in front of the Gathering you called that kind of antic "theatre".'

The soft laugh which came from the cage was a lot more disturbing than the snarling could ever be. 'My mistake, Abomination. You do grow. Perhaps you will yet share your aunt's desires and cunning.'

'The Gathering voted King Manokol to become the new War Emperor. You know what that means, don't you?'

'It is the start of the war which has been inevitable since Rothgarnal. Before too long, there will be a

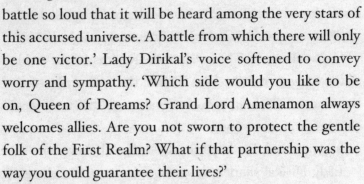

battle so loud that it will be heard among the very stars of this accursed universe. A battle from which there will only be one victor.' Lady Dirikal's voice softened to convey worry and sympathy. 'Which side would you like to be on, Queen of Dreams? Grand Lord Amenamon always welcomes allies. Are you not sworn to protect the gentle folk of the First Realm? What if that partnership was the way you could guarantee their lives?'

'Will you do that?' a worried Lantic asked.

'No, of course not,' Taggie said irritably. She'd encountered that treacherous compulsion of the Karraks once before, the way they could subtly enchant their voices to make everything sound so reasonable and appealing. Lantic clearly hadn't.

She gave Lady Dirikal a shrewd look. 'That's twice today

you've told me I'm going to die. You're very confident, my lady. Why is that? I'm beginning to think your Grand Lord sent those assassins just to provoke this war.'

'Believe what you wish, Abomination. It is no concern of mine.'

'I defeated your brethren before.'

'You were lucky before. Our soldiers will obliterate your armies.'

'Really?' Taggie asked. 'You fight against this universe because it is wrong for you. I know this, because I saw the changes you tried to make in the First Realm. You wanted to make it a place that doesn't constantly torment you. Why don't you forget war and go home to the Dark Universe? Why must you always attack the life we have built for ourselves?'

Lady Dirikal tilted her head to one side, the empty darkness within her eyes regarding Taggie with puzzlement. 'You know we cannot return. Mirlyn's Gate was lost after the Battle of Rothgarnal. That is the only way to pass between the universes. We can never go home.'

'I heard the legend,' Taggie said thoughtfully, trying to recall Mr Anatole's words. 'That the Grand Lord and the War Emperor declared a truce and together hid Mirlyn's Gate.'

'So you claim,' Lady Dirikal said. 'Our story of that day is different. After the pain and loss of the battle, our Grand Lord destroyed the Great Gateways that led to Rothgarnal so such a conflict could not be repeated, and in return the War Emperor agreed never to return to the Fourth Realm. After that the Grand Lord and the War Emperor united their powers to cast binding enchantments across Mirlyn's Gate. Both sides were terrified by the prospect of a full-scale invasion through Mirlyn's Gate, and sought to protect their home universe by closing it, thereby sacrificing all those who had already passed through to live in a place where they can never truly belong. After that, after the accord, your War Emperor murdered our Grand Lord.'

'Why would he do that?' Taggie asked.

'Because your kind are always treacherous and can never be trusted.'

'If the War Emperor didn't return from hiding Mirlyn's Gate, which we both agree on, isn't it more likely he was murdered by your Grand Lord?' Lantic said.

'Lantic,' Taggie said in annoyance. 'Not helping.' She was starting to regret the courage enchantment. The Lantic of yesterday would never have challenged a Karrak Lady.

'It matters not, now,' Lady Dirikal said softly. 'Mirlyn's Gate is lost.'

'But instead of fighting, why doesn't everybody concentrate on finding Mirlyn's Gate instead?' Taggie asked earnestly. 'Wouldn't that be better? You know our side will never invade the Dark Universe – those days are gone. You could go home knowing you were safe.'

'You have no understanding of such matters. A Grand

Lord and a War Emperor bound Mirlyn's Gate. Only a Grand Lord and a War Emperor can unbind it.'

'But if I can bring them Mirlyn's Gate they'd at least have to consider it, wouldn't they?'

Lady Dirikal shrank back from the wall of the cage. 'I adore your weakness, Abomination, for it will ultimately destroy you. It is matched only by Colgath.'

'Colgath? Who is he? I heard Golzoth and Jothran mention him.'

'Lord Colgath is the younger brother of Grand Lord Amenamon. A disgrace and a traitor. Nobody, no matter how high-born, should challenge the Grand Lord as he did. His rabble-rousing of the weak and the troublemakers among us condemned him to a life in jail. And for a Karrak that is a long time indeed.'

'So you don't all share the same view?'

'We do. He is insane. He turned away from our struggle against your kind, against this universe. A fool and a coward, he brings dishonour to all the Karraks, doubly so because he is Amenamon's blood.'

'If one of you can think conflict is pointless, so can others,' Taggie said with a note of defiance.

'You are mistaken. War is coming.'

'I'm going to find Mirlyn's Gate,' Taggie said softly. She could feel the excitement firing her blood. A determined smile spread across her face, for it was the answer to everything. 'I'm going to offer your people a way home. I am.'

Lady Dirikal stood to her full height, glowering down at Taggie. 'You sad and pathetic Abomination. Do you really think you can defy both our ancestors who were at the height of their powers when the fate of Mirlyn's Gate's was decided? It is lost forever.'

'Times change. That old War Emperor and the Grand Lord – they don't have the right to decide how we live today. We're the only ones who can do that. So I'm telling you now: I am going to find Mirlyn's Gate, and when I do, you will either go back through it freely, or we will expel you with all the force we have; I'll even help the War Emperor to make you go.'

Lady Dirikal's teeth extended to their full predatory length. 'Karraks do not wager,' she said. 'But if we did, I would gamble all I own on your impending doom.'

11

TAKING FLIGHT

Dusk was closing on Shatha'hal as Taggie left Lady Dirikal's cell. 'I need to think,' she told her friends abruptly, and headed up to the vast open roof of the upside-down pyramid. Her resolve was strengthened by knowing that the Gathering was preparing to anoint King Manokol as the War Emperor. Hopefully, everyone would be concentrating on that, so she would be able to sneak off without being noticed.

They joined the hundreds of Shatha'hal's residents who were strolling about through the palm trees and lingering by the fountains, taking advantage of the balmy evening. Stars were coming out across the cloudless sky, much brighter than those found in the Outer Realm. And two moons hung above the western horizon, one a ruddy red, the other a silver blue.

'They're beautiful,' Jemima said wistfully.

'Yes, they are,' Taggie agreed. She turned to face the gentle wind that was blowing in from the sea. There was just the faintest trace of salt in the air. She called the *Adrap* spellform into her mind. It was difficult, as always, but she concentrated hard, blocking out the chatter of her friends. And the spellform held true.

Now for the difficult part. She recalled the huge eagle soaring above the road outside Stamford; clicked her fingers. The memory and the spellform combined easily, and she felt the change begin across her body.

'Majesty?' Felix's voice was raised in alarm as magic swirled around her. But she held on to the clear memory of the eagle, which promptly curved round and flung a death spell at her.

The spellform broke as she instinctively ducked, trying to banish her recollection. 'Oww.' Tendrils of magic whipped out from her limbs. *I might have known even a memory of Katrabeth would ruin things!*

'Taggie!' Jemima was standing in front of her, hands on hips, chestnut hair hanging forward as she frowned. 'Were you trying to shapeshift into a bird?'

'Are you leaving us?' Lantic asked in dismay. 'Is this part of your search?'

'Search?' Sophie asked. 'What search? What did Lady Dirikal say?'

'Taggie is going to search for Mirlyn's Gate,' Lantic told them as he stared levelly at Taggie. 'That's what she decided after talking to Lady Dirikal.'

Taggie gritted her teeth. Never again would she give Lantic courage!

'Mirlyn's Gate?' Felix exclaimed loudly. The fur all over his body had fluffed out with indignation.

'And you were going to do it without us?' Sophie asked,

appalled. 'But, Taggie, we're your friends!'

'Majesty, you cannot attempt to find Mirlyn's Gate on your own,' Felix said.

'I was just trying the shapeshift spell,' Taggie said sullenly. 'It'd help us a lot if I could manage it, that's all.' She cringed from the four sets of eyes that were staring at her in disappointment. Thankfully it was dark, so they couldn't see the blush which shame had brought to her cheeks.

'Jemima, where's Mirlyn's Gate?' she asked abruptly.

'I don't know!'

'Ah well, worth a try.' She'd found Jemima's instinct was the strongest part of her ability: if she started thinking about things, the vision often wavered.

'Majesty.' Felix couldn't keep his head still; he was trying to keep a constant watch on the entire roof. 'This is not the place to talk of such things.'

'All right,' Taggie agreed.

So they all trooped back down the stairs into the palace. Lantic led them back to his chamber. 'You really shouldn't have tried to go off by yourself,' he scolded after the door closed behind them.

'I wasn't,' Taggie said sulkily. 'It was just a trial, that's all.' She couldn't bring herself to look at her friends.

'Ha!' Sophie snorted. 'If you can't even shapeshift to fly out of here, then you're definitely going to need our help.'

'And protection,' Felix said, his tail held stiff. 'Which is what I'm trained for.'

'I thought you'd want this war more than all of us,' Taggie said to the white squirrel. 'King Manokol promises to liberate the Fourth Realm.'

'But at what price?' Felix asked softly. 'No, I believe your way should be given a chance.'

Jemima's smile was pure defiance. 'Are you going to try and talk me out of it?'

Taggie hugged her. 'No. I wouldn't dream of it.'

'So do you have a plan?' Lantic asked. 'I've never been on a quest before, but I know you always need a plan.'

'It's not a quest,' Taggie said kindly. 'It's a . . . a . . .'

'A desperation,' Sophie declared.

They all laughed.

'I do have some ideas,' Taggie said.

'Go on,' Sophie said encouragingly.

'Lady Dirikal said that after Rothgarnal the Grand Lord and the War Emperor united to bind Mirlyn's Gate. So clearly, it's going to take a Karrak Lord's help if I'm going to unbind it.'

'Uh-oh,' Felix said, his whiskers twitching.

'You mean Lord Colgath, don't you?' Lantic said in amazement.

'Yes,' Taggie said. 'He's the only one of them we know who seems to be opposed to this conflict. At this point, he's our best shot.'

'You can't be serious.'

'Taggie's always serious,' Sophie said with a grin. Her wings were starting to flap slowly at the prospect.

'But we haven't got Mirlyn's Gate!' Lantic protested.

'There's no point in searching for it until Lord Colgath agrees to come with us,' Taggie said reasonably. 'Once we have him on our side we can start a proper search for it.'

'But we don't know where he is, either,' Lantic said.

'Not exactly, no,' Taggie agreed, beginning to wish he wasn't quite so forceful arguing against her. 'But we do know he's somewhere in the Fourth Realm.'

'In prison!' Lantic cried.

'If he's in a prison in the Fourth Realm, how's he going to help us?' a puzzled Jemima asked.

'Simple,' Taggie said. 'We have to break him out.' She smiled at the circle of astonished faces around her. 'Still want to help me?'

'I've got a lot of things here that would be useful,' Lantic said, staring round his chamber. 'The olobikes . . .'

'They're a bit big to be carrying with us,' Taggie pointed out. She welcomed his enthusiasm, and didn't want to slap down every idea he had, but really . . .

'You think so?' Lantic asked delightedly. He wheeled the first olobike over to a big cabinet, and shoved it inside. Several of his rings started to glow as he traced his fingers over the silver runes on the door. *'Kasalrath walax coramuth sevol.'*

Taggie was expecting the cabinet with its silver filigree to flash and flare with magical light. Instead, the silver darkened, then became blacker still, sucking light out of the air around the cabinet. Lantic waited until the silver regained its lustre, then opened the door.

'Where's the olobike gone?' Sophie asked.

'Look down,' Taggie told her. She'd recognized some of the enchantment, which was similar to the reduction spell in her charmsward. But she had to admit the whole magician's cabinet drama made it look a lot more impressive than when she cast one.

'Oh,' Sophie exclaimed. 'You've shrunk it.' She bent down and picked up the olobike which now fitted in the palm of her hand. 'That's so clever.'

'Do you have any weapons in here?' Felix asked.

'That coil of rope might come in useful,' Taggie suggested.

'Seespy birds.'

They spent the next fifteen minutes putting various items in the shrinking cabinet. Lantic finished up with a bulging satchel that he proudly strapped shut. 'Now what?' he asked in excitement.

'We have to get back to the First Realm,' Taggie said. 'We'll need somewhere to prepare without interference. Somehow I don't think the new War Emperor will welcome me trying to bring about a different resolution to this.' *And I know Queen*

Judith won't, she added silently.

'Shame we don't have a submarine,' Jemima said.

'Can you fly me to the Great Gateway?' Taggie asked Sophie.

'Sorry, no way,' Sophie said. 'I could probably lower you to the ground from this height, but you're too heavy to carry any real distance.' She shouldered the repeat-fire crossbow she'd bought in the city. 'Perhaps you can buy passage on a ship? You're the Queen of Dreams, you could buy a whole ship to take you home.'

'That wouldn't work,' Lantic said. 'The King's Air Cavalry would catch you before you cleared the city canals. Their pegasi are swift . . . Oh!'

'Could a pegasi reach Harrolas?' Taggie asked.

'Of course.' He grinned. 'And they are kept in the palace stables.'

She returned the grin. 'And you are a prince of the Second Realm. You can go anywhere at any time.'

'Yes,' he said, sounding surprised. 'Yes I can, can't I?'

'I thought these were fancy pavilions,' Jemima said as they headed across the roof of the pyramid towards an ornate white building with wooden lattice walls. The sky had become brighter than the first time she'd ventured out on the roof. It was the moons which caused it, rising almost to the zenith to throw out a bright radiance which cast eerie double shadows of slightly different colours.

'No, these are the royal stables,' Lantic said. 'The King's

Air Cavalry have been stationed here since Shatha'hal was built.'

A lone palace guard was on duty outside the stable gates – a giant with a spear the size of a small tree. 'Prince Lantic?' he said in a loud and baffled voice as he looked down at them. 'And the Queen of Dreams!' – spoken with delight.

Taggie looked up to give him her most welcoming smile. The charmsward bands aligned for an enchantment that would help him agree to them going inside. *Not courage!* Perhaps her grandmother's sleeping enchantment? But someone might see a snoozing guard and raise the alarm.

'I'm here to show the Queen and her entourage our pegasi,' Lantic said. 'They don't have them in the First Realm.'

'Sir, the stables have been closed for the night.'

'And I would like to see Onrith for myself. Is he eating properly now?'

'Oh, he does eat, sir, but not like he used to. The poor thing pines for your brother.'

'We all do,' Lantic said.

'I'd really like to see the pegasi. I've heard they are such wonderful creatures,' Taggie said, and got ready to cast the obedience enchantment again.

'Well, maybe a few minutes,' the guard said. 'But the pegasi have settled for the night now. If you could try not to disturb them, please.'

'Of course,' Lantic said.

Taggie knew her cheeks would be burning again. Some people were simply decent and helpful by nature. Only someone like Queen Judith thought to manipulate the whole world to get what she wanted.

The guard stood aside, and everyone trooped into the stables. The stalls were wider than Taggie was used to seeing horses kept in. As her eyes grew accustomed to the gloomy light inside, she could make out the shapes of the pegasi. Although they had shorter legs, their bodies were very similar to horses, except their noses tapered down and curved into sharp beaks, and their tails were more like fat pythons with a double fin at the end. But it was the wings she couldn't stop staring at. They sprouted from just behind the shoulders to fold down neatly along the flanks. She thought they'd be about twenty feet long when fully extended.

Lantic stopped at a stall. 'Hello, Onrith,' he said affectionately. 'How are you, boy?'

The pegasi hung its head over the stall door and looked at him, letting out a mournful sigh. Lantic scratched between its ears. 'I know. We all miss him.'

'Which one is yours?' Jemima asked.

'Mine?' Lantic said in surprise. 'I don't have a pegasi. Father didn't give me a commission in any regiment, let alone the Air Cavalry. He said my asthma disqualified me from military service. I'm the first prince in three hundred years not to serve in defence of the Realm.'

'So . . . do you know how to ride one?' Felix asked.

'Well, I have ridden one,' Lantic said defensively. 'Er, once.'

Jemima drew a sharp breath, closing her eyes as her head turned to face the doors. 'Someone's coming,' she said.

Taggie looked at the doors, which remained closed. 'Who?'

'It's Captain Feandez. Hurry.'

'Let's go,' Taggie said. 'Now!'

Lantic slid back the bolt on Onrith's door. The nervous pegasi stepped out. Sophie touched its face and emitted a long warble in the airsong language. All the other pegasi came to the front of their stalls; several of them warbled back at her. Onrith stomped impatiently.

'Get on Onrith,' Sophie instructed Taggie. 'He'll take you and Lantic.' She warbled away again. Several pegasi joined in. 'That one,' she said, pointing. 'Catlifrax. She will take Felix and Jemima.'

'I'm not sure . . .' Jemima said timidly.

Taggie briefly considered giving Jem a jolt of courage, but couldn't face the idea of an even bolder Jemima.

Someone started shouting outside the stables. There was the sound of running boots. The guard's voice rose, protesting.

Sophie's wings swept out. 'Go. I'll delay them.'

Taggie didn't need any more urging. She swung a leg over Onrith's back and Lantic jumped up behind her.

'Hold on tight,' he said. 'Please.'

She gripped Onrith's mane with both hands.

The door at the end of the stalls burst open. 'Hold!' Captain Feandez demanded. He raised a sword whose runes glowed a vivid blue.

Sophie moved her crossbow so fast it was a blur. The bolt was perfectly aimed, striking Feandez's sword and smashing it from his grip. Then Sophie zoomed towards him, her red contrail sparkling in the air as the crossbow's mechanism snicked another bolt into place. She warbled defiantly and the remaining pegasi were smashing down their stall doors, to follow her in a stampede towards Feandez and the horrified officers behind him. Panicked shouts filled the stable.

Onrith was charging in the other direction. Taggie ducked down under the doorway as the pegasi galloped out into the courtyard at the centre of the stable block. His great wings stretched out, and as they rose up on either side Taggie saw they were a kind of silky white membrane. Long, lean muscles bunched along the pegasi's body. Taggie drew in a gasp of apprehension. Onrith jumped into the air, and his wings swept down in a fast powerful motion. The air creaked in protest as the pegasi took flight.

Taggie couldn't help herself: she yelled in jubilation. It was one of the most extraordinary, exhilarating experiences she'd ever known. She loved it – despite the circumstances.

Onrith's wings flapped in a smooth regular motion now as he climbed steeply. Taggie risked a look back over her shoulder. Sure enough, Catlifrax was beating her way through the air not far behind them, with Felix and Jemima hanging on tight. She could just see a confusion of rampaging pegasi down in the stables; they spilt out on to the pyramid's roof, wings half flapping.

Then Onrith flew out over the edge of the roof, and the desert floor was a giddy distance below. Gusts of night wind thrown off by the walls of the massive pyramid buffeted them, and Taggie clung on. Hard.

Sophie soared up beside her, red hair churning as she smiled wildly. 'Nightflying is just fabulous, isn't it?'

'Get them to fly close together,' Taggie shouted. 'We'll be followed in a minute.'

Sophie nodded, and warbled at the two pegasi. Onrith banked gently, and Catlifrax rose up beside them. Taggie's charmsward bands spun. 'Jem,' she called across the gap. 'Cast a wardveil. Now!' She saw her little sister nod, though she didn't slack the rigid two-arm grasp she had round Catlifrax's neck.

'*Tolstemal*,' Taggie chanted – the spell for a shadecast. The air around her quietly went *pop*. Both pegasi and Sophie were now flying inside a long bubble of ghostly ripples which should have shielded them from questing eyes, just as Jemima's spell should have protected them from seers.

Sophie altered direction slightly, and the pegasi followed. Far beneath them, Taggie could see the meandering thread of the river Zhila glimmering in the light of the moons, which they began to follow out towards the sea.

12

EVERYONE HAS THEIR OWN PLAN

Captain Feandez had served his King loyally for his entire adult life. As an officer in the elite Blue Feather regiment he was completely familiar with life in the palace, encountering the royal family on a daily basis. But tonight, when Lady Jessicara DiStantona summoned him to the King's private office behind the throne room, he barely recognized King Manokol. His sovereign had changed; grown somehow.

For the past week King Manokol had seemed a tired shadow of himself in the wake of Prince Rogreth's murder. But now, after the anointment ceremony, here stood the War Emperor himself: a vital fellow with fierce bright eyes and a beard that seemed to crackle with energy. His dark purple cloak, fastened at the neck with a gold brooch, flowed about his shoulders as if it was a living wing. The crown of laurel leaves on his head were the most vibrant green Feandez had ever seen.

Captain Feandez went down on one knee. 'Sire.'

'At ease, Captain,' the War Emperor said.

Captain Feandez smiled to himself. The War Emperor's voice had sympathy and understanding, but it was also threaded with steel. The voice of a man used to exercising complete command over his subjects; the voice of a leader. Captain Feandez was very pleased to hear that again: the period of mourning for the murdered prince was clearly over. 'Sire.' Captain Feandez got to his feet. He was only mildly disconcerted by the sight of Queen Judith standing just behind the War Emperor.

'What happened on the roof, Captain?' the War Emperor asked.

'Sire, it was my fault. The Queen of Dreams escaped.'

'Come, come, Captain, the Queen of Dreams was my guest. You couldn't possibly foresee her taking the pegasi.'

'Thank you, sire, but I should have been more vigilant. She took Onrith.'

The War Emperor nodded solemnly. 'Indeed. And my son was with her?'

'Yes, sire.'

'Do you have any idea what in the blessed Heavens they think they're doing?'

'No, sir, I'm afraid not. But we assumed the Queen of Dreams would fly straight to Harrolas and back to her own Realm.'

'Youthful rebellion, my dear,' Queen Judith said in a kindly tone. 'The Queen of Dreams was opposed to the war right from the start. Such is the way of young romantics. And she is very young indeed. She doesn't understand the real duties a head of state must undertake. Why, even her own parents haven't allowed her to take the throne fully yet, despite all she did last year.'

'Yes,' the War Emperor said grudgingly. 'I suppose so.'

'And Lantic is no doubt under her thrall. Boys of that kind are so easily flattered if anyone shows them the slightest attention.'

The War Emperor snorted in derision. 'About time he started paying attention to what goes on outside his room. But this . . . it's a bad business.'

'I'm sure the captain here can help,' Queen Judith said pointedly.

'Ah. Yes,' the War Emperor said, returning his gaze to Captain Feandez. 'I have an assignment for you, Captain. A delicate one.'

'Anything, sire,' Captain Feandez said.

'You are to find these young royals before they cause any trouble. I don't want anyone mistakenly believing the Realms are anything but united on the war which is to come.'

'I understand, sire.'

'Bring them back here by whatever means necessary. You will be given my warrant to operate as you see fit within any Realm to fulfil these instructions. It is humiliating that my first official act as War Emperor is to arrest my own son before he spreads any sedition!'

'Necessary, my dear friend,' Queen Judith murmured reassuringly.

'It certainly is,' the War Emperor said. 'And let us be clear, Captain, both the Queen of Dreams and her sister are to be brought back as well.'

'The Blossom Princess, sire?' Captain Feandez asked in surprise.

'She has a Third Realm heritage,' Queen Judith murmured. 'Even if it is not apparent yet. We cannot risk her being at large.'

'Absolutely,' the War Emperor agreed. 'The squirrel and the skymaid I don't care about, but those three must be stopped at all cost.'

'Yes, sire,' Captain Feandez said earnestly.

'But discreetly,' Queen Judith said. 'Nobody wants a martyr.'

'You have the authority to take whoever you want with you on this mission,' the War Emperor said. 'And the Royal Armoury is completely open to you, whatever implements you need.'

'Thank you, sire. I will return the miscreants to you, I swear.' Captain Feandez saluted, and withdrew from the study.

Outside, in the broad cloister with its high lightstones, he let out a long, relieved breath. His worry that he would be disciplined over the shambles in the stables had proved false. This new mission was a sign of the War Emperor's confidence in him. He smiled grimly and adjusted his tunic, ready to gather his most reliable fellows for the mission.

'Captain Feandez?'

Captain Feandez bowed deeply. 'Ma'am.' He hadn't seen Queen Danise standing behind the study door.

'I understand my husband has asked you to bring back our son?'

'Yes, ma'am. The War Emperor has honoured me with that task.'

'My husband is having a difficult time, he has been given a great responsibility when he should be grieving properly.'

'We all miss Prince Rogreth, ma'am,' Captain Feandez said, because he couldn't think what else to say.

'Good, because I do not intend to grieve for my other son. I'm sure poor Lantic thinks he has something to prove to us all, for he has never been given the attention and respect Rogreth had. That is my fault as much as anyone's. But that tragic mistake ends now. You will make sure that he is brought back alive. Do you understand me, Captain? Alive.'

He'd never seen the Queen with such a fierce light in her eyes. In some ways she was more imposing than the War Emperor. 'Yes, ma'am,' he gulped. 'I understand.'

'Good. Then may you have the blessing of every star in the Heavens on your quest, Captain. I suspect you're going to need them.'

While Captain Feandez hurried down to the storage chambers below the palace, Lieutenant Bromani was in his quarters on the amphitheatre side of the palace, getting changed into his full dress uniform. He was rather flattered by the invitation he'd received, but not entirely surprised. After all, officers of the palace guard were hugely popular among the daughters of the nobility. Along with his fellows, he was always receiving invitations to the various parties and grand balls that were thrown almost nightly in Shatha'hal. What had startled him was the messenger. He'd been on duty outside the Hall of Council during King Manokol's anointment as the War Emperor, when he turned to find an old woman standing right behind him. She was wearing a black dress that somehow made him think of crow's feathers, and seemed very stooped. A veil hung over her face, obscuring her features.

'My Queen's daughter, Katrabeth, invites your attendance in her mansion after the anointment is over,' she said in a croaky voice.

'She does?' Bromani said. He and his fellow officers had spent the past few days observing all the foreign princesses at the formal welcoming parties and dances thrown by Shatha'hal's aristocracy. Some of them were remarkably pretty. But none, they all agreed, were quite as beautiful as the daughter of Queen Judith. 'She wants to see me?'

'Indeed,' the old woman said, as if she herself didn't understand why. 'It is unwise to disappoint her,' she added sourly.

'I will do no such thing,' Bromani said. He turned to see if any of his fellows were nearby so he might brag to them. Sadly, none were within earshot. When he turned back, the old woman had vanished. A cold gust of air brushed past him, making him shiver.

Bromani and his squire spent a long time adjusting

his elaborate dress uniform until it looked absolutely perfect. He was desperate to impress the gorgeous young sorceress. When he arrived at the mansion on Shatha'hal's upper level he did indeed look tremendous, with his bright scarlet tunic sporting a wide and elaborate strip of gold braid down the front, his sharply creased trousers of a deep blue, and the knee-high black boots polished so they appeared almost silver. A curving ceremonial silver sword hung from his waist.

The old woman led him to a drawing room on the first floor, hobbling stiffly up the grand curving stairs. Katrabeth was waiting for him, smiling lightly as she took in his uniform. She rested a hand delicately on the base of her neck. 'My, my, Lieutenant, how marvellous you look.'

'Thank you, ma'am.' Bromani couldn't take his gaze away from her intense brown eyes. They seemed capable of looking straight into his very thoughts. For the first time, Bromani wondered if he might just be falling in love. 'How may I help you?'

Her laugh was a delight, so sweet and light. 'Oh dear, didn't Nursy tell you?'

The woman wrapped in her black dress bobbed awkwardly. 'No. Sorry.'

Katrabeth sat on a settee, and patted the cushion next to her. Not quite believing his good fortune, Bromani hurried over to sit beside her.

'I'd like you to tell me things about this wonderful city of yours,' she said.

'It will be my pleasure, dear lady.'

'Oh, goodie!' Katrabeth giggled. She leaned forward, and before Bromani realized what was happening, her exquisite lips brushed teasingly against his own. Bromani wanted to run his finger along his collar to let out some of the heat his inexplicably hot skin was producing.

'She's a funny old thing, my Nursy, wouldn't you agree?'

Bromani gave a cautious smile. He didn't want to seem discourteous to the old woman, even though her continued presence in the drawing room was slightly unnerving.

'You know, she's looked after me since the day I was born,' Katrabeth continued. 'Of course, Nursy punished me when I was little. She said I was a naughty girl. She punished me a lot. Then one day I learned how to punish her back. Mummy was so proud of me.'

Bromani's smile was forced now. He couldn't take his eyes off the old nurse's gauzy veil, wondering just what it covered up, and why. 'Perhaps you could tell me what you wish to know of Shatha'hal,' he said, attempting to change the subject to something more agreeable. That was when he tried to stand up. He found his legs didn't work any more.

'I . . . I can't move,' he said, in rising panic. When he lifted his arm, it seemed to be made of lead.

'Yes, I know,' Katrabeth said lightly. 'My kiss has that effect on people. Your chest is tightening up as well, isn't it?'

Bromani gasped, which made him realize how hard it

had become for him to breathe. Each breath was more difficult than the last. The numbness was slowly spreading across his whole body.

'Now then, my dear Bromani,' Katrabeth said pleasantly. 'Before you become completely unable to breathe at all, I'd like you to tell me exactly – and I do mean *exactly* – what my lovely cousin the Queen of Dreams talked about with Lady Dirikal. And don't you be a naughty boy and leave anything out.'

13

NO GOING BACK

Dawn shone a warm glow across the sea as the pegasi flew into the fjord where Harrolas's waterfall thundered down the cliff face. Taggie looked round, but she couldn't see anyone in pursuit. Certainly not a flock of Air Cavalry pegasi.

'I am the Queen of Dreams, and I wish to return to the First Realm,' she said into the rushing air. Onrith descended below the top of the cliffs, lining up above the waterfall. Sophie flew alongside, while Catlifrax brought up the rear.

The huge waterfall began to part in the middle, revealing the dark nothingness behind. Its roaring was ferocious as they passed through. A heavy squall of rain drenched them. There was a momentary flash of blackness, then they were out into the welcome gold sunlight of the First Realm.

Jemima grinned back at the darkness behind the waterfall as it began to close. 'Thank you,' she told Harrolas. Once more a twinkling light winked at her.

Hours later, the pegasi landed between the canal station and the doorway in the hillside that led to Arasath. Sophie alighted beside them, smiling round in satisfaction and stretching her arms wide. 'I haven't flown so far in a long while,' she said. 'An occasional flight like that does you good.'

When she slid down off Onrith, Taggie saw the poor animal was exhausted. She stroked his flank in thanks. Catlifrax had to sit on the grass as soon as Felix and Jemima dismounted. Lantic couldn't stop staring up at the land curving overhead. 'This is a wonder beyond any in our Realm,' he muttered in awe. 'And the land is so green. How soft on the eye. You have an amazing Realm, Queen of Dreams.'

'Can you thank the pegasi for us?' Taggie said to Sophie. 'You can tell them they'll be looked after at the palace.'

Sophie nodded, and began a quiet warble to the spent animals. Taggie could understand some of the airsong language, but knew she'd never be able to speak it herself.

'Majesty,' Felix said apprehensively. 'I didn't get time to ask before, we were all so involved trying to leave Shatha'hal—'

'But do I know how to find Lord Colgath?' Taggie finished for him.

Felix's black nose twitched. 'Yes, Majesty.'

Taggie saw the way everyone was looking at her, waiting. 'Well . . . no,' she admitted. 'Jem, do you know where he is?'

Jemima gave her a long disapproving look before she took the purse of runes out. She shook the little black stones and let them fall on the sweet grass amid the flutterseed stalks. 'That's strange,' she said, crouching over the rune stones. 'Everybody knows. He's in a tower overlooking water.'

'What do you mean, everybody knows?' Felix asked.

'Everyone in the Fourth Realm. It's not a secret there.'

'So where exactly is the tower?' Taggie asked.

'I don't know,' Jemima snapped. 'I'm not a satnav app! We need to ask someone from the Fourth Realm.'

Everyone swivelled round to stare at Felix.

'I was born in the *First* Realm,' he protested, with his sharp little teeth chittering away. 'The Fourth is my heritage, but not my home.'

'We knew we'd have to go there anyway,' Lantic said. 'This changes nothing.'

'But how do we get there?' Sophie said. 'We'll have trouble travelling between Realms without someone seeing us. Everyone is going to be watching for us – especially you, Taggie.'

'Lord Golzoth managed it,' Jemima said with a note of resentment.

'Managed what?' Lantic asked.

Taggie gave Jemima a sympathetic glance, remembering all too clearly their last encounter with that particular Dark Lord. Golzoth had come very close to killing them – especially Jemima – before Mum finally dispatched him. 'She's right,' Taggie said. 'Last year, Lord Golzoth followed us about very easily. We never did find out how he managed that.' The memory of her showdown with the Karraks in the palace returned to chill her again. 'Remember when we broke into the palace to rescue Dad? Right at the end, in the throne room, Golzoth turned away and left just before I cast the spell to bring sunlight back into the First Realm.'

'He had an escape route,' Sophie exclaimed.

'Maybe it was a Gateway!' Jemima said. 'Perhaps he had his own version of a Great Gateway, one that could take him wherever he wanted? That's why he was always turning up right behind us.'

'I've never heard of a Great Gateway like that,' Lantic said cautiously. 'And their history is a required part of the Royal Society's study.'

'When you need to know something, always ask an expert,' Taggie said primly, and indicated the wooden doorway set into the hillside.

Sophie clapped delightedly. 'Oh yes! Come on.'

After a minute walking along the curving brick-lined tunnel, the five friends came to the iron-bound door.

'I am the Queen of Dreams,' Taggie announced to the dark wood, 'and I would ask you a question, Arasath.'

'A question?' the Great Gateway's deep voice said behind her. 'I do not answer many questions. I open. I close. That is my purpose.'

'Nonetheless, this is important.'

'Then by all means ask, Queen of Dreams.'

'Is there a Great Gateway that can open anywhere it wants?'

The air in the tunnel moved gently as if sighing. 'Oh,

how I remember such talk,' Arasath said. 'Fierce we were back then, impassioned with the flame of youth and determination! So long ago it was.'

'Who? Who talked about it?'

'All of us. Every mage in the Universal Fellowship desired to open across the universe at will. Alas it was beyond all of us. We can only open between two fixed points. Once established, they cannot be changed.'

Taggie's eyes narrowed to study the door. She knew from bitter experience how tricky Arasath could be. 'So if the Universal Fellowship failed, did someone else succeed?'

The air gusted again, sending strands of Taggie's hair wafting about. It might have been a laugh. 'There was another Fellowship, in another place. They too learned to pass between their Realms, but in a different manner to us. Their gates were smaller, and free to move.'

'The Dark Universe where the Karraks come from,' Taggie said instinctively.

'Yes.'

'Were any of those Gateways brought through Mirlyn's Gate, into this universe?'

'Those of us in the Fellowship who survive, we hear things, whispers out there in the void between Realms. Whispers that are not ours. They are faint, and they are few.'

'So the Dark Lords do have their own version of Great Gateways?' Taggie mused.

'We believe so.'

'I have one last question.'

'You are impulsive, Queen of Dreams. Impatient and curious. I suppose that is admirable in one such as yourself.'

'You said, "Those who survive." Is Mirlyn one of those survivors?'

'He is the unheard now. Together, Light and Dark bound him; together, Light and Dark closed him; together, Light and Dark feared him. But they could never silence him. In the end he was too strong for their spells to break. All they could do was take him to a place where his voice cannot escape.'

'And nobody knows where that is?'

'We have listened for our lost fellow since the day of Rothgarnal. We have not heard him.'

'Thank you,' Taggie said with satisfaction.

'You are always welcome, Queen of Dreams. In you, we hear hope. Small though it is.'

'I'd like to pass into the Outer Realm now.'

'Of course.'

The iron-bound door swung open.

'And please don't allow anyone to follow me through for a day,' Taggie added as an afterthought.

'As you wish.'

After Nursy had dragged a trembling, sobbing Bromani out of the mansion's rear door, Katrabeth opened an ancient wooden box the size of a thick book. Inside, a circle of crystal similar to a magnifying glass sat amid folds of imperial-purple silk. The darkness it revealed was flecked by slivers of eerie green light that appeared round its edges and sank away somewhere in the centre, as if there was a hole there. She clicked her fingers at it.

The green flecks reversed their fall, bringing with them the image of a single room, easily as big as the mansion she was staying in. It was poorly lit, with iron braziers on the wall stuffed with a few glowing coals on the verge of extinction. However, she could just make out a large seat in the middle: an odd seat indeed, made from many bones, all twisted together. Grand Lord Amenamon was sitting on it, his smoke cloak writhing round him like a tormented living thing.

The mouth on his skeletal face opened slowly. His teeth were like small flickering ice-blue flames burning just

behind the thin lips. 'Katrabeth,' he growled in loathing, the teeth-flames flickering from his breath.

'Grand Lord,' she replied levelly.

'You risk much. The anamages of the Second Realm are ingenious, and your seeing crystal is a powerful magic. Their contraptions may detect your enchantment reaching for me.'

'Much is at risk this day.'

'What has happened? Was King Manokol anointed War Emperor as we wanted?'

Katrabeth gave him a confident smile. 'He was. All royalty present at the Gathering transferred their authority and no small portion of their power to him, even the Elven King. However, the Queen of Dreams did not take part in the ceremony. She is setting out to find Lord Colgath. I didn't know you had a brother.'

The roar of fury that came from Amenamon's mouth was so powerful, so full of hate, that it was all Katrabeth could do not to sway back. 'I have no brother any more,' he finally snarled. 'Colgath is a traitor and a fool. Why does the Abomination seek him?'

Katrabeth took a moment, mainly so the Grand Lord could calm down. It was like dealing with a spoilt five-year-old, she thought. 'She visited Lady Dirikal. They talked about finding Mirlyn's Gate. My ridiculous cousin wants to open it. She thinks that if she does, you'll all go back to the Dark Universe, or failing that she will join with the War Emperor to force you to return there.'

'Mirlyn's Gate must not be found. My father died so it would remain hidden, and our home universe would be safe from invasion. He had no choice. The Trakal did not work on Mirlyn's Gate.'

Katrabeth tipped her head to one side as she frowned at the seeing crystal. 'The what?'

'The Trakal. My father and the Congress of Lords created it before the Battle of Rothgarnal. It is a magical weapon of enormous power, designed with one purpose; to destroy the Great Gateways. It worked on them, as Rothgarnal proved, but even it could not destroy Mirlyn's Gate.'

'You mean you have a weapon that can kill the Great Gateways?' Katrabeth asked in surprise.

'We did.'

'Why didn't you use it to rid yourselves of the Great Gateways that open into the Fourth Realm? If you sealed yourself off, the other Realms would never be able to invade you.'

'My father might well have done that upon his return. After the Battle of Rothgarnal he joined the War Emperor to take Mirlyn's infernal Gate to a place where no one would ever find it. I remember that day well, for I pleaded with him to be the one who accompanied Mirlyn's Gate to its hiding place. He told me it was his responsibility alone. He was a true Grand Lord, and even today I strive to honour his memory.'

'But they never came back,' Katrabeth said slowly.

'No doubt your War Emperor betrayed and murdered my father. And soon my vengeance for that crime will be felt across every Realm.'

'Then you're not worried about my cousin and your brother becoming allies? Together they would be formidable.'

Grand Lord Amenamon snarled. 'Ha! Not even Colgath would ally himself with the Abomination.'

'Very well, then,' Katrabeth replied. 'Our agreement remains intact.'

Again the flames that were the Grand Lord's teeth flickered brightly as air hissed from his mouth, as if he was uncertain. 'If the Abomination were to find Mirlyn's Gate it would . . . distract my people, especially now on the eve of the war. I cannot tolerate that. I require the Lords and Ladies to be fully united behind me to defeat the War Emperor.'

'Then you must make very sure the two of them never meet,' she said, trying not to make it sound too patronizing. 'Where is Lord Colgath?'

'He is imprisoned in a tower without doors.'

'Impressive. So there is no problem, is there?'

'No.' Grand Lord Amenamon's mouth opened wide, the teeth-flames growing longer and brighter. 'We know of every Grand Gateway into the Fourth Realm, even those that have been closed for centuries. We will watch for the Abomination. I will enjoy meeting her in person before her death.'

14

THE OLDEST SHOP IN THE WORLD

It was night when Taggie and her friends walked up out of the roundadown. Mum's grey Range Rover was parked outside Orchard Cottage, where they'd left it a week ago. It had a keyless lock system, and of course Mum had the fob in her handbag, which was back in the First Realm. Taggie concentrated on creating a new spellform, one that was a lot simpler than the shapeshifter one. She clicked her fingers. The doors unlocked and the inside lights came on. 'Yes!'

'Is this one of the new steam cars?' Lantic asked.

'It has a combustion engine,' Taggie told him. 'Like the submarine.'

He climbed in to the back seat. 'This is your royal car? It is most luxurious.'

'Nobody knows I'm a Queen in this Realm. This is an ordinary car – for people who can afford it. Jem, show him how the seatbelt works.'

'You're not going to drive us, are you?' Jemima asked in dismay.

'It's an automatic. All I have to do is steer. I know the way to Mum's house, it's night, and I'll use magic on any police that try to pull us over. What can go wrong?'

Jemima looked like she could name quite a lot of things, but held her tongue.

Taggie crafted an enchantment to start the engine, and clicked her fingers. Nothing happened. The fifth spellform she came up with worked, and the engine purred into life.

'Oh, glorious Heavens,' Lantic said. They drove out of Melham and Taggie risked accelerating up to forty miles an hour as she peered over the top of the steering wheel. 'We're faster than the very wind itself. Is this full speed?'

'Yes,' Taggie said.

'Nowhere near,' Jemima said. She showed Lantic how to use the iPads clipped to the back of the headrests. He goggled in amazement, and started asking questions. Then Jemima made the mistake of bringing up a games app. For the rest of the trip Taggie thought his head was going to explode.

Breakfast was late. It had taken Taggie over an hour to drive to Mum's house. By then she was exhausted, and they all stayed in bed until mid-morning. Taggie showed Lantic how to use the shower. Taggie and Jem politely ignored the yipes of delight which came from the bathroom as he discovered shower gel and fluffy towels and the electric toothbrush. Even more embarrassing was when he figured out the toilet flush.

'Outer Realm engineers are amazing,' he exclaimed when he finally showed up in the kitchen. 'Can you get me

plans of the toilet's water mechanism?'

'I'll look into it,' Taggie mumbled, and started cooking him scrambled eggs.

'Oh, bravo!' Lantic started applauding as the toast came popping up out of the toaster. 'A cupboard of coldness!' Taggie had opened the fridge to get the butter out.

Taggie just laughed, which made him hang his head. She hadn't intended to be mean.

'So what shall we do?' Sophie asked. She was sitting at the breakfast bar drinking a smoothie, and wasn't as impressed with everything as Lantic. She had visited the First Realm before, during Taggie's last half-term. Taggie had had a great time showing her round, though Sophie had been pleased to get back home. She wasn't allowed to fly anywhere in the Outer Realm in case someone saw her – everyone's phone had a camera, it was too risky.

'We need to find Golzoth's gate,' Jemima said. 'Obviously.'

'Golzoth came here,' Taggie explained, 'to this actual kitchen, to try and kill us. So the dark gate would have delivered him somewhere close by. And he would have planned to slip back through it as soon as he was finished, so its entrance should still be open somewhere. We just need to find it.'

'I have spent a year guarding you at this house,' Felix said. He was sitting at one end of the work surface, nibbling a bowl of nuts and sliced banana, with some milk in a smaller bowl. 'I have cast exposure enchantments to uncover dark spells, I have searched with my revealor glasses, I have set alarms and traps. There is no sign of any kind of magic in this village nor in the surrounding fields. Your mother is also extremely vigilant.'

Taggie sighed. 'Well, we have to start somewhere.'

'But we don't even know what it looks like, or how big it is,' Lantic complained. 'It's a needle in a haystack when you've never seen a needle before.'

'Whatever it looks like, it will contain a great deal of magic,' Taggie said. 'That's what we're seeking. So let's split up and search the area. Jem, I'm relying on you now.'

Taggie wished she hadn't said that. Later that afternoon, when they all returned to Mum's house, tired and short tempered from finding nothing, Jemima looked particularly miserable, moping about and saying sorry so many times that Taggie had to give her a big hug. 'I'm probably wrong about the whole thing,' she said.

'No, you're not,' Jem said. 'I was thinking about it. And it makes perfect sense.'

'Then we'll look again tomorrow,' Taggie said. 'Golzoth must have hidden it somewhere.'

Lantic was slumped on a stool, his head resting on his arms as he watched the electric kettle start to boil with a rapt expression. 'Your pardon, Taggie,' he said. 'But another day spent searching open countryside is going to get us nowhere. Golzoth wouldn't have hidden the entrance of the gate where someone could stumble across it by accident. It must be somewhere perfectly secure, yet at the same time a place that he could easily reach at any time and without attracting attention. Is there such a place nearby?'

'A million,' Taggie complained. 'Old barns, sheds, outbuildings. And Stamford has a lot of disused buildings. Any one of them would do.'

'Then something must make one of them special to a Karrak Lord. How would we find that out?'

Taggie and Jemima looked at each other. 'Mr Laural,' they chanted.

Sophie had to wear a light plastic raincoat to cover her wings, which she didn't like, but it was the only way she could move about the Outer Realm unnoticed. A big broad-rimmed hat kept most of her undulating hair contained.

Lantic was more of a problem. Nothing Taggie had fitted him, even if she could have convinced him about wearing a girl's T-shirt. She had to rummage through Mum's gardening outfits, and use a belt to hold up some worn jeans. The shirt she pulled out of the drawer flapped about like a sail on his skinny chest.

Jemima thought she'd got away with it, but Taggie insisted she continue to wear her *athrodene* armour under a dress with a long skirt. 'Because you can't cast shielding enchantments like the rest of us,' Taggie said when her sister moaned. Felix nestled down in a big canvas carryall bag which rested on Taggie's knees for the short journey.

'This place looks so old,' Lantic said as the bus chugged along through the usual slow procession of traffic snarling up Stamford's ancient streets. 'I thought everything in the Outer Realm was new.'

Taggie, who never normally paid the town centre much attention, realized that just about every building was stone, with lopsided roofs and walls that bulged in odd places. 'It's only new around the edges,' Taggie said. 'Some things don't change, thankfully.'

'So who is Mr Laural?'

'A shopkeeper,' Taggie explained. 'A Jannermol who came here from the Fifth Realm originally. They say that was four hundred years ago. He started his shop when more magical folk visited to the Outer Realm. If anyone knows about special secret places around here it'll be him.'

'What sort of shop is it?' Lantic asked.

'Delicacies mainly, foodstuff from every Realm. He's quite famous in that respect, even though there aren't many magical folk left in the Outer Realm these days. Mum buys things from him.'

'Dad uses the shop as well,' Jemima chipped in. 'It's where they first met.'

'I wonder if Rogreth ever visited him?' Lantic asked.

'Possibly,' Taggie said. 'If he did, Mr Laural will remember. He remembers everything.'

The bus parked in the big station at the top of Sheep Market. Taggie held the canvas bag carefully as they disembarked.

'It's so noisy here,' Lantic said. Cars drove up and down the small hill alongside the bus station, engines revving as they climbed the slope.

'There's noise everywhere in this Realm,' Sophie said disapprovingly.

Taggie walked down to the bottom of Castle Street and started along St Mary's Street in the middle of the town. The road was narrow and busy, with pavements that weren't wide enough. Lantic kept flinching at how close the vehicles passed.

Thankfully they didn't have to go far. She was looking for Cross Keys Lane, which was so small it was easy to miss. It began in the gap between a quaint Tudor building and the sturdy stone-built Georgian block next door. The Tudor building overhung the entrance, producing a narrow rectangle that looked like a doorway that had no door.

Taggie turned into the tiny alleyway. The stone walls on either side were dark with age and dirt. After about twenty paces they were past the buildings and the open sky was above them. On her left, the wall had two columns of larger stone blocks set into it, indicating where a doorway used to be centuries ago. Old stonework now sealed off the opening.

Taggie placed her hand in the middle, and took a furtive look round before speaking the password. There was no one else in the alleyway. 'Uncross keys.'

The stones between the door columns turned to phantoms. Taggie quickly stepped through.

Mr Laural's shop was a small room with floor-to-ceiling shelves covering every wall that were completely full of jars and clay pots and tins. An oak counter stood at one end, black from age, with balancing scales and a stack of paper bags on top. Lightstones glimmered orange on brackets in each corner, cloaking the shop in a warm twilight glow. The air was heavy with the aroma of fish and spice.

'Mr Laural,' Taggie called out. Given his age, the shopkeeper spent a lot of time sleeping. 'Mr Laural, It's me, Taggie.' She raised her voice. 'Mr Laural!'

Behind the counter, what looked like a four-foot-high egg, with a lot of wispy grey hair, rocked slightly. The top of the shell lifted up, revealing a head with a skin of pale-blue scales below the shell cap. Mr Laural's flat, lizard-like face kept rising on a thick neck. Then two circles on either side of the shell popped out, revealing themselves to be the top of pincer hands. His arms slid out of the holes like snakes emerging from a nest. Somewhere at the bottom of the shell, Mr Laural's four legs must have come out, because the whole shell rose up until the top of his head almost touched the ceiling.

'Hello there, young Majesty,' Mr Laural said pleasantly in his creaky voice. 'What can I get you and your fine friends this day?'

'I'd like some razormint chocolates, please,' Taggie said. 'And half a dozen colcal eggs boiled in raspberry juice.'

Mr Laural's wide eyes blinked slowly. 'An excellent choice, Your Majesty.' He turned and reached for a big glass jar full of glittering green razormints.

Jemima tugged at Taggie's sleeve. 'Dandol sticks!'

'Oh yes, and some dandol sticks as well, please, Mr Laural.'

'Indeed. And how are you today, dear Blossom Princess?'

'Fine, thank you, Mr Laural.'

'Mr Laural, did my brother, Prince Rogreth from the Second Realm, ever visit your shop?' Lantic asked in a shaky voice.

'Oh, now let me see,' Mr Laural said as his rubbery arm slowly wiggled round to take the box of dandol sticks off a low shelf. 'I do recall the Prince Rogreth. Yes, I do. And you are his brother, you say? Yes. I see the resemblance. He was a most polite young man. I was sorry to hear of his death. My condolences.'

Lantic sniffed, his eyes started to water. 'Thank you. What did he buy from you?'

'I believe he selected a carton of jellied antropine seeds. He said you couldn't get them in the Second Realm, and there was a young lady he wanted to impress.'

'Please may I have a carton of them, as well?' Lantic said, fighting to hold back tears.

Taggie put her arm round his shoulder and gave a reassuring squeeze.

Mr Laural began looking round the shelves for jellied antropine seeds, his movements slow and sinuous.

'I have a question, Mr Laural,' Taggie said. 'No one knows this area better than you, so I was wondering, is there a safe place for magical folk round here? A secure place that someone who perhaps used dark magic could leave something they held precious for safekeeping?'

'Whatever would you want with such a place?' Mr Laural asked, his large eyes blinking slowly. 'You are the Queen of Dreams. I'm sure your mother would be shocked that you asked such a thing.'

Taggie pushed a gold half-sovereign back across the counter at him, enough to buy six months' worth of razormint chocolates. 'Mr Laural, it's because I'm the Queen of Dreams that I need to know of such a place. I have a duty to keep the peace.'

'Indeed you do, Majesty,' he said, closing his leathery pincers deftly around the shiny coin. 'In which case I would suggest the old munitions dump would serve the purpose you describe.'

'What munitions dump?' Jemima asked.

'During the Outer Realm's Second World War, a large cavern was excavated under Burghley Park. Originally it was a gnome warren, although they hadn't used it for over a century, not since King George III ran his not-very-successful campaign to purge them from the land. The British army extended the warren so ammunition could be stored there without fear of it being seen and attacked by enemy planes. A small side passage was dug to it from the main railway tunnel, so trains could load and unload in complete secrecy.'

'I didn't know that,' Taggie said.

'It has a tragic history. There were several cave-ins during the excavation, and more than one miner was killed. Outer Realm men claimed it was cursed. It was an unpopular posting. After the war it was abandoned, and the side passage bricked up. But I know it has on occasion proved useful to certain . . . reprobate types who wish to avoid the attention of the sheriffs and Black Garter Knights who seek them.'

'And the entrance is in the train tunnel?'

'Yes, Majesty.' Mr Laural's thick pincer hands slid a large paper bag across the surface of the counter. 'Your provisions, Majesty. I trust they will be satisfactory.'

'Everything we get from your shop is satisfactory, Mr Laural.'

15

A TUNNEL INSIDE A TUNNEL

Taggie emerged back out into the tiny alleyway, squeezing her eyes against the bright sunlight. She led her friends down the slope to the Meadows. Five minutes later they were standing on the eastbound platform of Stamford's railway station. It was a lovely little station, with the booking office built out of the same mild yellow sandstone as the rest of the town. The waiting room on the other platform was a Victorian wooden cabin with a canopy roof supported by iron pillars. At the end of the platforms an iron footbridge straddled the tracks. Taggie and her friends gathered there, looking along the tracks to the entrance of the tunnel, barely four hundred metres away. It was a simple rectangle at the end of a brick-walled cutting, with two slim, arched road bridges between them and it. A train had just left the station as they arrived. Now there was nobody left on either platform.

'Come on,' Taggie urged. 'Before someone sees us.' She jogged down the ramp at the end of the platform and started along the side of the track. Felix scampered past her, holding his tail horizontal as he always did when he ran. Their feet crunching on the loose-packed stone seemed to make far too much noise inside the high cutting, with every footfall echoing guiltily between the dark-blue brick walls.

They ran under the first road bridge, then the second. Sophie took her coat off as they reached the tunnel entrance itself, then kicked her oversized boots away. Her wings began to flap, and her feathered feet unfurled. She hovered a few inches above the tracks.

'Oh, that's better,' she sighed. 'Those clothes were like being in chains.'

Taggie grinned and took her friend's hat. Sophie's red hair expanded outward and floated about placidly in the air.

They were poised on the edge of the shadow cast by the tunnel entrance. Unseen above them, a lorry growled along the road. Taggie realized they were all waiting for her to step inside. With a shrug she started forward again. It would be another hour before the next train. Their schedule was very regular.

Felix, who had expanded up to waist-height, put on his purple-lens revealor glasses. Lantic noticed him do it, and rummaged round in his satchel for a similar pair. Jemima made a show of putting on hers. Felix did a quick double-take. Jemima's smug expression halted any comment he might have made.

Unlike the cutting outside, the tunnel seemed to absorb sound. They moved forward cautiously. Felix held up his paw, and rich yellow light shone out from his ring, casting a pale circle of light. The tunnel entrance shrank away behind them.

Liquids dripped unseen in the darkness. The air was a lot colder. Lantic shivered, and not entirely from the chill. He made his way over to Felix. 'I wonder if I might ask you a question?' he asked quietly. 'It is a delicate one.'

Felix's nose twitched. 'Bodyguards are fully familiar with discretion, Prince.'

'Uh, right then. Er, do you happen to know if Taggie has a particular boy? One she's keen on?'

Felix grew several inches taller. His stare was unnervingly direct. 'As I said, Prince, bodyguards are discreet. So you can rest assured that is not a question I would ever answer.'

'Ah. Um. Yes. Right, of course,' Lantic said, backing away, his head bobbing nervously. 'Thank you.'

Felix's little teeth grinned in the tunnel's gloom. He pulled his revealor glasses back down and examined the filthy brick wall. 'I think this might be it,' he announced.

When Taggie went over to the squirrel she could see the brick was different where his forepaw was indicating. 'Are there any doorway enchantments?' Her question seemed to be sucked away by the tunnel air.

'A small one,' Lantic said. He was peering at the grime-coated wall through his own revealor glasses, his nose mere inches away from the bricks.

'Do you know anything about them?' Taggie asked. Her method of opening locked doors was mainly blasting them with a destruction spell. She didn't fancy doing that in the confines of the tunnel.

'Not much,' Lantic said. 'And certainly not this one, for I believe this is Karrak wizardry.' He fumbled for a small notebook and started flicking through. After what seemed an age, he murmured, 'A-ha,' and began to wave his hands over the tunnel wall while chanting softly. Green runes glowed faintly within the bricks. Lantic took a couple of steps back and held his fist out. '*Toraku*.' A gem on one of his rings twinkled a dull purple. Nothing happened. 'Oh, Heavens be cursed,' he grumbled, and twisted the gem until it turned aquamarine. '*Toraku*.' This time a spark leaped out and struck the centre of the glowing runes.

A circle of bricks clattered loudly to the ground, exposing a black hole behind.

'Wait! I've got an illuminious,' Lantic said, and dived into the satchel again to produce one of his small anamage birds. Blue-white light shone brightly out of its eyes like miniature headlights, and it darted into the opening, revealing a much smaller tunnel beyond.

Felix drew his sword, which glowed green. Sophie cocked her crossbow and aimed it at the opening. The tip of the bolt glinted with the disturbing violet tinge of bad magic.

'Jemima?' Taggie said. 'Is there anything dangerous in there?'

'There's certainly dark magic present somewhere close,' Jemima said, staring at the gap in the bricks. 'But it's old. I can't see much else.'

'I'll go first,' Taggie said. She spun a tough shield enchantment round herself, then waited until the charmsward bands had aligned correctly for a destruction spell. As ready as she'd ever be, she edged cautiously through the opening.

Nothing jumped out at her. No guardian spell tried to kill her. 'Come on through.'

Ten metres on the other side, a set of rusty railway tracks led away down the tunnel. Somehow the darkness outside the light cast by the illuminious bird seemed deeper. They followed the bird closely, as it flew above the curving rails. Before long, they came to the munitions dump's tiny station.

The tunnel widened out to accommodate a slim

platform. Old iron trolleys were lined up along the wall, rusting slowly away into oblivion. Red-brown flakes lay around them like puddles of autumn leaves. There was a big archway leading back from the middle of the platform. They all peered round the edge to find a wide corridor whose far end was beyond the beams of light thrown by the illuminious bird. Alcoves on either side opened into the old ammunition storage rooms.

'There's magic down there,' Jemima said.

Felix craned forward. 'I see none.'

'Let's be careful,' Taggie said. With Sophie flying at her side, crossbow held ready, they advanced down the dingy corridor a few paces behind the illuminious bird. The first five ammunition rooms were completely empty. Then Sophie gave the sixth a puzzled look. 'Look at this.'

The room had a miniature table and chairs in the middle. Equally small dishes and cups were scattered about. They clearly hadn't been used for a long time.

'Gnomes,' Felix declared.

Taggie shivered, she was glad the horrid creatures had moved on. Gnomes were the one magical folk she couldn't bring herself to accept. Wicked and malicious, they'd been the first folk of the Realms to ally themselves with the Karraks.

She kept going.

'There are crates in here,' Jemima said.

Taggie risked a quick glance into the storeroom her sister was staring at. She saw some open wooden crates lying about. They were all empty. 'Nothing there,' she said. 'Keep going.'

'Taggie, wait. Those are the same kind I saw being put on the submarine.'

'What?'

'I'm not joking. They're the same.'

Taggie cursed under her breath. She didn't need Jemima's sight or Felix's glasses to feel some kind of dark enchantment up ahead, waiting in the gloom. It had to be the dark gate, she was sure of it. 'Felix, go with her. Take a look at the crates.'

The squirrel held up his paw so his ring's golden light shone out, and he accompanied Jemima into the storage room. Taggie moved on.

At the eleventh door she stopped again. There was an ancient oil drum in the middle of the storeroom, and the light from the illuminious bird glinted on an object resting on top. It glinted gold.

'Oh yes,' Taggie said eagerly. She took a step towards the door. A huge figure stepped out in front of her. Taggie yelled, half in shock, half in fright. It was a soldier gol, bigger even than those guarding Lady Dirikal. And it was swinging something very large at her.

She ducked fast, and a heavy sword whistled over her head to clang into the wall, cutting deep into the brickwork. Sophie aimed her crossbow quickly, an excellent shot that sent a bolt slamming into the soldier gol's elbow joint. The bolt must have caused some damage wedged in there, because the arm didn't work so well now, slowing down and emitting grinding sounds as it moved.

That really wasn't much use, Taggie saw as she scuttled backwards along the ground, because two more soldier gols had appeared behind the first. They must have been waiting in the storeroom, out of sight behind the door.

Taggie's arm shot out. '*Droiak!*'

The red blaze of her destruction spell smacked full into the second gol's chest. She might just as well have thrown a handful of feathers for all the effect it had. The soldier gol kept on coming.

Taggie scrambled to her feet. 'Lantic! What do we do?'

'Er, a counter-charm. Reorder them.' He started to chant. Two of his rings glowed brightly as the soldier gols lumbered forward. Sophie fired another crossbow bolt. It was perfect shot, jabbing into a knee joint, which started to make the harsh grinding noise, but didn't slow the thing down much. The gol bent over and tugged the bolt out.

Slivers of magical light wove out of Lantic's rings to coil round a soldier gol. But it slashed its sword down, slicing the enchantments, and blasting a fantail of sparks up from the concrete floor where the tip struck.

'Oh great Heavens,' Lantic gulped.

'Bring the roof down,' Sophie shouted. 'Bury them.'

Taggie didn't see any alternative. She pointed her hand up, and chanted '*Droiak*', trying to restrain the magic, to make it cleave into the vaulting bricks at an angle. That way the entire place wouldn't come crashing down.

A barrage of shattered bricks came thundering down on top of the first soldier gol, pummelling it to the ground. Taggie aimed again. '*Droiak.*'

Thick clouds of choking dust billowed along the corridor. She squinted through it all at the vast pile of broken brick and rubble she'd brought down on top of the gols. There was a gap above it they could still scramble over to reach whatever had glinted.

'Well done,' Sophie said, waving the dust away from her face.

Felix and Jem peered round the corner of the room they'd been investigating. 'What happened?' Felix asked. He held a firestar in one paw, ready to throw it.

'Soldier gols,' Sophie said. 'They were waiting for us. Don't worry, Taggie got them.'

'I don't understand what enchantments control them,' Lantic said in a muffled voice. He was holding a handkerchief over his nose and mouth. 'It shouldn't have been able to resist my reorder.'

Taggie grinned at him. Every inch of his clothes and skin were caked in dust, and she knew she'd be looking equally silly. 'That's the thing about magic. You never know—'

Something went *crunch* behind her. She spun round. Another *crunch* came from the pile of rubble. Several bricks tumbled down the side. A sword stabbed up into the dusty air.

'Oh no,' she groaned. They'd have to run for it. And that

meant soldier gols charging round Stamford, their swords slicing through anything and anyone who got in their way. 'No. No. No!'

Lantic was scrambling desperately through the satchel.

'Run!' Taggie yelled. She knew she'd have to bring the entire branch tunnel down behind them, and hope that would stop the soldier gols.

'No,' Lantic said. He was stumbling towards the pile of debris as a gol's arm punched up. 'We have to stop them.' He coughed, sucking down a laboured breath.

'We have to leave,' Felix shouted. 'Now!'

'Lantic,' Taggie squealed fearfully. 'Come back.'

A huge section of the rubble heaved apart, and a gol's head and shoulders emerged. Taggie was horrified. She'd have to trap Lantic in here with the soldier gols.

'Come back!' she yelled.

Lantic was coughing constantly. 'Wait,' he implored. Finally he found what he'd been looking for in the bulging satchel. His hand pulled out an anamage spider the size of a field mouse.

A second soldier gol burst out of the rubble. Lantic hurriedly dropped the spider, then fished out a second. The third soldier gol bulldozed its way free. Lantic lobbed a spider at it, and half fell back down the rubble. Then he tripped. Taggie screamed. Sophie shot another bolt into the shoulder joint of the formidable clay arm that was slamming down to crush him. It slowed, emitting a screech she thought would puncture her ears.

'*Ti-Hath*,' Taggie cried. A protective shield of air curved over Lantic, instantly solidifying. The soldier gol's fist bounced off it.

'Get out,' Sophie shouted.

Lantic didn't need any urging. He scrambled forward, his whole face red as he tried desperately to breathe. Behind him the soldier gol raised its arm again. Then stopped. Its blank head tipped forward in confusion. One of the anamage spiders was racing round and round its legs, moving with astonishing speed. A slim gossamer thread spun out behind it. The soldier gol tried to swipe the annoyance off its legs. And missed. The gap between its legs was rapidly vanishing under a web of gossamer. It swiped again and again, missing each time. Then it stopped trying to catch the spider, and tugged at the gossamer binding its legs. The gossamer was too strong, it didn't snap or tear. And the spider was now spiralling about the gol's torso. Behind it, the other two soldier gols were struggling inside the gossamer cocoons that were swiftly engulfing them.

It took another minute, but the spiders completely swaddled the soldier gols. They tumbled over, becoming motionless statues of soft white silk.

'Lantic,' Taggie said in the silence that followed. 'That was amazing.'

'Very useful indeed,' Sophie conceded.

Lantic wheezed down a breath. 'Asthma,' he choked out.

Sophie and Taggie grabbed an elbow each, and hauled

him out of the cavern and back down the tunnel until the air was clear of dust. He sat with his back to the wall, trying to recover, with Jem and Sophie fussing over him. Taggie and Felix made their way cautiously back to the munitions dump station.

'Majesty,' Felix said awkwardly when they reached tiny platform.

'What?' she asked, a little sharply – but then the munitions dump made her very nervous.

'It is not my position to offer comment. However, do you think Prince Lantic would have been quite so eager to risk himself under ordinary circumstances?'

'I hardly think this qualifies as ordinary circumstances,' she said, waving round the station. At the same time she could feel her embarrassment growing.

The squirrel swished his tail about. 'I was referring to the courage enchantment you used on him earlier.'

'Oh.' Taggie flinched. She certainly hadn't realized Felix had seen her do it. 'Felix, I really had to talk to Lady Dirikal.'

'I appreciate that, Majesty. But were there no other options?'

She wanted to say, 'No quick ones,' but that would make her sound even more selfish. 'Probably,' she mumbled, wishing she didn't feel so bad. *I got what I needed at the time*, she thought. And right there and then, when she really didn't need it, up from her memory came the image of Queen Judith in the Hall of Council: arrogant and victorious as she won the argument about who was behind the assassins, manipulating everyone for her advantage. Taggie pulled a face at the vision. It was a horrifying thought that she might turn out like her aunt.

'I won't be doing it again,' she said firmly. 'And anyway, I don't think it lasts this long.'

'You might be right. The prince may well believe he has something to prove. To someone,' Felix said primly. And with that he scampered off over some of the rubble.

Frowning at the squirrel's somewhat enigmatic statement, Taggie followed him over the rubble. She gave the immobilized soldier gols a wide berth as she scrambled into the storage room the contraptions had been guarding. The shiny object on top of the oil drum was a fat ring, measuring just over a foot in diameter, made from thick strands of gold and ebony twined together. She picked it up cautiously, feeling the dark magic it contained. It was a very potent artefact, she could tell, but it didn't react to her touch.

Her charmsward bands turned. '*Evoloor*,' she chanted: an exposure charm, which should show her the nature of the dark magic she could sense in the ring. Except the charm didn't work on it. Whatever the ring contained, it wasn't giving up its secrets easily.

Lantic was looking a lot better when she got back to him.

'You have asthma and you went deeper into all that dust?' Taggie reproached him. 'That was mad.'

He coughed again and spat out some dust. 'The gols had to be stopped. I knew my spiders would do the job.'

'Thank you. It was also very brave, but please don't do it again.' She hoped she didn't look as guilty as she felt.

He smiled weakly. 'What did you find in there?'

Taggie held up the ring for them all to see.

'Is that a dark gate?' Jemima asked.

'I've no idea,' Taggie admitted.

16

A QUICK TRIP TO THE FOURTH REALM

By the time they'd walked back to the railway station they still had forty minutes to wait until the next bus back, so they all trooped into Cafe Black on the corner of Stamford High Street and Ironmonger Street. It was a light, airy establishment, with modern white tables and chairs. All of which made Taggie conscious of how grubby they looked. They sat at a table near the back, and put Felix's canvas bag on the floor.

'Banana milkshake, please,' a smiling Jemima said to the waitress behind the counter. She'd learned a while ago that if she was polite, the staff added marshmallows to the shake for her. She and Taggie called it the 'Felix Special' – he did so adore marshmallows.

'Hot chocolate, with marshmallows,' Taggie said. 'Do you have ice cream in your city?' she asked Lantic.

'Er, no, I don't think so,' he said, which earned him a strange look from the waitress.

'One strawberry ice cream,' Taggie ordered, hoping that would go some way to making up for the courage enchantment.

'Two,' Sophie said quickly; ice cream was one part of

the Outer Realm she thoroughly approved of.

After the waitress brought their orders over, Felix poked his head up out of the canvas bag, twitching his nose about. 'So what exactly are soldier gols doing guarding Lord Golzoth's left luggage?' he asked.

Jemima and Taggie automatically started giving him their marshmallows.

'Someone in the Second Realm must be smuggling gol parts out,' Lantic said with an expression of disapproval. 'But I cannot believe any battlemage house would be so corrupt as to sell them to the Grand Lord.'

'Maybe not directly,' Sophie said. 'But Golzoth certainly wound up owning some soldier gols – today proved that. The Karraks will be using minions to do their dirty work as always. Greedy people who don't care who they trade with as long as they make a profit.' She popped some ice cream in her mouth and smiled contentedly.

'They weren't enchanted with any normal animation magic,' Lantic admitted glumly. He gave his scoop of ice cream a suspicious sniff, and put a tiny piece in his mouth. 'Oh wow! It's freezing, and it's delicious!'

Taggie grinned at him as he started scooping up more strawberry ice cream. The sight of him enjoying himself made her feel a lot happier.

'Those crates in the munitions dump were definitely the same as I saw in Shatha'hal,' Jemima said thoughtfully.

'What was in them?' Sophie asked.

'Nothing,' Jem said with a sigh. 'They were empty.'

'This is not good, Majesty,' Felix said. He used a forepaw to scrape some sticky marshmallow from his tiny teeth. 'Karrak Lords deploying squads of soldier gols would be a formidable adversary in any battle.'

'And that metal attachment Jemima sighted was definitely from this Realm,' Lantic said, giving his empty bowl a forlorn look. 'But what could it be for?'

'They're up to something,' Taggie said. 'Assassinating young royals and smuggling weapons from various Realms is all too much for a coincidence. The Grand Lord is deliberately provoking this war. He must believe he's capable of winning it.' She gave her friends a pensive look. 'I'm really concerned about what the Grand Lord is planning on equipping his army with. Lantic, you've no idea how awful Outer Realm weapons can be.'

Felix finished the last marshmallow. 'We'll never find out just by sitting here, Majesty. Perhaps you should consider informing the War Emperor about this development before we venture into the Fourth Realm? You have the right to address the Gathering of Kings and Queens. They could launch an inquiry.'

'We have no proof,' Taggie said. 'Jemima's sight through a sealed crate, more empty crates turning up here, and some leftover soldier gols that shouldn't be in this Realm. That isn't enough – not for the Gathering. I know that now,' she said bleakly. 'They'll laugh me out of the Hall, them and their clever slippery words. The next time I face them, it will have to be with something nobody can deny.'

'So we're going to the Fourth Realm, then?' Sophie asked with a gleam in her eye.

'Probably,' Taggie said. She glanced down at the bag with the gold and ebony ring which hung round her neck. 'If we can just find out what this thing actually is.'

'It is a gate which came from the Dark Universe,' Arasath told them when Taggie held the ring up in front of the door at the bottom of the roundadown.

'Really?' Taggie said eagerly. She and Sophie high-fived, while Jem and Lantic grinned broadly. 'So I was right. This is how Golzoth followed us all those times.'

'He was seriously tricky,' Jemima said bleakly.

'But we've got it now,' Sophie said triumphantly. 'We can be the sneaky ones.'

'Indeed.'

'How does it work?'

'I will talk to it,' Arasath said. 'Bring it to me.'

The handle-less door swung open, Instead of the usual brick tunnel, it now revealed a cupboard with a single shelf. Taggie put the ring on the shelf, and backed away as the door swung shut. Then she was left waiting expectantly for longer than she hoped.

'It is locked, of course, which is why it would not respond to you,' Arasath said eventually. 'Golzoth placed it under his authority. A moment . . . It has been an age since I dabbled in such enchantments. None of the Universal

Fellowship have ever talked to a gate of the Dark Universe before.'

'What's it saying?' Jemima asked impatiently.

'Ah, it has nothing to say for it is not as we are. This is more anamage contraption than living soul.'

'Oh.' Taggie didn't know if she should be disappointed or not. The door opened, and Taggie retrieved the ring. It didn't look any different. 'Can we use it?' she asked.

'The dark gate is ancient, beyond even my years,' Arasath said. 'And so tired that I feel fatigued simply by talking to it. Though it is not alive, it is near the end of its life. The Dark Lords did not treat it with respect. However, I have now released it from Golzoth's servitude. So, in order for it to serve you, you must have a clear picture of the place you wish to travel to. Show your destination to the dark gate using a portrayal enchantment. Once you have done that, use the ordinary opening enchantment, and it will take all those who are holding it.'

Taggie gave the Dark Gateway an admiring look. 'Is that all?'

'Yes. But you must give it a precise picture of your destination; and I do not believe it is capable of opening more than three or four times before it is finally spent.'

'I understand. Thank you.'

'You are welcome, Queen of Dreams. Do you wish to return to the First Realm?'

'No thank you. Not right now.' She bowed in thanks, and made her way up the roundadown.

They sat in a circle in the middle of the orchard. Above them, bees buzzed lazily between the blossom. More of the tiny white petals burst open eagerly in the presence of the Blossom Princess.

'We can go anywhere we want,' Lantic said with satisfaction. 'Anywhere at all. How fantastic is that?'

'But only three or four times,' Sophie said soberly.

'We can only rely on three,' Taggie said. 'So we must be very careful which destinations we choose.'

'Getting into the Fourth Realm without the Karrak Lords knowing has to be the first,' Lantic said.

'Yes,' Taggie agreed cautiously.

'Arasath said we have to know the place we want to travel to,' Jemima insisted.

'I know. Felix, can you think of the best place in the Fourth Realm for us to start?'

The squirrel became very still. 'Majesty, I have never set foot in the Realm my family fled from.'

'You must have seen pictures.'

'Well yes. There is a painting of our old family home in the house I grew up in. It hangs above the fire in our parlour.'

'That'll have to do, then,' Taggie said.

'Er, I've heard it's cold in the Fourth Realm,' Lantic said.

'Very cold indeed, now,' Felix agreed.

'Perhaps some preparation, then, before we depart?'

Taggie and Jemima went into the cottage, where

the caretakers made up sandwiches and flasks of hot chocolate for everyone, which Jemima packed into their old school lunchboxes. Then the sisters went through the hall wardrobe, picking out a selection of winter coats and boots. By the time they'd all put them on in the orchard, they were hot and sweaty.

'Everybody ready?' Taggie asked. She held up the dark gate.

One by one they gripped the ring.

Felix closed his eyes. His pointed nose twitched as if he was smelling something. '*Caravaz el thrain,*' he chanted softly.

The middle of the ring glowed with a hazy light. Taggie thought she was looking through a thin grey mist at a lovely long house. There was a lawn in front of it running down to a river, and the slope behind was covered by an oak forest.

It certainly seemed like a real place.

The charmsward bands slid round, the door aligning with a puff of wind. '*Seseeamie.*'

The orchard started to rotate around them. Jemima gasped at the sudden movement. Then the mist was rising out of the ring to envelop them, turning the orchard distant. Sunlight dimmed as if evening had rushed up on them, and now there was nothing visible beyond the mist.

Taggie realized the image in the ring was now the orchard. Her head came up. The mist was withering away. When she exhaled, her breath was white in the air. And breathing in revealed just how cold that air was. She was looking at the house Felix's portrayal enchantment had summoned up. Except the light and life had been drained from the real thing. The house had faded to grey, its windows black and cracked, with a roof which had sagged under a thick mantle of snow. More snow enveloped the flat area at the front which had been the lawn. The river was frozen. On the slope behind, the oak trees were reduced to melancholy ice sculptures, sad shadows of their former vibrant selves. They were also slimed with tendrils of frost fungus which had swamped the entire woodland with insidious sallow fronds. Clusters of grape-sized spores hung from the branches, pulsating slowly.

'Urrgh,' Jemima said, her nose wrinkling up in dismay at the sickly growths that had insinuated themselves everywhere. 'I'd forgotten how much I hate that stuff.'

Taggie glanced up at the sky, which was a uniform grey cloud. She couldn't even guess where the sun was. 'I'm so sorry, Felix.'

'You didn't do this, Majesty,' he said. 'And if we succeed, all this will be banished.'

Jemima walked over to the house, and put her gloved hand on the frozen climbing rose that covered the front wall. It took a long while, but a single stem stirred, pushing a bud through its coating of frost and slushy fungus. A topaz rose bloomed in front of her determined face. 'There's life here, Felix,' she said. 'The Fourth Realm isn't dead. Not yet. It sleeps under this terrible blanket, but all is not lost.'

All of them stood there, staring at the rose. They gradually realized it was the only speck of colour in the whole world.

A clap of thunder rolled across the frozen landscape. Taggie couldn't see any lightning flashes. Then a wind rose from nowhere to brush against her face.

'We should go,' she said.

17

THE DREAMER AWAKES

The dream had lasted as long as the sylphwitch's cold, cold sleep. She dreamed of times long past, when the Realm was warm and bright, when gold sunlight poured out of a sapphire-blue sky all day long. Outside the dream her world had fallen to bitter cold white, a white that caged her trees as fast as any jail.

Then, long years after she'd given up any hope of throwing off the blanket of ice, Jatheldorn the sylphwitch felt a tiny surge of life out there among the frozen branches of her precious trees. A tiny pulse of warmth and life that caused a flower to bloom.

In the midst of a cocoon-like bed that looked like a mesh of a million silky root strands, Jatheldorn opened her eyes. She took her first breath in over two years, and smiled. A fair magic had returned to the Fourth Realm. A tiny glimmer, alight like a candle flame in the midst of her forest, but burning with so much warmth. Jatheldorn launched herself eagerly out into her slumbering trees.

There was a track through the woodland behind the house. They trooped along it, boots squelching on the tapering grey strands of frost fungus that wove a loose carpet over the frosted grass.

'How far to town?' Sophie asked. They'd been walking for ten minutes, and were still climbing up the slope.

'Aurestel is supposed to be a hour's ride from the house,' Felix said.

As one, they looked at the track ahead of them. They couldn't even see the crest of the hill. Up ahead, the trees were taller, their branches starting to merge together to form a grey tunnel through which tendrils of mist hung motionless in the air.

A white fox slipped across the track. It had a white vole in its mouth, and gave them a quick look before vanishing into the ice-rusted bracken.

'I could fly up and take a look,' Sophie said.

'No,' Taggie said.

'It would only take a minute.'

'There's nothing else in the air,' Taggie said. 'No birds, no insects. You'd be the only thing moving.'

'Except for the rathwai,' Felix said. 'The air hounds of the Dark Lords rule the air here.'

'I'll stay with you,' Sophie said in a small voice.

It wasn't long until the slope flattened out. The big trees on either side were smothered in tangled ropes of frost fungus. There was no sound as they trudged on, apart for a few bursts of thunder from the unseen sky above.

Flakes of ice began to sprinkle the ground around them, as if it was snowing. But when Taggie glanced up, the grey sky was threaded with a few strands of darker cloud, nothing that looked like snowclouds. Then she saw speckles of green on the branches curving over the path.

'Jem,' she said cautiously.

'I know,' Jemima whispered in a subdued tone. 'I can't help it.'

'What's happening?' Lantic asked.

'The trees are greeting the Blossom Princess,' Felix said.

'I'm sorry,' Jemima said.

'Don't be,' Felix said. 'Please. This is proof that all the ruin the Dark Lords and Ladies have brought here cannot defeat the Fourth Realm. It is wonderful.'

Jemima actually blushed despite the cold, he sounded so grateful.

Taggie was wrong about nothing else moving in the air. They saw a big white eagle alight on a frozen oak further up the track. It made no sound as it studied them.

'A snow eagle,' Felix said reverently. 'They were rare even before the Fourth Realm fell. To see one now is indeed a stroke of good fortune.'

Taggie stared back at the big bird, feeling immensely sad that something so magnificent should be trapped in a world like this, never knowing clear skies or the touch of warm sunlight. But even so it retained a dignity that even the eternal winter couldn't banish.

It took off and flew over their heads. She smiled as it went.

Eventually the trees began to thin out, and the track

opened into a broad clearing just as the ground started to dip down. They crept forward to an ancient tree that had fallen, and crouched behind it. Taggie could see across a vast plain below them. Snow-covered ground merged with the uniform grey sky at some unknown distance. The only thing that broke up the bleak winter landscape was Aurestel, which nestled just beyond the foot of the hill.

Taggie was surprised. After seeing the Weldowen family house she'd been expecting Fourth Realm architecture to be a little more elaborate. But the town was comprised entirely of dark cubes, most of which had tall chimney stacks rising high out of their flat roofs. There weren't any small houses or shops. It was a city of factory blocks, she thought.

'This Realm used to have homes and halls and taverns and schools,' Felix said bitterly from behind her. 'There were squares and parks in every town, our cities had

a gentle grandeur. Now look. They have torn down everything we built since the First Times to put up their soulless travesties of buildings.'

'I'm sorry,' Jemima said. She gripped his forepaw tight. 'This must be so hard for you.'

'Don't concern yourself about me.'

'We do, Felix,' Taggie said firmly. 'What they've done here is awful. One day, the King in Exile will return and everything you've lost will be rebuilt.'

'Aye,' he said grimly. 'One day.'

'Is that a railway line?' Jemima asked.

Taggie looked harder at what she'd assumed was a road: a perfectly straight black line cutting across the plain. Something was moving on it, a row of carriages with a big engine at the front, puffing out smoke and steam.

'The Fourth Realm never had railways,' Felix said. 'This is new.'

'The Karraks must have built it,' Lantic said.

'In those factories, presumably,' Taggie mused, eyeing the smoking chimneys with suspicion.

'If they're factories, where do the people live?'

'There are no other buildings,' Felix said uneasily.

'But . . .'

Jemima abruptly stood up and turned round. 'You can come out now,' she said in a clear voice. 'We won't hurt you.'

A breeze swept across the clearing. And a figure in a grey cloak was suddenly standing five metres behind them. It was all Taggie could do not to let out a squeak of surprise. The hood made her nervous: she couldn't see the figure's face. It could have been a Karrak Lady, except now she looked closer, the cloak was no longer grey; it seemed to shimmer on the verge of all colours.

'A sylphwitch,' Felix muttered in amazement, and bowed deeply.

The figure pushed her hood back. An astonishingly pretty young woman with skin as black as midnight smiled back at him. 'A Weldowen,' she said, smiling in return. 'Welcome home.'

Taggie blinked. The sylphwitch didn't look young any more; her face was aged with wrinkles and her raven hair had faded to silver. It was as if her face was a blank mask upon which different features were projected at random.

'Who are you?' Lantic asked.

'My name is Jatheldorn. I am the guardian of these woods, and you woke me.'

'I'm sorry. We didn't know . . .'

Jatheldorn laughed a young girl's spry laugh, but it was an ancient woman who spoke. 'Not you, foreign princeling.' She turned to Jemima. 'I talk to you, Blossom Princess of the First Realm.'

'You know who I am?' Jemima asked.

'I know what you are.' Jatheldorn held up the yellow rose. 'Who else could do such a thing?'

'Sorry,' Jemima said, with a shrug that wasn't particularly modest. 'I just wanted to show my friend his Realm wasn't completely dead.'

'Don't be sorry, little one.' And now Jatheldorn was barely older than Jemima. 'It is a wonder to behold, when I thought such things were long behind me. Unfortunately –' her finger pointed upwards – 'they don't agree with that sentiment.'

Sophie's head snapped up, her gaze darting across the bleak sky. 'Rathwai,' she said, and shuddered.

Taggie was trying hard to see the creatures that so upset her friend. In the distance over the town, a couple of black dots were slowly rising. She squinted. 'Is that . . . ?'

'Yes,' Sophie said. 'And if I can see them, they'll soon be able to see us.'

'They are hunting you,' Jatheldorn said. 'I have a home nearby. You'll be safe there. Follow me.'

The door to Jatheldorn's home was a wide crack in a centuries-old oak that had lost its upper branches in some storm long ago. Once they squeezed their way in, earthen steps took them down to a cosy room ribbed by the oak's roots. Even without a fire it was warm, as if the air had somehow held on to the last of a distant summer's heat. Lightstones in the soft crevices produced a green-tinged glow.

'Why are they hunting us?' Felix asked. 'How did they know we're here?'

Jatheldorn, now a handsome middle-aged woman, held up the rose. 'I plucked this so the rathwai would not see such a magnificent spark of colour. Without evidence of

190

the Blossom Princess's touch they might have gone back to their stables. Alas, the Blossom Princess is more powerful than I realized. My trees shake off their sleep to greet her, so heartened are they by her presence.'

'Oh,' Jem grunted, and studied her boots. But there was a smile playing over her lips.

'I told you not to be sorry,' Jatheldorn said. 'You broke their enchantment, Blossom Princess. An act the Dark Lords and Ladies fear more than any war or rebellion. They believed their mastery of this poor Realm to be absolute. You have shown them it is not. Small wonder they hunt you.'

Taggie groaned in dismay. 'This was supposed to be a quiet little expedition.'

'Do not worry, Queen of Dreams,' Jatheldorn said. 'My forest was in a sleep that grows deeper with every passing day. Even I had thought the trees were lost to life. Now their sap rises to greet you and their spirits stir. I had resigned myself to sleeping away my remaining years. You have brought hope to us. And hope is the most precious gift of all.'

'So what are you?' Lantic asked.

'The sylphwitches are the guardians of the forests and woodlands of the Fourth Realm,' Felix said.

'I have that honour,' Jatheldorn said. 'And what of you? A Weldowen, the Queen of Dreams no less, a Second Realm prince, and a lady-in-waiting from the skyfolk of Air. Such a strange group of friends. Stranger yet is your arrival here. Why have you come?'

'I need to see someone,' Taggie said. 'I'm hoping you can help.'

'If I can, I will. I mourn deeply for the summers denied my poor trees. There is nothing I will not do to see their return.'

'There's a war coming,' Taggie explained. 'A terrible, pointless war that will see thousands dead. We are trying to stop it. But to do that, I must visit a Karrak Lord I've heard about who may be able to help. Do you know of Lord Colgath?'

Jatheldorn diminished to a woman of incredible age, and laughed for a long time. 'Do you know there is water in the seas and rock in the mountains? Of course I know of Lord Colgath. He is the one who led his filthy brethren to enchant the air and clouds when the Karraks first came here. He is the banisher of seasons, the bringer of the cursed winter. Yes, I know Lord Colgath well.'

'He's in a tower,' Jemima said suddenly. 'A tower overlooking water. I can see him sitting inside a black ball.' She blinked and gave a cheerful glance round the room. 'Did that help?'

'The armies of Darkness will surely tremble before you, Blossom Princess,' Jatheldorn said with a teasing smile. 'I don't know where this tower is, but others will. Rest here this night, and I will search out a friend I recall who may be able to help you.'

18

CATCHING THE TRAIN

Taggie woke to find Jatheldorn gone. All they had for breakfast were the jam sandwiches in their plastic lunchboxes, which they tucked into hungrily.

'Do not concern yourself about the sylphwitch,' Felix told the rest of them. 'The forest guardians are among the oldest peoples to live in this Realm; legend says they were the first to be brought here by the angels. She would never betray us to the Karrak Lords.'

Sure enough, Jatheldorn returned just as they were talking about going up the stairs to look round outside. She brought an old man with her, wrapped in a coat that was so tattered it was more like a cloak of rags.

'This is Novarl,' Jatheldorn said. 'His ancestor was mayor of Aurestel when it fell to the forces of the Dark Lords and Ladies.'

The old man blinked as he looked round the room, as if he couldn't quite see everyone properly. 'Legends,' he whispered. 'Bright strong legends standing before me. Oh, to have lived to this time. I never truly believed, even though the sylphwitch visited me when I was young. They made me confess she was a dream, a nightmare. I never repeated the story. For that I am ashamed.'

'The fault is mine,' a now-youthful Jatheldorn told him kindly. 'I wasn't aware for how long I have slept.'

'We're not legends,' Taggie said. 'We're just people. Really.'

Novarl frowned, and walked over to the table in the middle of the room. He reached out to the yellow rose that was sitting in a small glass of water. But his hand drew back fearfully before he touched it. Then tears were running down his cheeks.

'Please,' Jemima said anxiously. 'Don't cry. There's nothing wrong.'

'I have never seen such a thing before,' Novarl said. 'It is beautiful. A living plant that isn't grey and foul. A miracle from the past.'

'It's only a flower,' Jemima said. She picked it up and gave it to him.

Novarl held it up in front of his incredulous face. 'Even I had begun to doubt,' he said, and coughed. 'People who have magic to match the Karrak wizardry no longer dwell in this poor Realm. But now this: plants that grow and bloom. Leaves budding on the trees again. Real. All of it real, after all. My grandsire told me of those days, as his grandsire had told him. I listened to the ancient tales of the time before the sky turned grey and winter became the one eternal season. But we always knew it was true from the ruins that still lie around the outskirts of New Aurestel. Things were different long ago.' He looked around at them hopefully. 'Is that why you are here? Are you to return us to those lost times of warmth and colour and joy?'

'I don't know the future,' Taggie said, deeply moved by his reaction to something as simple as a flower. 'But I hope to change what is happening here and now. It won't be quick, nor easy. But if it can be done, I will do it. You have my word.'

Novarl bowed to her. 'A Queen indeed.'

'But we do need some help.'

'Yes. Jatheldorn explained to me. You seek Lord Colgath?'

'We do.'

'He is imprisoned in Red Loch Castle, beyond the reach of even his own kind.'

'Red Loch Castle?' Felix exclaimed, his tail fluffing out. 'Curse their arrogant sacrilege.'

'You know it?' Taggie asked in surprise.

'Yes indeed, Majesty,' Felix said. 'It was built by King Yovonin at the end of the First Times, when wars and conflicts still raged across the Fourth Realm. He decreed an impregnable fortress be built to safeguard his family in case the wars went badly for him. It was never used then, of course, but it became a symbol of his fortitude, and that of his line. King Ornalo, the last king of the Fourth Realm, made his final stand against the Grand Lord's forces there.'

'Aye,' Novarl said. 'Well, now it is the impregnable prison of the Grand Lord.'

'There were too many bold words spoken to describe

it,' Felix said grimly. 'It was broken before, so it can be broken again.'

'Let's hope so,' Taggie said. 'Novarl, how do we get there?'

Novarl reluctantly took his gaze away from the yellow rose. 'By train. The eastern line from Aurestel passes close to Red Loch. You can get off when it stops at Valaran station to take on water and coal. From there it is an hour's ride on a stout horse.'

'All right. Can you get us to the station?'

'I will try.'

'The Karraks have sent their minions into the forest to hunt for whatever is spoiling their enchantments,' Jatheldorn said. 'As they come, they are taking their iron axes to the trees which have dared defy them by opening their buds.'

'No,' Jemima cried in distress. 'The trees were just saying hello to me. They can't chop them down for that, that's so evil.'

The sylphwitch shimmered to a twenty-year-old with a fierce expression. 'Like Novarl they have forgotten why they never ventured into the forest in the time of the cold darkening. I can take you past the intruders, and as we go I will remind them why they should stay away from my trees.'

Novarl had brought with him a sack full of coats. Everyone in New Aurestel wore one, he explained, they'd be able to pass through the streets without drawing attention to themselves.

The bundles he produced were similar to his coat – old and raggedy, their original colour lost beneath decades of oily stains. And they smelt.

'Like an Ethanu,' Jemima decided as she pulled one on over her own coat and fastened the laces up the front.

'You know the Ethanu?' Novarl asked.

'Oh yes. I know the Ethanu. Are they here?'

'Yes,' the old man said. 'They run the town for their Karrak masters. Let us hope they don't discover you.'

'For their sake,' Taggie said firmly as she pulled the coat's hood close around her head.

Outside the ancient oak, Jatheldorn held out her arms. 'I will carry you all,' she told them.

'How?' Jemima asked brightly.

'On the breath of the wind, of course,' Jatheldorn said. 'For the wind is swifter than all things.'

Intrigued and a little apprehensive, Taggie took one of the sylphwitch's hands, with Sophie holding her free hand, and Novarl holding hers. Jemima took Jatheldorn's other hand, with Lantic holding on to her, and carrying Felix in the crook of his arm.

'Away,' Jatheldorn said, a word the wind captured and took with it as it gushed around the big old oak trunks of the forest.

Taggie gasped, then giggled as she found herself drifting just above the ground. She felt a very strange (but not unpleasant) magic washing around her. Jatheldorn was indeed carrying them all, swishing round the trees, and gliding above the snow-coated undergrowth.

Eventually Taggie caught a glimpse of several Ethanu through the trees ahead. The Karrak's faithful lieutenants were the same here as they had been when she encountered them last year. They wore long leather coats, and a trilby-style hat whose brim cast a deep shadow over their head. The only visible part of their faces were the silver circles of their wire-rimmed glasses. Just behind them were smaller figures in distinctive red armour.

'Nobody mentioned Rannalal,' Sophie muttered sourly. The little four-legged knights were the ones wielding axes, holding them high, ready to bring them down hard against the bark of trees that were sending green buds pushing through their crust of ice and mushy frost fungus.

'They're going to see us any second now,' Lantic said in worry.

'They cannot see that fast,' Jatheldorn assured him.

That was when Taggie realized

the Ethanu and Rannalal were motionless: the axes weren't being raised in readiness, they were poised in mid-swing – frozen like the Realm around them.

They drifted out into a small clearing where all the trees were threaded with vibrant green. Jatheldorn halted right in the middle of the statue-like group of Ethanu and Rannalal. Everyone's feet touched the ground again.

'Have you enchanted them?' Jemima asked cautiously.

The sylphwitch laughed lightly. 'Oh no. It is not they who are enchanted this moment. We move too quick for them. Now let us make mischief before we leave.'

Taggie thought she understood. The sylphwitch had somehow made time speed up for them, leaving the rest of the Realm standing still by comparison. 'I never heard of magic like this,' she said.

Jatheldorn took hold of a Rannalal's axe, and pulled it decisively, turning the sharp head away from the tree he was trying to fell, and bringing it down just above one of his feet. His hairy face with its pig-like snout never flickered as she adjusted his swing. 'The angels taught the art to my ancestors when they brought us down from the Heavens,' she said, her face now ancient again. 'It is almost lost now.'

Taggie grinned at the rearranged Rannalal. When he moved again, the axe would go slamming into the ground right between his feet.

Suddenly everyone was laughing as they ran across the little clearing, tugging axes about, tilting the sharp blades, prising fingers off the handles so the axes would fly free.

Manipulating the Rannalal was like manoeuvring them through thick liquid.

Jatheldorn held out her arms again, and everyone took hold. They glided silently out of the clearing. Taggie really wished she could stay and watch in real time, but it was not to be, she admitted reluctantly.

The sylphwitch took them to the edge of New Aurestel, and they touched the ground again. Sounds and movement burst around them like a wave on the shore. 'I can carry you no further outside my forest,' she told them.

So amid the ruins which surrounded the town, they put poor Felix into the sack where nobody would see him. Then Novarl walked on confidently, leading them to the train station.

The cube-buildings were bigger than Taggie had realized. Their chimneys belched out a yellow-tinged smoke which layered the still air, slowly sinking to the ground rather than wafting away.

Ethanu (always in sixes) marched their strange slow march along the roads. It was all Taggie could do not to let loose a destruction spell when they passed by. Her charmsward bands were aligned ready for one.

Rannalal patrols were everywhere, parading about in their red armour, making everyone else scurry out of their way.

'There's more of the dark folk than there are humans,' Lantic observed.

'Very few of us have children now,' Novarl said. 'Who

would want to bring a child into this Realm, this life?'

Now he'd said it, Taggie couldn't see any children anywhere.

'That man is looking at us,' Jemima said.

Taggie glanced in the direction her sister was indicating. The man seemed little different from anyone else using the road, except for his coat, which had a fur lining.

'Who is?' Taggie asked.

'I don't know him,' Novarl said. 'He's not from Aurestel.'

Now he'd seen them looking at him, the man turned away and walked round the side of a building.

'I didn't like that,' Jemima said. 'No one else is curious about us.'

'People are as suspicious as they are fearful,' Novarl said sadly. 'Everyone makes it their business to know everyone else's business. Most people here would turn you in to the Dark Lords for better sleeping quarters or just the price of a decent meal. Please don't judge us too harshly. It didn't used to be like this.'

'Nobody is judging anything,' Taggie assured him. She gazed up curiously at the big square wall they were walking past. A low hammering sound was constant now. 'What do they make in these places?'

'The centre of each block contains a furnace. All day and all night we bash out metal shapes for the Karrak Lords.'

'What sort of shapes?' Lantic asked eagerly.

'For the last few years my home foundry has made

nothing but lead balls, no bigger than the tip of your finger,' Novarl said. He pointed to another of the big cube-buildings. 'They're taken there, where Ethanu and other mages imbue them with bad magic. I don't know what happens to them after that.'

'Taggie glanced at the cube he indicated. She could feel dark guardian enchantments circulating slowly within the walls, alert and suspicious. 'But I'd like to find out.'

'You cannot,' Jatheldorn said. 'You risk much simply by being here. Do not submit to raw folly simply to satisfy your curiosity.'

'I know,' Taggie said. 'What about sending one of your seespy birds inside?' she asked Lantic.

'And if it gets seen?' he queried. 'The Ethanu are accomplished mages, and the Karraks already know something is badly wrong here.'

Taggie pressed her teeth together. She knew her friends were right, but she also desperately wanted to know what scheme the Karraks were pursuing. In the end common sense won. 'All right. Next time.'

'I wasn't planning on coming back here,' Sophie retorted.

It took them a good quarter of an hour to walk across the joyless town to the station. There was a train waiting at the single platform. Its engine was a great iron beast, twice as big as any Taggie had seen before, with greasy steam jetting out from a dozen vents and valves amid the wheels and pistons, while black smoke chuffed noisily out of its funnel. It was pulling half a dozen passenger carriages and two dozen trucks. As they waited on the platform with the other passengers, they could see men loading big crates from carts into the trucks while Rannalal guards stood around listlessly.

'You should go home now, Novarl,' Taggie said.

'But—'

'Please. You have been a tremendous help. I don't want you to come to any harm because of what we do.'

'I will stay with you for a while,' a young Jatheldorn told Novarl. 'My pardon, Queen of Dreams, but I cannot stray far from my trees for long. I would see that no harm befalls Novarl. Perhaps I should say hello to others in the town. I feel bolder now.'

'Don't be too bold,' Taggie told the sylphwitch. 'I cannot guarantee my success.'

'You may have doubts,' Jatheldorn said, now heavily wrinkled with age, but possessing a kindly smile. 'Those who know you do not.'

Taggie touched Novarl's arm. 'It is your task now to tell the stories of the old times again, to keep the hope and memory of this Realm alive. You must not forget who you were, and who you can be again.'

'I understand.'

'Show your friends the rose,' Jemima said brightly. 'If I can come back, I will. And when I do I'll show you what a whole Realm full of flowers is like.'

'I will not forget you,' Novarl said solemnly, and turned away so his tears would not be seen.

'He's back,' Sophie said quietly.

Taggie hissed as she glanced round casually. Sure enough, the man in the fur-lined coat was standing at the far end of the platform. She didn't believe in coincidence. 'I don't want him seeing us get on the train,' she told the others.

'We need a distraction,' Lantic said.

Taggie gazed back at the nearest cube-building with narrowed eyes. 'Perhaps I can shake things up a bit.'

'You'll be too much,' Jemima said with a knowing smile. 'I'll do this one.'

The station had been built on one of Aurestel's original parks. When the rail line was laid, no one had bothered to clear the remaining trees away. There was no point. So there they stood, around the station and the metal rails, like sentries left behind from another era, clad in white snow and smears of slimy grey frost fungus. Nobody paid them any attention any more.

So passengers and railway workers alike frowned and turned to stare when one of the biggest trees in the old park started to make odd crackling sounds. Their amazement grew as they realized the sounds were made by the mantle of crusted ice shattering. Sharp crystals cascaded down from the branches, ripping the frost fungus with it. People crept forward to gape in amazement at the spectacle.

As if the tree shrugging off its snowy winter coat wasn't

enough, the dark buds exposed on the branches began to swell. For the first time in centuries, astounding pink and blue flowers burst open. Cries of wonder went up, and the crowd surged forward, sweeping everyone on the platform along with them. Sweet yellow bananaberries started to fruit in the middle of the petals. The Rannalal didn't know what to do about the phenomenon. Whistles were blown, and harsh angry grunts ordered people away. They were ignored.

More Rannalal arrived, their armour jangling as they ran to help their beleaguered colleagues. They started hitting people with their batons and sword hilts the way they always did. But just this once, under the towering altar of colourful flowers and ripening fruit, the cowed sullen human residents of New Aurestel didn't meekly slink away. And the Rannalal were reminded exactly how strong people twice their height were, and how angry they could get.

It was only when the Ethanu began their slow inexorable advance on the station that people finally scampered away. Behind them, small four-legged figures in red armour lay on the ground, unmoving.

The driver of the great engine was keen to prove he was loyally following orders and departing on schedule. As the Ethanu arrived, the train let out a piercing whistle and slowly pulled out of the station with a lot of clanking sounds as metal pistons growled and strained.

*

Taggie watched the chaos through a window at the end of a carriage as they pulled away from the platform. The man in the fur-lined coat was nowhere to be seen. 'I think we're OK,' she said. 'That was cool, Jem.'

Jemima shrugged, trying not to look too pleased with herself.

A narrow corridor ran along each railway carriage. Taggie and her friends found a compartment in the third carriage that was empty. As soon as the door was shut, Taggie opened the sack. Felix bounded out, shaking his fur and complaining a lot. He grew tall enough for his nose to reach Jemima's elbow.

'How long did Novarl say the trip would take?' Sophie asked.

'Nearly a day to get to Valaran,' Taggie replied. 'But I think there are a couple of stops on the way.'

Jemima examined the old school lunchbox they'd packed back at Dad's cottage, which now contained a single sandwich and a couple of chocolate digestive biscuits. She pulled a face and settled back on the wooden bench.

Sophie pressed her face to the window, watching the icy land slip past. They were rolling across the desolate plain at a surprising speed. New Aurestel was soon lost behind them. Long, straight snow mounds marked hedges that separated fields which hadn't seen a crop for centuries. Occasional trees were black cracks against the grey sky. Nothing moved across the vast expanse, no people, no animals. She couldn't see any buildings, not even ruined farmhouses. It was all very disheartening.

The silence that had claimed the compartment was depressing, as if the flat defeated lands were sucking their humour away. Sophie looked over at Taggie, seeing a miserable expression on her friend's face. 'You really want to know what they were making in those factories back there, don't you?'

Taggie nodded. 'It simply has to be connected to the Grand Lord's plan to win the war. It might even be the proof we need to convince the Gathering to reconsider.'

'I can find out for you,' Sophie said. 'It's easy enough for me to fly back to the trucks and see what's in those crates.'

Taggie gave her a hopeful look. 'If someone sees you . . .'

Sophie grinned. 'They won't, you know they won't. I'll fly directly above the carriages. If there's a guard on the trucks I'll come straight back down. If the coast's clear I'll dive down on to the last truck and open a crate. Come on, Taggie, it's not the kind of thing the Karraks will be expecting. There are no skyfolk in the Fourth Realm any more.'

'Well . . . if you're sure.'

Much to his annoyance, they left Felix behind in the compartment as the rest of them edged down the corridor. The other passengers had all drawn the blinds on their doors, so no one saw them passing. The door at the end of the corridor opened on to a small metal platform between the carriages. Freezing air blowing through the gap made everyone's raggedy coats flap about.

'All clear this way,' Taggie said, looking into the next carriage.

'Nobody following us,' Lantic announced, keeping watch on their carriage.

Sophie hurriedly unfastened her coat, letting out a sigh of relief as her wings were freed from the grungy fabric. She strapped her crossbow across the front of her tunic, grinned reassuringly at Taggie, then took off, soaring straight up.

The wind hit her as soon as she cleared the carriage roofs, shoving her about. She got a mouthful of disgusting smoke from the engine, making her cough and blink the stinging vapour from her eyes. But she kept going straight up. First and always she scanned round to check for rathwai. There weren't any.

When she was three hundred metres above the train she levelled out. It took a surprising effort to keep up, the train was travelling so fast. Which made it easy to gradually drop back, watching the carriages slip past below. She gave the end platform of the last carriage a careful examination, but there was no one there.

Sophie slowed down, allowing the long line of trucks to pass below her. The smoke from the engine cast a raggedy tail along most of the train, reducing visibility. That was good. That would help keep her approach unobserved.

Slowly she began to lose height, dropping back into the tattered streamers of smoke. She held her breath as the thin fumes churned around her. Then she was below the cloying murk, and the last of the trucks was directly below her feet.

Sophie landed in a crouch on top of some crates, drawing her crossbow in a swift motion to hunt round for targets. She waited for a few seconds, but there didn't seem to be any alarm raised on the train. But there was a lot of bad magic close by; she could feel it leaking into the air like a unhealthy smell, making her shiver in foreboding.

She slung the crossbow back across her chest and took out a dagger. The tip was shoved into the end of a crate, where the wooden boards were nailed together. She wormed it deeper into the crack. When she pushed down, the plank began to creak upward. She worked the gap for a minute, loosening the thick iron nails, then the board sprang up.

The inside of the crate was packed with smaller boxes, all wrapped in tinfoil. Her dagger cut it open easily. Sophie frowned at the contents, she'd never seen anything like them. Yet instinctively she was cautious. The boxes held clips of brass cylinders the size of her thumb, with a lead ball wedged tight into one end. The lead was infused with the menacing violet glimmer of bad magic.

Sophie took a couple of the clips out, surprised by how heavy they were, and stuffed them into her belt pouch. Then she carefully pushed the board back into place, and used the hilt of the dagger to hammer the nails back down, enough to pass any casual inspection. One final check round to make sure no one was watching, and she took off through the wispy smoke.

She flew in a high arc back to the gap between the third and fourth carriages where everyone was waiting for her. Hovering ten feet above them, she waited for them to give her the all clear. Taggie stuck her thumb up, and she shot down on to the platform. Lantic was holding her coat ready.

'Oh no,' Jemima cried. She suddenly opened the door to the fourth carriage. 'Stand in front of the glass,' she told Taggie, and rushed into the corridor, slamming the door shut.

Sophie folded her wings down tight, and shrugged into the coat. She could hear Jemima's muffled voice above the noise of the train.

Taggie was peering through the window. 'Someone's in the corridor. Jemima's bumped into them. Hurry.' She took her gloves off, and pulled her coat sleeve up, exposing the charmsward. Its bands were turning slowly.

Sophie fastened several laces on the coat as fast as she could, then soothed down her twisting hair, and pushed it inside the coat's hood. Lantic was on his knees, helping her into her boots.

'Finished,' Sophie sang out.

Lantic opened the door into the third carriage, just as Jemima backed out of the fourth. 'Sorry again,' she called as she closed the door behind her.

Everyone scurried back into the third carriage. Taggie

turned back for one last check, and draw a breath in dismay.

'What is it?' Sophie asked.

'It was the man in the fur-lined coat,' Taggie said. 'I saw him at the far end of the corridor.'

'Did he see me?'

'No. Not your wings, anyway. But he certainly saw Jemima causing a commotion.'

They hurried back to their compartment and shut the door.

'What happened?' Felix asked.

'The man in the fur-lined coat,' Taggie said. 'He might be a problem after all.'

They all stared at the door, waiting to see if the man in the fur-lined coat would open it.

'This is silly,' Lantic announced. He twisted a ring so that its gaudy jewel glowed a sullen scarlet. Then he pulled the door open and stepped out into the corridor. 'Nobody here,' he said.

Sophie let out a long breath in relief.

'What did you find?' Taggie asked eagerly.

Sophie quickly untied her coat laces and opened her belt pouch. She took the clip out gingerly, making sure she didn't touch the lead balls. 'These. I've no idea what they are, but there's thousands of them.'

'Oh, great Heavens!' Taggie exclaimed in shock. 'They're bullets.'

19

CUTTING LOOSE

It took Taggie a good quarter of an hour to explain bullets and guns to her alarmed friends.

'Will they work in the Fourth Realm?' Jemima asked uncertainly.

'Bullets use simple chemicals,' Taggie said. 'Gunpowder is going to explode no matter where it is.' She held up one of the horrible bullets Sophie had retrieved, its sickly violet glow was almost invisible in the daylight. 'And the Karraks have given them tips of bad magic. I doubt many enchanted shields can withstand them. No wonder they're confident enough to start a war.'

'There are thousands of them in those crates,' Sophie said in a troubled voice. 'Tens of thousands. And this is but one trainload.'

'We should blow them up,' Jemima said. 'Sabotage the Karraks' war. Taggie, all you have to do is hit one crate with your destruction spell. That'll set off the rest, they'll all explode.'

Taggie had to admit it was extremely tempting, but . . . 'That's not why we're here,' she said reluctantly. 'I know it would damage the Karraks' plans – a little. But there will be more ammunition in storage somewhere. Not to mention all the guns to fire them. We have to prevent the war from ever starting.'

Jemima looked disappointed, but nodded agreement.

'What do guns look like?' Lantic asked. 'I assume from your description they're made of metal?'

'Yes,' Taggie said. 'Why?'

'I'm thinking of the gol arms Jemima saw back in Shatha'hal. The attachments were for machines from the Outer Realm. Enchanted bullets have to be made here, but it sounds like guns need a lot of precision moving parts. They would have to come from experts in producing such things.'

'Outer Realm weapons companies,' Taggie said in dismay. 'They'll make anything for anybody who has money. Oh my, the Karraks are going to fit Outer Realm guns to an army of gols.' She shivered at the terrible notion.

'We have to warn the War Emperor,' Felix said. 'He must be told the armies of the Realms are walking into a trap. Majesty, we cannot allow soldiers with enchanted swords and shields to go up against gols with machine guns firing these bullets. They'll be slaughtered.'

Taggie's hand went to the dark gate she was carrying in a bag hanging from her neck. 'You're right. We do have to warn them. But we can always escape this Realm at any time. I'm still going to try and talk to Lord Colgath. If it looks like we're in trouble, then we'll use the dark gate to leave immediately, I promise.'

The train raced on across the frozen plain for hours. It was mid-afternoon when they all heard a blast from the engine's whistle.

'We're slowing down,' Lantic said. 'Is this Valaran already?'

'No,' Taggie said. 'It's too soon.'

'So why are we stopping here?' Sophie asked with an anxious edge to her voice.

'Novarl said there would be other stops,' Felix reminded them.

'I see a station,' Jemima said, her eyes tight closed. 'There are passengers waiting on the platform.' She flinched. 'Some Karraks live here.'

'That's all we need,' Felix grunted.

'Jemima, cast a wardveil,' Taggie said. She opened her bag and took out the gold and ebony ring. 'Everyone take hold. If they find us, the dark gate will take us away in a second.'

There they stood, in the middle of the compartment, each gripping a section of the ring as the train slowly came to a halt beside a long platform. The town, whatever it was called, could have been New Aurestel, but for the missing hills behind. The big cube-buildings were identical, as were the squads of Rannalal knights marching about. A group of Ethanu stood at one end of the platform, with a few passengers keeping their distance from the dark creatures. A rathwai cried high overhead, and Sophie shuddered.

'It's OK,' Taggie reassured her friend quietly. 'It can't see you. And we can be gone in an eyeblink.'

Sophie nodded her thanks.

'I can see some people getting off,' Lantic said, pressing his face to the broad window. 'People getting on. Only a couple in our carriage.'

After a minute the engine blew its whistle. Doors began to slam shut.

'Oh,' Lantic said.

'What?' Sophie and Felix asked together.

'The fur-coat man. I see him.' Lantic twisted, trying to look right along the platform. 'He's talking to the Ethanu.'

Taggie clenched her teeth. The charmsward bands turned, and she prepared a portrayal enchantment. All she had to do was decide the location: her palace in the First Realm or Mum's house. *The palace would be best*, she thought. *I am Queen there. Perhaps I can still do something about the war, and we have the bullets as evidence now.*

The engine whistle sounded again. Wheels and pistons started clanking. They started to creep forward.

'I can't see the Ethanu,' Lantic said in frustration.

'They got on,' Jemima said. Her face was white with fright. 'They're in the last carriage.'

The train began to pick up speed. Wisps of smoke churned past the window.

'We have to go,' Sophie said. 'We'll never get to Valaran now.'

Everyone looked at Taggie.

'Jem? Can you see what the Ethanu are doing?'

Jemima gave her a resentful look. She threw the runes on to a bench, and studied them for a long moment. 'Questioning people,' she said. 'They're making their way along the compartments.'

Taggie looked down at the gate ring. She could feel the magic stirring in it, as if it knew it was about to be called upon. It wasn't fair! They'd come this far against all the odds, and they knew where Lord Colgath was. Just a few hours away now.

'Taggie!' Sophie said. 'There's six of them.'

'I know,' Taggie said. 'But six isn't a problem, not really.'

'You can't be serious, Majesty,' Felix said. 'We're barely outside the town. There are Karrak Lords here.'

'That's right,' Taggie said slowly as an idea came together in her head. 'So we need to wait until we're as far away as we can be.'

Felix went first, speeding along the corridor to the second carriage, keeping well below the windows on the other compartments so no one saw him. Taggie brought up the rear, just in case the Ethanu caught up with them.

By the time they reached the second carriage, the train was back up to full speed, and the desolate countryside was a white blur outside. They went through the second carriage and into the first.

'Jem?' Taggie asked.

'They're still in the last carriage,' Jemima said happily.

'Right then.'

The door at the end of the first carriage was locked. Lantic adjusted one of his rings and muttered a soft enchantment. The lock broke with a loud snap.

Outside on the little metal platform the noise of the engine was a constant roar. Smoke swirled in the gap between them and the high blank wall of the coal tender in front.

'Here you go,' Lantic said, and handed one of his anamage spiders to Felix.

The squirrel nodded and sprang down on to the thick coupling. Wind flattened his white fur as he scampered along, three feet above the tracks. Then he was climbing the tender wall, claws grabbing the rivets. Taggie couldn't believe he could do it so easily. But in less than a minute he was on top. A single slender gossamer thread stretched out between the carriage platform and the spider he held.

When he put it down, the little contraption began to clamber back along the thread, spinning another behind it.

Jemima shook the runes in her hand, and examined them. 'They've arrived at the fifth carriage,' she announced.

'That's the Ethanu I remember,' Taggie said wryly.

'Slow and methodical. And never giving up.'

'You were right, then, we have plenty of time,' Lantic said, and now even he was relaxing. 'This isn't quite as frightening as I thought it was going to be.'

Taggie grinned. 'So how scared are you?' She tried to make it sound light so he wouldn't realize how scared she was.

'Oh. Badly.' He grinned back. 'You know, my father will want to throw me into the deepest dungeon below the city when we get back. But even he will have to admit he never expected me to do anything so reckless. Not even Rogreth sneaked a visit to the Fourth Realm.'

'You're not doing this just to prove something to your father, are you?' she asked anxiously.

'No. Taggie, I absolutely believe we're doing the right thing. That's why I'm here with you.' His grin grew sheepish. 'Mind you, showing my father I'm not the useless ana-nerd he thinks I am is a pretty good bonus.'

'I'm just glad you're with us,' she told him truthfully.

In three minutes the spider had woven a net like a sagging ladder between the carriage and the tender. Jemima was first across, swaying from side to side as she scrambled up the mesh. Then she was on top of the coal, and smiling brightly back at Taggie. 'Easy,' she taunted.

'Go on,' Taggie told Lantic.

While the prince was crawling gingerly across the mesh, Taggie helped Sophie take off her coat and boots.

The skymaid simply flew over to the coal tender, carrying the bulky coat.

Taggie was last across. Seeing how easy it had been for the others didn't necessarily make it easy for her. The train was hurtling along at a terrific speed. The track was a smear below her, and the gossamer impossibly thin to be holding her weight. The wind was constantly whipping her rag coat about, and she swayed from side to side a lot more than Jemima had. It was cold, too, making her fingers stiff.

But she made it over and joined the others sitting atop the coal as the engine's grubby smoke swirled around them. Together they watched the spider unwind the mesh.

Jemima looked up from the runes in her hand. 'They've reached the fourth carriage,' she announced.

Taggie looked across the countryside, trying to work out distances. It had changed since leaving the last town. No longer a flat empty plain. Undulations were gradually getting bigger. She could see hills and valleys on both sides of the track. Somehow the dismal grey sky seemed lower.

They were miles from the town. It would take hours for anyone to walk back, especially the Ethanu.

'OK, they're in the third carriage now,' Jemima announced. Then later: 'Second carriage.'

They'd been sitting on the tender for at least forty minutes, which by Taggie's reckoning put them at least sixty miles past the town, when Jemima finally said: 'Here they come. First carriage.'

'Let's go,' Taggie said.

Felix, who was now as tall as her elbow, drew his sword. The blade shone a bright green through the acrid vapour streaming past them from the engine's funnel. Sophie cocked her crossbow. Lantic turned two rings until they glowed a bleary amber.

Taggie knelt on all fours and looked down at the coupling. The charmsward bands spun round. '*Droiak*.'

She'd been expecting the tender to lurch about when the coupling disintegrated. But it was made from iron and was still two-thirds full of coal. Something that heavy barely quaked as it broke free from the carriages and trucks. The change in speed as it began to accelerate was quite noticeable, however.

Felix sprang nimbly across the coal, while Sophie flew alongside. The engine driver and the fireman who shovelled coal into the firebox had just started to realize something was wrong when Felix jumped down into the engine's cab. The fireman, who was so big he could have been a troll, lifted up his huge shovel, ready to swipe at the intruder. Felix calmly pointed a forepaw behind him. The fireman turned his thick neck to find a fierce-looking skymaid with wild red hair flying just outside the cab, her crossbow aimed unwaveringly at his head. His shovel clattered on to the metal floor, and he joined the driver in raising his hands.

There was some talk about what to do with them. Lantic expanded the rope in his satchel, and used it to tie them both up. They sat with their backs to the coal tender, looking miserable as their fate was discussed right in front of them.

'We can't just stop the train and chuck them out,' Jemima said. 'They'll freeze to death out here.'

It was hot in the cab, with the coal in the firebox glowing like lava, throwing out a huge amount of heat. They'd even taken off their Outer Realm coats.

'We can't take them with us,' Sophie exclaimed.

'Taggie!' Jemima cried.

'We'll not tell anyone,' said Losovan, the driver. 'Honest. Will we, Jarley?'

'Not say nuffink,' Jarley the fireman agreed. ''Oo are you, anyways?' He couldn't stop looking at Sophie. 'Never seen a flying girl before.'

'Not say anything?' Lantic said in exasperation as he examined the cab's multitude of dials and levers. 'We've stolen your train and left the carriages behind. Do you think the Karraks won't notice that?'

'We won't say who, though,' Losovan promised desperately.

'Yes you will,' Taggie said. 'You'll answer every single question they ask you as best you can. Don't lie to them. Don't hide anything from them. Understand?'

'Gorrit, miss,' Jarley said.

Swarz was the next town on the line, Losovan told them – the only scheduled stop before Valaran. So Taggie and Lantic and Sophie took it in turns to shovel coal into the firebox, while Felix and Jemima kept watch.

The huge engine roared through Swarz at a scary eighty miles an hour, with Felix letting off a long blast on the whistle as they zoomed past the platform.

'Sorry,' he muttered, his teeth chittering unrepentantly. 'Always wanted to do that. And it should confuse the station staff.'

From the smeared glimpse she'd managed, Taggie hadn't even seen any Ethanu waiting on the platform. Now station and town were vanishing fast behind them.

Taggie told them to stop the big engine a couple of miles outside Valaran. Everyone put their coats back on and stepped down on to the track while Losovan and Jarley gave them a baleful look. Lantic threw several levers in the cab, turned some valve stopcocks, and the pistons hissed and pumped. The engine began to roll forward. Lantic jumped down. They all watched it pick up speed and charge off down the track. Without any more coal added to the firebox, it would loose pressure and slow down soon enough.

'I hope it *is* only two miles,' Sophie said. The grey sky was starting to darken. Nightfall was near.

'It is,' Jemima said.

They walked down the track until they saw the lights of Valaran ahead of them, then crept off to one side. Valaran was a fishing village nestling in the cliffs above the sea, with a big stone harbour curving out into the dark waters below. Here at least the houses were ordinary, with small cottages clumped together in a maze of narrow streets. Several dozen ships bobbed about at anchor inside the safety of the harbour walls.

From their vantage point on a small hill behind the village they could see a lot of activity at the tiny railway station. People were running round frantically.

'This is my job,' Felix announced. 'Wait here. I'll go into town and find some horses.'

Taggie's instinct was to object, but she couldn't actually think of a good reason. Felix was right, he was the perfect person to creep into the village without being seen. So they waited in the frozen bushes at the base of the hill, stamping their feet as the cold slowly soaked through their two layers of coats.

It took him an hour. But he eventually returned riding one horse and leading another. Taggie hid a smile at the extraordinary sight of a squirrel on horseback. Jemima giggled hysterically.

20

BY THE LIGHT OF THE RED LOCH

It was a two-hour ride along a narrow coastal road. Their horses' hoofs made little sound on the snow. Above them the immovable sheet of cloud glimmered faintly from the light cast across its upper surface by whatever moon and stars roamed this Realm's Heavens. But it did provide just enough light to make out the road and a few dark shapes in the distance.

Taggie was starting to worry they'd missed Red Loch altogether. Then she saw a red glow up ahead, as if a ruby-coloured sun had just set behind the horizon.

Red Loch was twenty miles at its longest stretch, and over eight miles wide in the middle. It had a rocky island a mile offshore, which was where King Yovonin had decided his impregnable fortress would be built. A thin bridge with innumerable supporting arches stretched out between the shore and the island.

Taggie looked at the water in confusion. It glowed a dull red, as if the loch's bedrock was a giant seam of dying lightstone.

'Amazing,' Lantic said. 'A sea of light.'

'Is it enchanted?' Sophie asked.

'Not quite,' Felix said. 'It has been like this since an angel fell from the stars in the First Times and crashed to the ground forming the loch. Some say it is the angel's blood that mingles with the water.'

'That means nobody's going to sneak up on the castle,' Sophie said in dismay. 'Not in this light.'

'No, they're not,' Taggie agreed. 'But the loch's not too bright. We should manage to get over the bridge OK.'

The bridge only began thirty metres out from the low cliff which ran along the side of the loch. Once, long ago, there had been huge guard-towers on either side. They must have contained a drawbridge that could be lowered to cover the gulf between them and the cliff. Now the towers were razed to mounds of stone smothered in rotting frost fungus. The drawbridge was gone, obliterated in King Ornalo's doomed last stand.

In its place was a rickety-looking ramp of wood. A long lodge had been built on top of the cliff where the ramp started. Its windows shone with the orange light of a fire burning in its hearth. The glow of the loch revealed several armed Rannalal knights patrolling outside.

'Now what?' Lantic asked as they reined in their horses and studied the lodge from the shadows.

'I'll take care of them,' Taggie said. She dismounted and walked along the beaten-down strip of snow that was the road.

When she was fifty metres away, one of the Rannalal lifted its snout and sniffed the air. It let out a growling cry, summoning more from the lodge. They lined up across the road, bristling with sharp enchanted weapons. Taggie kept walking; she didn't even hesitate when she saw the tiny shape of gnomes scurrying about between the legs of the Rannalal.

'Stop,' the Rannalal commander shouted as she stepped forward into the meagre splash of light from the lodge's open door.

'Of course,' Taggie said. She held her hands up, and the coat sleeve fell away from her wrist. The symbols on the charmsward bands were already lined up. '*Wonfi al turon*,' she chanted softly, and her grandmother's gentle enchantment sent the Rannalal and gnomes falling into a deep sleep.

'That. Is. Amazing,' Lantic said as he came up behind her, and stared at the shapes snoring on the ground.

'They'll stay like that for a few hours,' Taggie said. 'We'd better carry them back into the lodge. It's too cold out here.'

Once the unconscious knights and slumbering gnomes had been dragged back inside, Taggie stood at the edge of the ramp and looked along the narrow bridge to the island that rose from the expanse of rippling luminescent water.

'Is it safe?' Lantic asked in a quiet voice. The bridge was barely wide enough for a cart to travel along. There would be no hiding on it if someone came the other way.

'Jem?' Taggie asked.

'I think so. I can't see anyone on the bridge.'

'Do we ride down it?' Lantic asked.

'No,' Taggie said. 'We don't know what's at the other end. The horses could be a problem. We'll leave them here.'

'I thought you'd say that,' he muttered.

Taggie, Jemima, Felix and Lantic stepped on to the ramp. Sophie flew beside them, her crossbow held ready for any trouble.

King Ornalo's final battle must have been ferocious. It wasn't just the ramp that had been built to make the bridge useable again. As they walked along they found big sections of the road missing, as if a monster had taken bites out. Beams and planks had been used to fill the gaps in the crumbling stone, and by the look of it they'd been repaired and replaced many times since. Long lengths of the low walls running along each side were also missing. Somehow the spindly rails patching them up didn't seem much use.

It was tough going. They didn't trust the repairs, and had to test every wobbly plank before they trod on it. Someone had to watch out behind in case anyone appeared at the end of the bridge and gave chase. Sophie was constantly worried rathwai would fall upon them from the sky, and held her crossbow ready the whole time.

When they were two-thirds of the way across, they could finally make out the ruins of the castle in the vermilion gloom cast by the loch light. Huge blocks of stone had been smashed down and strewn across the ground. A single tower remained, standing black against the rose-tinted sky. Its smooth surface tapered gradually, then flared out in an onion shape eighty metres above the ground.

'No need to ask where Lord Colgath is kept, then,' Sophie muttered.

'A tower overlooking water,' Taggie said. 'Well seen, Jem.'

'Where are all the jailers?' Lantic asked.

Taggie eyed the lone tower uneasily. It seemed to radiate dark wizardry into the cold air. 'I don't think he needs them,' she said. 'Those Rannalal were there to keep people out, not him in.'

As they reached the end of the bridge, a couple of yellow lights became visible amid the colossal avalanche of rubble. A couple of shacks had been built from the smaller stones. The light they were seeing was creeping out of crude shutters. Beside them were pens of goats and pigs who snuffled softly.

'Is anyone else around?' Taggie asked Jemima.

'No. I can sight three men and a troll in the shacks, but that's it.'

Taggie craned her neck back to look at the bulbous top of the tower. 'What about up there?'

'Sorry,' Jemima said. 'It's chock-full of wardveils and shadecasts.'

'The tower has a lot of enchantments besides wardveils,' Taggie said. 'The Karraks have done something odd to the tower itself, I can feel it.'

'They'd need to use some potent wizardries to hold one of their own,' Lantic said. 'The brother of the Grand Lord is going to be formidable.'

Keeping a nervous watch on the shacks, they made their way across the broken stone and drifts of snow.

21

THE THING IN THE TOWER

Eventually the children and Felix came across a well-worn track that stretched between the shacks and the base of the tower. They followed it to the tower itself, which loomed ominously over them. Walking a complete circle round the base, the only opening they could find was a small metal cylinder set into the smooth stone at shoulder height, barely two feet high and one in diameter. There was a keyhole in the middle of it.

Lantic peered at the inset cylinder. 'Whatever this is, it can't be the way in. Yet it's the only gap in the stone. This is a sore puzzle.' He waved his hands across the metal, chanting softly. 'Hmm, that's very odd. My lock-breaker enchantments don't have any effect. It's as if the magic stopped working.'

'Let me try,' Taggie said. The charmsward bands spun, axe symbol aligning with door and wind. They glowed a dark amber. '*Zothron*,' she chanted, which was a much stronger opening spell than the one Lantic had used. She felt the magic flash out of her hand, only to be sucked away into nothingness by the stone.

'Oh Heavens,' she said with a shudder at the unsettling

effect, and looked up at the tower with a newfound dismay and respect. 'The Karraks have enchanted it to kill magic. That's how they're keeping Lord Colgath inside. He can't escape because his wizardry doesn't work in there.'

'So how do we get in?' Jemima asked.

'Sophie,' Taggie said, still looking at the bulging top of the tower. 'Can you fly up there and see if there are any windows?'

The skymaid took off and zoomed upward. Barely a minute later she was back down. 'Five windows,' she said breathlessly. 'They're narrow, like slits in the stone, but you could get in if they didn't have iron grilles set across them. I didn't see any light inside, but I did try calling his name. If Colgath is in there he's not answering.'

'Then I'll ask him a little more firmly,' Taggie said with determination. She formed the complicated *Adrap* spellform in her mind, visualizing the eagle she wished to become: a beautiful bird, sleek and powerful, with huge wings spread wide, just like Katrabeth achieved. She held her arms out. Clicked her fingers. Excited by the idea of racing Sophie through the air, which was . . .

The spellform twisted, and magic flared out of her feet into the ice-covered rocks. 'Oww.'

'Taggie!' Jemima groaned in exasperation.

'I can do this,' Taggie snapped back. Once again the *Adrap* spellform. Then the visualization. She thought she'd got both of them right as she clicked her fingers, but the two together were too much. Magic sizzled away. She stamped her foot as much in frustration as pain.

Felix flicked the tip of his tail from side to side. 'Lantic, if Sophie takes the spiders up there can they weave a ladder down to the ground for us?'

Taggie was about to protest, to tell them to stop, that she could shapeshift. Except the doubts in her heart made it hard to form the words. She wasn't going to sniffle at her repeated failure, though. Definitely not.

Lantic gave the tower a thoughtful look. 'I can do better than that,' he said, and retrieved the three spiders from his satchel. He chanted several instructions to them before giving them to Sophie. 'Take them to the very top and place them on the stone,' he told her.

Sophie took off again.

She was back down quickly. 'I called for Colgath a few times again. Nothing.'

'Do you suppose he's dead?' Lantic asked.

'He wasn't when I sighted him,' Jemima insisted. 'It wasn't that long ago.'

'How long will the spiders take?' Taggie asked.

'Should be down in a minute or so,' Lantic told her.

'Really?'

He gave her a mischievous grin. She couldn't help but smile back. This Lantic was so different to the one who'd greeted her off the royal barge back in Shatha'hal. Easy to be around . . .

Sure enough, each of the spiders descended on a single strand of gossamer a couple of minutes later.

'It's going to take forever to weave a ladder,' Jemima complained.

'Who said anything about a ladder?' Lantic asked.

He made Jemima stand still and ordered a spider to scurry round and round her, weaving a simple harness of gossamer.

'Oh!' Taggie said. A spider wound an identical harness round her, and Lantic kept hold of Felix as the third spider spun out his harness.

'Ready?' Lantic asked.

Suddenly the door on one of the shacks slammed open. They could hear the voices of two men in the night air.

'Go,' Taggie urged.

'*Morool*,' Lantic whispered.

The three spiders began to crawl back up the gossamer they'd spun down from the top of the tower, lifting Taggie, Lantic and Jemima up with them. Taggie felt a disquieting tingle down her legs again as she dangled on the end of gossamer thinner than a strand of cotton, sliding relentlessly up into the sky with nothing beneath her feet. She turned as she rose higher and higher, spinning ever so slowly, so that one minute she was staring at the featureless stone wall of the tower, then the next the loch slid round into view.

When she glanced down she saw the men from the shacks holding lanterns as they walked along the path to the tower. Sophie fluttered past, quieter than a moth and holding her crossbow ready. All the men had to do was glance upward and the game would be up. The light of Red Loch might be faint, but it made them very visible.

The men walked to the bottom of the tower. Their harsh voices laughed about something. By then, Taggie was a good thirty metres directly above them. She saw one slide a key into the metal cylinder. The cylinder must have opened, because the other one put his hand inside. He seemed to be pulling at something. There was an odd grinding sound, as if stone wheels were rolling around inside the tower. Then the cylinder was shut and locked, and they were walking away again.

Taggie hadn't even realized she was holding in her breath until she exhaled in relief. The tower wall slipped round in front of her once more. Taggie looked up. The bulging room at the top of the tower was a lot closer now.

Five minutes after leaving the ground, Taggie and the others were clinging on to the metal grid that covered one of the window slits. Sophie hovered in the air a few metres away. Up here, there was a lot more wind blowing off the loch. It made Taggie's grip seem very precarious.

'Lord Colgath,' Taggie called nervously. 'I am the Queen of Dreams from the First Realm. Please, I must talk with you.'

Peering in past the iron grid, there was only darkness to be seen. Nothing moved. There was no sound. 'Please!' Taggie growled as loud as she dared. 'Colgath. I can get you out.'

'Why won't he answer?' Jemima whined.

Holding on to the harness, Taggie put her feet flat against the vertical wall of the tower room, and straightened her legs. She stood at right angles to the wall, which redoubled the tingling in her legs.

'What are you doing?' Jemima squeaked.

'Breaking in.' Taggie prayed the enchantments within the tower's stone didn't also work in the iron grille. The bands on her charmsward slipped round. She pointed her finger, and summoned her full magical strength. '*Droiak!*'

The purple-white magical light flashed out of her finger, smashing into the grille. The glare immediately flared wide, as the tower's enchantments sucked the magic away. But the grid had buckled and twisted under the impact of the destruction spell.

'*Droiak!* . . . *Droiak!* . . . *Droiak!*'

Finally the tough iron gave way, leaving a hole just big enough for Taggie to wiggle through.

'I think the men down below might have heard that,' Sophie said drily. 'The door on one of their shacks just opened.'

Taggie growled in annoyance and carefully pulled herself through the wrecked grille. The window was a sloping hole cut through the tower's thick stone walls. Taggie slithered helplessly down, then felt herself falling, and flung her hands out in front.

It was only a few feet, but the impact made her squawk as pain flashed up through her wrists. She crumpled inelegantly on to the floor.

'Taggie, are you OK?' Lantic called.

'Yes, fine.' She could see the pale red rectangle of the window slit above her, and slowly stood up. 'Lord Colgath?'

It was a single room; in the distance she could just make out four other rectangles of scarlet luminescence that were the other windows. Somewhere close by she could hear running water – which was odd. She instinctively tried to search through the charmsward's memories for an illumination spell. There were no charmsward memories. The wizardry in the tower's stone really did kill any magic inside.

Taggie did what she'd done a hundred times in the Outer Realm when she got caught outside at night, and pulled her mobile phone from her pocket and switched it on. As there was no magic inside the tower that could interfere with the device, the little screen lit up right away, casting a reasonable blue-green light across the circular room. She peered round. The room itself was normal. Definitely a jail cell for someone important. There were several bookcases full of big leather-bound tomes; a stone basin with water running into it from a spout just above; what she assumed was a toilet – a low stone cylinder with a hole in the top. And also the remains of a wooden bed and desk which someone had carefully dismantled.

The furnishings didn't interest her at all. Instead she stared in bewilderment at the mechanism that had been built across the floor. It was like a big chunk of clockwork, but made out of wood and leather, with cogwheels, and rollers, and rope pulleys, and a slim conveyor belt running through the middle.

'What in in the sweet Heavens . . . ?' Taggie gawped.

'Taggie?' Lantic hissed. 'The men are coming, and the troll as well. They'll see us in a minute. What's happening? Is he there or not?'

'No, he's not here. You'd better come in.'

Lantic was first. Taggie helped catch him before he tumbled on to the ground. Jemima was next, looking round curiously. Then Sophie wiggled in. Felix appeared in the grille, and began to slide down the stone. He started to grow. Fast.

Taggie was so surprised, she took a half-step back, letting out a yelp.

Felix landed on the floor, and slowly clambered to his feet in the hazy light of the mobile's screen. Taggie, Sophie, Jemima and Lantic simply stood there, staring at him.

Felix gazed round them in concern. 'What?'

'Felix,' Jemima said in wonder. 'Felix . . . it's you.'

Felix brought his hands up, gazing at them. He wasn't a squirrel any more, but a boy of about fifteen years, with long white hair that reached halfway down his back. 'Oh my,' he gulped.

'There's no magic in here,' Taggie said quietly. 'The curse can't work when you're inside the tower.'

Jemima walked over to him as if in a trance. She reached up and touched his face, then broke into a glorious smile.

'It *is* you. You were at the quayside. You saved me from the gols.'

Felix gave a lopsided grin, and shrugged.

'And you didn't tell me who you were!' Jemima shouted crossly.

'I was just doing my job watching out for you,' Felix said sheepishly. 'You're always getting into trouble.'

'Am not! And, anyway, how come you weren't a squirrel that day?'

'*For each day outside my birthday and while snow falls on oak,*' Felix quoted softly. 'That is the curse placed upon my family.'

'It was your birthday,' Jemima said sadly. 'I forgot.'

'I never told you,' he said. 'I don't wish you to see me like this.'

'Why, Felix? Why?'

He gave her a mournful look. 'Because you will pity me for the rest of the year. I thought it best you think of me only as what I appear the rest of the time.'

'I wouldn't pity you. I *won't* pity you,' Jemima said solemnly.

'Thank you.'

They shared a tentative smile.

Taggie turned away, slightly embarrassed as Felix started to examine his arms with a childlike curiosity. He was right: once they were back outside she'd never stop thinking of him as he was now. She held up the mobile, shining it round in an attempt to take her mind off the cruelty of the curse.

'So what happened to Colgath?' Lantic said.

'He escaped somehow,' Taggie said. 'We need to find out how.'

'Then why are those men in the shack below, and Rannalal guarding the bridge?' Sophie asked.

'I don't know,' Taggie replied. 'We need to find something, some clue that tells us where he's gone.' She spotted an oil lantern beside the remnants of the desk. There were some matches next to it, the box covered in dust. But they still worked, and she soon had the lantern lit. It cast a pale yellow light across the tower room.

'What in all the Heavens is that thing?' Jemima said,

looking at the bizarre wooden mechanism.

'I don't know,' Taggie said. 'But it has to be connected with his escape, somehow. Lantic, can you see what it does?'

'Not really.' He walked over to the stone basin, and touched a small wheel next to it. 'This looks like a miniature waterwheel, but it should be under the water. I think it can hinge round. Perhaps if I . . .'

He stopped as a faint metallic growl sounded. They all looked at the other end of the mechanism as the noise became louder. Set into the wall was a small metal cylinder identical to the one at the bottom of the tower. Wooden struts, carved from the desk, extended right up to the curving metal. Something like a piano hammer rested against it.

As they watched, the cylinder turned. A hole in the metal slid into view. The little hammer fell into it. Strings and pulleys attached to the bottom of the hammer moved, tugging at parts of the mechanism. Cogwheels clicked round. The small waterwheel swung under the water running out of the spout, and began to turn. Then every pulley and belt was rotating.

A hand-like scoop reached into the open cylinder with a whirring sound and tugged out a plate woven from dried reeds. It held a pile of raw meat. The plate dropped on to the conveyor belt and trundled across the room to the stone toilet. The belt tipped the plate and meat into the hole. There was a brief clattering as they fell down into oblivion.

The metal cylinder turned shut, pushing the hammer back out. Strings jerked the waterwheel back. The whole mechanism became still.

Lantic stared at it, open-mouthed. 'Oh, by the sweet Heavens! That . . . *that* is the most utterly brilliant thing I've ever seen. I love it!'

'The lift comes down empty every time,' Taggie said, and even she felt a burst of admiration for the Karrak Lord's ingenuity. 'The guards think he's still up here eating the meals. They don't know he's escaped.'

'How long since he left?' Felix asked.

'Years, probably,' Lantic said in excitement. 'And this is a sturdy mechanism. It'll probably last for several more years. When they do finally realize he's gone, the trail will be colder than the Grand Lord's heart.'

'Right then,' Taggie said, scanning round the bookshelves. 'Something in here should tell us where he's gone.'

'No it won't,' Sophie contradicted sharply. 'Come on, Taggie. They sealed him up in an anti-magic cell eighty metres up in the air. And he's smart enough to break out of it. He's not going to leave clues where he went!'

'Not deliberately, but . . .' Taggie broke off as a fierce animal screech sounded outside the tower.

'Rathwai!' Sophie exclaimed in fright. 'Heavens protects us, rathwai have come.' She ran over to one of the windows and grabbed at the grille, pulling herself up until her face was against the iron. 'I see them. A whole flock of the monsters being ridden by Karrak Lords. They're circling the tower.'

Lantic had gone to the window Taggie had broken. 'Oh no,' he groaned in dismay.

'What?' Taggie squeezed into the little stone nook beside him to look down. The bridge was alive with vivid orange light. What looked like an entire army was marching along it, with every soldier holding a blazing torch aloft. Enough soldiers to stretch three-quarters of the way back to shore. The shore: where even more columns of troops were drawn up, waiting to cross.

She let go and slid numbly back into the room. Her hand went to the bag hanging round her neck, feeling the shape of the gate ring inside. 'It won't work,' she whispered, aghast. 'There's no magic in here. We can't get out. We're trapped.'

Her mobile started to ring.

22

A PRISONER'S ONE PHONE CALL

They all stared in disbelief at the phone in Taggie's hand. She slowly brought it up to her face. Signal strength showed one bar. The screen display read 'UNKNOWN CALLER'.

Taggie pressed the 'accept call' icon. 'Hello?'

'Queen of Dreams.' A deep voice reverberated out of the mobile. 'So sorry to have missed you.'

'Who is this?'

The bass voice chuckled. 'Lord Colgath.'

Taggie sank to her knees in frustration. 'Where are you?'

'Thankfully, a long, long way away from Red Loch Castle. I found its hospitality somewhat disagreeable. I'm sure you appreciate that.'

'How did you escape?' Taggie cried.

'Ah. Now you see, this is where I face an unfortunate dilemma. My dear brother believes I'm still a prisoner in that tower with you. And that is the Grand Lord's own personal army you can see marching over the bridge, with him at the head no less. I believe he brought them through his private gate to deal with you, whom he has named

"Abomination". He will be extremely unhappy to discover I am gone.'

Taggie turned to the window. 'You can see the army? You must be close.'

'Alas, I am observing through a seeing crystal, which is also how I can send a mobile signal all the way back to the tower. Because, you see, I'm actually sitting a long way away here in my rather comfy new home, with my feet up, eating some delectable strips of jellied volpas as I watch your escapade unfold in the crystal. It is most enjoyable entertainment. A "guilty pleasure", I believe it's called.'

'The tower is impregnable. Amenamon will never know you and I have escaped. Please tell me!'

'Nothing is forever, Queen of Dreams. Even you and I will turn to dust. You sooner than I, of course.'

'I came here to stop a war,' she shouted. 'You can help me. Doesn't that mean anything?'

'Stop a war? The war that Amenamon has spent decades plotting and preparing? You seem intent on setting me against him. However, his wrath is not something I wish to face again. I'm sorry, Queen of Dreams. Your intention is noble, but doomed.'

'Why have you called, then? Is it just to mock me?'

'Certainly not. I was curious whether you actually live up to your reputation. I am glad to see you do. It's a shame you are about to die. The likes of you and I, who deplore the stupidity of violence, are few and far between in these sad days. Soon there will be none of us left. But I will remember you for as long as I can. Goodbye, Queen of Dreams.'

'No!' Taggie howled at the mobile. But the call had ended. There were no signal-strength bars left. Lord Colgath must have closed up the seeing crystal. She couldn't call anyone else for help.

Taggie started crying. She slumped on the floor of the tower room, letting the tears run down her cheeks, no longer caring who saw. It wasn't just that she was about to die, but that her death would mean no one else would stop the war. Thousands would die because she had failed.

Her friends gathered round, hugging her, murmuring such words of comfort they could manage. Eventually she dried her tears and smiled a weak thanks at them. 'I'm sorry I brought you here,' she told them in a small voice.

'If Colgath got out, we can get out,' Lantic announced defiantly. 'Perhaps he weakened one of the window grilles?'

'How would that help?' Felix asked. 'We've already got an open window and we're completely trapped.'

'He must have had old friends, or supporters,' Lantic said thoughtfully. 'Once he broke the grille, they could have brought a rathwai for him to fly away on.'

'Still not helping us,' Felix said.

'If we could just climb out, we could use the dark gate.'

'If you stick your head out there, the rathwai will eat it,' Sophie said scathingly.

'Your crossbow will work if you hold it outside the grille,' Lantic told her.

'I will go if that is what we have to do,' the skymaid said, struggling against her fear. 'But I cannot hold off an entire flock of rathwai while the rest of you climb out behind me.'

'No,' Taggie said. 'It's a silly idea. There must be another way.'

'The room is sealed, apart from the lift mechanism,' Lantic said pedantically. 'And the lift isn't big enough – not even for Felix if he became a squirrel again.'

'There's the toilet,' Jemima suggested. 'That has to lead down through the tower somehow.'

They all turned to stare at the raised circle of stone with a hole in the top.

'We don't know how wide the sewer pipe is,' Felix said.

'Do you have a better idea?' Sophie asked.

Felix gave her an apologetic grin. 'No.'

'We have to get the top off,' Lantic said.

'How?' Jemima asked reasonably.

'That's why Colgath didn't use the sewer to escape,' Felix said. 'There's no way to shift the stone.'

They all fell silent as they heard a new sound from outside: a drawn-out howl of an angry beast snarling as if in pain. Something in the howl told them it was a big animal making it. Very big. Another howl began. As one, they rushed over to the windows.

On the shore to one side of the bridge, seven barges were drawing up beside a small wharf. Long lines of torch-bearing soldiers were assembling to greet them. Each barge had a very large cage resting on top. The light from the loch's water wasn't bright enough to reveal what was inside the cages.

More of the beasts were howling and snorting now. The cries were loud in the tower room, and Taggie couldn't imagine what it was like down there on the wharf.

'What's in the cages?' Jemima asked in a scared voice.

'My grandmother told stories of the Zanatuth,' Felix said. 'Great beasts that came through Mirlyn's Gate with all the other wretched creatures from the Dark Universe. There were not many of them, for even the Karraks are supposed to be afraid of them. Bigger than elephants, more savage than rathwai. They cannot be tamed or controlled, only goaded. In battle, even the mightiest of the Fourth Realm's knights fell before them.'

One by one, they backed away from the windows in subdued silence.

'We really need to see what kind of sewer pipe is under that toilet,' Sophie said.

Lantic knelt down beside it and held the oil lamp over the hole, peering down. 'It does seem to get a lot wider below the floor,' he said, and rapped on the stone with a knuckle. 'This stone is solid, though, and set into the floor. Do we have anything we can use to crack it? Maybe even chip at it?'

Sophie immediately produced her dagger, and tried scratching at the stone with its point. 'Granite, or harder,' she proclaimed in frustration. 'I think the knife would wear down before I could make a mark.'

'Is there any way we can overcome the dark enchantments?' Felix asked. 'We need but one of your destruction spells, Majesty. You're easily strong enough to blast this chunk of stone apart.'

Taggie and Lantic looked at each other. He shook his head slowly. 'This is a prison that explicitly prevents magic,' he said. 'The enchantments in the stone can only be countered from outside where magic still works.'

Taggie gave the stone toilet a thoughtful look; something Felix had said was nagging at her.

'So the Grand Lord and his army will cancel the enchantments,' Jemima said hopefully. 'Maybe Taggie can hit it with her destruction spell as soon as they do. Before the Zanatuth charge. We've only got to smash the top bit.'

'That's right,' Taggie said abruptly, and smiled. 'Yes! An explosion, that's what we need.'

Felix gave her a very curious look. 'An explosion?'

Taggie grinned round at them, her hope returning fast. 'Yes. A non-magical explosion. Sophie, give me the bullets.'

Oh, brilliant, Taggie!' Jemima said. 'Of course! The gunpowder.'

They tipped the lamp's oil out, and poured the gunpowder from the bullets carefully into the little metal canister. Taggie used every bullet except one, and tapped down the gunpowder, screwing the canister's cap back on tight. There were more than enough leather straps in Colgath's mechanism to lower the canister down the toilet until it was just below floor level. Then Taggie said, 'Get down.' She lit the fuse: a length of string they'd soaked in oil.

Cowering together beside the wall, they waited as the blue flame sped across the floor and into the hole. Outside, the incensed cries of the Zanatuth rose as if they sensed they would soon be let loose on their prey.

The gunpowder exploded with a blast even louder than the ferocious beasts outside. A sun-bright flame stabbed up from the toilet hole, licking the stone ceiling above. The floor shook.

When Taggie got back up to examine the toilet stone by the light of her mobile's screen she saw a giant crack running up the side and along the top. Lantic wrenched a long pole of wood from the mechanism, and jabbed it into the hole. All of them tugged – hard. Taggie grinned at the unusual sight of Felix straining away beside them, his long white hair waving about. She was afraid they'd snap the wood, but then came the fabulous sound of stone grating against stone, and the pole shifted. They shoved it back in, and pulled again.

A couple of minutes later, they'd levered the two halves of the stone apart, and were looking into the circular opening below. The screen's light revealed a stone tube covered in slimy green algae. The basin obviously drained into the sewer as well. Water trickled along the bottom of the tube, which curved away at a steep angle, but at least it wasn't a vertical drop. On the ground below, the Zanatuth were bellowing as they were let out of their cages.

'Who goes first?' Sophie said.

'We really don't have time to debate this,' Felix said. 'I have a sword and know how to use it.' He swung his legs over the edge of the exposed tube, and gave them a mischievous wink. Then he pushed off, and was gone. They could hear him sliding for several seconds.

From outside came the dull thud of something massive hitting the side of the tower. Taggie half expected to feel it tremble.

'Me next,' Jemima said keenly. She dropped down the opening.

Sophie followed, then Lantic. Taggie waited as long as she dared so he could get clear, then let herself fall into the blackness, just as the second Zanatuth hurled itself against the tower.

23

WHAT LIES BELOW THE FLOOR

The sewer tube spiralled down the tower. Its wet, algae-slimed walls made it horribly slippy. Taggie pushed her elbows out against the rough walls to try and reduce her speed but it was painful, so she had to do it sparingly.

There was the tiniest warning the tube was coming to an end. She thought she heard a splash echoing up through the darkness. Then that was definitely Jemima squealing – but not in terror. A small red glow appeared beyond her feet.

All at once, she shot out into open air, and fell. She was in a small cave with red water filling the bottom. Her friends were splashing about in it. There was just enough time for her to take a breath and close her mouth as she hit the water. It was deathly cold, stabbing into her body like a thousand small blades of ice. She floundered about for a frightening couple of seconds, completely disorientated.

Her head came back up into the air, but the thick layers of clothes she was wearing immediately threatened to drag her back down again: they were so heavy from all the water saturating them. She kicked hard to stay afloat.

'Where . . . ?' Salty water flooded into her mouth, and she coughed.

'Taggie!' Jemima shouted.

'Here,' she called out. 'Lantic?'

'I'm OK.'

'Sophie?'

'Up here.'

'What?' She tipped her head back to see the skymaid hovering above the glowing water. 'Oh. Felix?'

'I hate water. Squirrels can't swim, you know.'

Taggie was slightly disappointed he'd transformed back into a squirrel. She'd liked having him as a human boy rather than the bundle of soggy fur that was now thrashing about.

He wasn't the only one struggling. The cold was actually making her ache. She had to get out fast.

'Taggie!' Jemima yelled in panic as she kicked up a big spray of glittering red droplets. 'I can't keep afloat. The armour's too heavy.'

'Hang on,' Sophie said. She skimmed across the water and grabbed Jemima by her collar, towing her to the edge of the cavern. Then she came back for Felix.

Jemima was still coughing water up on the rock when a sea serpent thicker than her leg, with glistening dark-green skin, reared up out of the water and snapped its jaws shut around Jemima's ankle.

Everyone screamed at once. The serpent writhed and its jaws sprang open quickly. Broken fangs fell out.

The *athrodene* armour, Taggie realized. Nothing could

get through it. Jemima squirmed up the rock, screaming and trying to get away from the luminous water.

Sophie dived down and snatched Felix clean out of the water.

'Move!' Sophie bellowed as she dropped Felix on the rocks next to Jemima.

Taggie and Lantic started swimming desperately for the rocks at the edge of the cave. Sophie hovered overhead, her crossbow aimed down at the water as she stared down intently.

Every stroke was a huge effort. Taggie could barely move her arms, they were so cold and heavy. Her saturated clothes added to the difficulty, but sheer panic kept forcing her to push one arm ahead, then another, in what amounted to a feeble paddle.

A crossbow bolt streaked down into the water barely a foot from Taggie. Something brushed against her leg. She screamed, and forced her leaden arms to move a fraction faster. Bubbles erupted behind her.

A serpent's head reared up next to Lantic.

Felix flung a firestar. The bright circle expanded as it

flew through the air and sliced into the serpent's skull. Blood spurted out. The ruined thing sank below the surface.

Long dark shapes produced slick ripples as they raced towards it. Then the water churned vigorously as they began their feeding frenzy.

Taggie was almost at the rocks. Her feet touched something solid, and she was scrambling up out of the freezing red seawater, sobbing in relief.

Sophie fired her crossbow again. Then Lantic was crawling up out of the glowing water, shaking so badly his limbs almost didn't work.

'Use the dark gate,' Sophie shouted. 'Get us out of here.'

Taggie just grunted. Her teeth were chattering so much she couldn't talk. Numb fingers scrambled at the bag hanging round her head. She couldn't even pull the crude lace fastenings open. Jemima leaned forward and simply sliced through the fabric with a small dagger. Taggie managed to pull out the black and gold ring with frigid fingers. Sophie sank down out of the air and grabbed hold. Everyone else gathered round.

Taggie thought about Mum's kitchen. '*Caravaz el thrain*,' she groaned.

The middle of the black and gold ring blinked to show the wonderfully familiar room with its shiny cupboards and polished floor.

Two serpents emerged from the water and began to slither up the rocks. All Taggie could think of was how unfair that was. They were sea serpents!

Felix flung another firestar. It was so bright Taggie could barely see anything.

'*Seseeamie.*'

The five of them landed on the kitchen floor amid a spray of icy water and sea-serpent blood. They lay there for a moment like fish that'd been emptied out of a trawler's net. Water started running out of their clothes, forming a huge puddle that spread right across Mum's pristine tiles.

Taggie groaned with all sorts of dismay. Then she was fumbling with the laces on the Fourth Realm coat, desperate to get her icy clothes off. Felix was shaking himself like a dog, scattering droplets everywhere, much to everybody's consternation.

'Everyone OK?' Taggie asked. Something about how ordinary the kitchen was made it seem as if she'd simply woken from a bizarre dream. One second she'd been in fear of her life fleeing Karraks and Zanatuth and sea serpents in a dark frozen Realm, the next she was at home with the warm afternoon sun flooding through patio doors.

'Well,' Lantic said as he wheezed down some air. 'At least we know why Lord Colgath didn't use that escape route.'

Taggie shuddered. It was the closest she could come to a laugh right now.

'Bags me the shower first,' Jemima said through chattering teeth.

24

SIGHTED

An hour later Taggie joined everyone else back down in the kitchen. They'd either had a hot shower or a decent soak in a hot bath. Lantic and Jemima had covered the tiled floor in towels while Taggie made everyone hot chocolate.

'So now what?' Lantic asked as they sat on the stools along the breakfast bar.

Jemima found a packet of biscuits, and started handing them round. She showed Lantic how to dunk them in his hot chocolate.

'Now we make Lord Colgath an offer he can't refuse,' Taggie said as she sipped from her mug. She hadn't felt like this before. Now the fear had faded, there was a flame of anger deep inside her that powered a determination greater even than the time she'd faced the usurper Lord Jothran to battle for the throne of the First Realm. She wasn't going to creep about meekly any more as if she'd done something wrong.

'Er, what sort of offer?' Sophie asked.

'Me, or his big brother and the War Emperor,' she said without hesitation. 'His choice.'

Sophie nodded in approval. 'Nice one.'

Taggie looked round the kitchen to see if anyone objected. Lantic and Jemima gave her a thumbs-up; Felix twitched his wet black nose, sending his whiskers swishing about.

So Taggie picked up her mobile and made the call.

'Taggie!' Prince Harry exclaimed. 'Heavens above, what have you been up to?'

'Trying to stop a war,' she replied levelly.

'Ah well, no wonder you're so unpopular. You know Manokol has practically accused you of treason? Andrew's told us the Gathering has issued a proclamation that you appear before them to answer their questions.'

'Oh really? I'd like to see them try and make me.'

'That's the spirit. So as you're sort of persona non grata, as it were, I definitely should not be telling you to be careful. There's a lot of magical folk stomping about the Outer Realm looking for you.'

'No, you'd better not tell me that at all.'

'I won't then, because there's a lot of them, and some of them really aren't pleasant. Filthy tempers and no manners, and that's just the ones on our side.'

'I can imagine.'

'So what can I not do for you?'

'I don't need a favour,' Taggie said. 'Just over an hour ago someone called my mobile number. I really don't need to know exactly where that call came from.'

'I'd better not tell you then. I won't call you back in five minutes after MI1 hasn't run a trace through the phone company records.'

They got ready while they waited for Prince Harry to call back. Not that there were a lot of clothes left in the sisters' wardrobes. Taggie put on jeans and a dark sweatshirt, then combed back her hair and wove it into a thick braid.

'We're being sighted,' Jemima said suddenly. 'I can feel it. A seer is searching for us. Do you want me to cast a wardveil?'

'No, not yet. And why are you wearing Mum's sunglasses? It's going to be dark in a couple of hours.'

Jemima who had chosen combat trousers baggy enough to cover her *athrodene* armour along with the black denim jacket she always wore for Laser Quest (complete with all her game badges), gave her a defiant look. 'There'll probably be a big fight when we find Colgath. And action heroes always wear dark glasses.'

'Fine. Whatever.'

Sophie was wearing yet another of Taggie's oversize fleeces, along with a disgruntled expression as she folded her wings and shrugged into it. Lantic had to make do with a pair of Mum's jeans – Jemima cut a few inches off the bottom of the legs and promised him frayed edges were fashionable in the Outer Realm, just like belts holding the waist up.

'I've got good news and bad news,' Prince Harry said when he phoned back.

'Go on,' she told him.

'Well, the good news is we tracked the call to a mobile

here in London; it was made from Canada Square in Docklands. The bad news is that the phone was bought for cash eleven months ago, there's no record of who bought it.'

'Can you send me the address?' she asked.

'Texting it to you now.'

'Thank you, Harry.'

'No probs. Do you need backup?'

'No. But I do need to keep the police away if anything goes wrong. I don't want ordinary people getting hurt.'

'Leave it with me.'

Taggie drove to Stamford station in Mum's second car, an ancient Mercedes A-Class. She was a lot more confident behind the wheel now.

Just as they turned into St John's Street a police car started following them. Taggie watched it in the mirror for a minute, then clicked her fingers. All four of the police car's tyres burst simultaneously, and it veered into a row of parked cars.

At the station she stood in front of the ticket machine and used Mum's spare credit card to buy four first class tickets to London.

'Do you want me to cast a wardveil?' Jemima asked as the machine spat out the tickets.

'Not yet,' Taggie told her.

'But we're still being sighted.'

'Trust me.'

They climbed aboard the next local train to Peterborough station. Fifteen minutes later they got off at Platform 5, and made their way up the stairs to the bridge that spanned all the platforms. 'Now you can cast that wardveil,' Taggie told Jemima. 'There are trains going all over the country from here. No one will know which one we take.' A couple of minutes later, they caught the express down to King's Cross station in London.

There were lock spells and trip enchantments and Second Realm spygems, even an ordinary Outer Realm house alarm. Katrabeth simply glided past all of them, disabling them with her own powerful magic.

She stood in the middle of the kitchen and frowned in disapproval at what she saw. The floor was covered in soaking wet towels, smelling like seawater. Strangely, they seemed to be glowing a very faint red.

Katrabeth wrinkled her nose up in disapproval. 'See what you can find,' she told Nursy, who was hovering behind her.

She found Taggie's bedroom easily enough. Her eyebrow lifted in scorn at the frilly lace trim around the chest of drawers, the pink duvet and matching pillowcase, the childish blue ceiling with its painted clouds. She held up a flower-print skirt from an open drawer, and didn't even bother to compare it with the scarlet silk dress she was wearing, it was so inferior. There were pebbles and shells lined up on the windowsill, obviously collected from various seaside holidays. She picked them up one by one, examining them, trying to gather the magical scent of her prey. There was one thing: a daisy chain in a scuffed toy jewellery box. It was old and dry now, but Taggie had obviously put a lot of effort into making it some distant summer, and she'd kept it. She had considered it precious at one time.

'Oh, Nursy,' Katrabeth called loudly.

The old woman shuffled into the bedroom, her stiff dress rustling like dry leaves as she moved. She stopped abruptly when she saw the daisy chain dangling from Katrabeth's finger. 'Find her for me, Nursy, there's an angel.'

'No no, my sweet one,' Nursy said fearfully. 'Don't make me do that. Please. The little princess has cast a wardveil around them. You know how it burns when I break through.'

Katrabeth's expression hardened. 'Nursy, darling, you're the very best seer in the Third Realm. If you can't break a child's wardveil, then what use are you to me?'

The old woman seemed to stoop further down as she shuffled over to Katrabeth. She took the daisy chain, and wrapped it round her arthritic fingers. A soft muttering emerged from behind the veil as she rocked slowly from side to side. After a while, Katrabeth could hear sobbing.

'Well?' she asked impatiently.

'A train,' the old woman whimpered. 'They're all on a train to London. It travels like the wind. They are confident. Happy. They talk of seeing Lord Colgath in the city.'

'Thank you, Nursy. You see, you are the best.'

The old woman swayed, and crumpled on to the bed. Katrabeth ignored her and took out the ancient wooden box with the seeing crystal inside. The slithering green specks it contained flowed back to reveal the Grand Lord brooding on his chair of bones.

'Have you found her?' Amenamon asked.

'She's on a train to London to meet your brother.'

'So that's where he is.'

'Apparently.'

Amenamon let out a long growl. 'Before the Abomination came to the tower without doors she may have visited New Aurestel. The trees are struggling against our winterfall enchantments. Something awoke them.'

'Jemima!' Katrabeth spat.

'Most likely,' the Grand Lord said. 'It has encouraged my subjects in the town to become troublesome.'

'I'm sure you can deal with a simple rebellion.'

'Yes. But New Aurestel is where we manufacture the bullets.'

'What! You mean Taggie knows about them? If she tells the War Emperor . . .'

'It is unlikely she discovered them,' the Grand Lord barked. 'However, we cannot take the chance.'

Katrabeth tilted her head to one side. 'We?' she asked sweetly.

The Grand Lord's teeth-flames burned a dangerous blue-white. 'Do not mock me! If you do not accomplish this, then my agreement with your mother will be over.'

'It wasn't an agreement, as I recall, but a bloodbound promise, and not even you can elude that.'

'We shall see. Eliminate the Abomination before she finds Colgath. Those who accompany her must also be dealt with. No word of the bullets must escape.'

'London is a hundred miles away, and *we* don't have much time. You have more connections to wealthy individuals and companies in this Realm than I do. You'll have to arrange some fast transport for me.'

'Very well. My Lords Quinadox and Laythal are in the Outer Realm overseeing delivery of one of our contracts. I understand the company we deal with produces flying machines of some kind. They will collect you.'

'Thank you.'

'And Katrabeth, I will instruct them to escort Lord Colgath back to the Fourth Realm. We do not require your assistance in that matter.'

'Whatever you say.'

'Now this is what I call a train,' Lantic said as they sat in the big padded chairs around a table in the first class carriage, watching the flat Cambridgeshire countryside flash past. 'Though I would like to be driving, like I did the steam engine.'

The guard who came to inspect their tickets frowned at them. 'No pets,' he said, his finger pointing accusingly at Felix. 'Especially no pets sitting on the chair arms. That thing should be in an authorized cage in the luggage car.'

'How about I put you in a cage?' Felix snapped back.

The guard's jaw dropped in astonishment.

Jemima grinned happily as he fled down the carriage; he didn't come back.

'Yes,' Lantic said. 'This is definitely how trains should be.'

Jemima's smile suddenly dropped away, and she gasped. 'Someone's seen us,' she said fearfully.

'What do you mean?' Felix asked. 'That guard is hardly going to tell anyone what happened.'

'Not that,' Jemima said. 'A seer broke through my wardveil. They saw us. They know we're on this train, they know where we're going.'

'Who can do that?' Lantic asked.

'A very powerful seer,' Taggie said uneasily. 'Can you see them?' she asked Jemima.

Her sister shook her head, looking thoroughly miserable. 'There's just . . . dead daisies.'

'Dead daisies?' Felix asked in bewilderment.

'Yes. That's all I can see. I'm sorry.'

Taggie put her arm round Jemima. 'It doesn't matter,' she said. 'They were always going to find us at some point. But we're only thirty minutes away from London. That doesn't give anyone time to do anything about us now.'

A TOWER OVERLOOKING WATER

It was dark by the time the escalator brought them up out of Canary Wharf station to a long plaza facing a line of hirebikes. The children gazed up at the skyscrapers and modern glass buildings standing around the plaza, which were all lit up from within to form tall mosaics of light against the night sky.

There were quite a few people walking about, going in and out of the curving glass entrances to the huge underground station. Just about all of them seemed to be talking on their mobiles. Taggie spotted a couple of Ethanu. As she watched, one of them raised a mobile phone into the shadow below his silver glasses.

'Come on,' she said. 'We're not going to have long.'

They hurried up the broad steps at the north end of the plaza, and crossed the road to Canada Square. The little park of grass and trees looked sad and out of place amid the huge skyscrapers around it. A strong wind was being channelled by the concrete and glass canyons, plucking at their clothes. Several people were leaning into it. Taggie opened the canvas bag she was lugging round, and Felix hopped out. Standing beside the weird blue disc sculpture in the middle of the grass, they all looked up at the forty-five-storey glass tower on the other side of the road. Even tipping her head back as far as she could, it was hard for Taggie to see the top. She consulted the screen on her mobile. 'Prince Harry says the signal came from the upper floor,' she said.

'A tower overlooking water,' Lantic said.

'Told you,' Jemima said with a sniff.

'Now we just have to get up there,' Sophie said. 'Easy for me.'

'Let's try the obvious first,' Taggie said, and they set off to the foot of the tower.

The entrance lobby was in a smaller building on the side of the main tower. It had a set of three revolving doors guarded by three security guards and two full-size bronze lion sculptures. The security guards scowled at everybody who walked past.

Jemima scurried up to one of them, a woman with a thoroughly disapproving expression.

'Hello,' Jemima said in her sweetest voice. 'I was wondering, is there a public viewing gallery at the top? Somewhere I can look out across the river?'

'What?' the guard snapped in annoyance. 'This is an office block. People work here.'

Jemima widened her eyes to make herself utterly adorable. 'Yes. So?'

'So, you cannot go up.'

'You're having the top floor redecorated, aren't you?

How long has that been going on?'

'Five years now,' the guard said, then frowned, as if she didn't understand where that reply had come from. 'You go away, now. People work here. Hard work.'

Jemima stuck her tongue out and walked away.

'You are a cheeky girl,' the guard called after her. 'Don't let me catch you here again.'

'Jem!' Taggie groaned despairingly when her sister rejoined them.

'What? I found out he's definitely up there. And he's been here for five years at least.'

'That's not the point . . .' She broke off. On the other side of the lobby's thick smoked glass wall, not ten metres away, a dozen Ethanu were lining up, facing her. Beneath their hats, circular glasses glinted silver.

'How come the tower has Ethanu inside?' Jemima asked in alarm as everyone started backing away along the pavement outside the tower.

'They only ever have one master,' Felix said. 'So they'll be Lord Colgath's guards, I expect.'

As they watched, the Ethanu extended black fingernails as long as their fingers as they edged closer to the glass wall.

'Maybe we should find a better place to think about this,' Lantic said apprehensively.

They quickly walked round the corner into Upper Bank Street, struggling to stand against the wind, which seemed to be building in strength. Taggie looked up at the sheer glass face which this side of the tower presented. It was easily more than twice as high as the jail tower at Red Loch Castle. 'I don't want to fight our way up through forty-five floors of Ethanu,' she said. 'Lantic, could the olobikes get to the top?'

Lantic gazed up the imposing cliff of glass and pulled a face. 'Well, yes. It's rather high, though.'

'Yes, I sort of noticed that myself.'

They shared a grin, and he took the tiny olobikes from his satchel. Taggie watched them grow as he cast the counter-spell. Within a minute the two full-size olobikes stood ready on the pavement.

'I know said it before,' Taggie said, 'but that is *so* cool.'

Lantic smiled with pride.

'I should be able to catch you if anything goes wrong,' Sophie said quietly as Taggie took hold of the handlebars, trying to nerve herself up for the ride.

'Thanks.' She smiled at her friend.

Jemima suddenly turned round, her eyes tight shut as she faced the end of the road, the wind whipping her hair across her face. 'Uh-oh. Captain Feandez just arrived.'

'Tell us what can you see, Jem,' Taggie said.

'He's at the underground station with a whole gang of Blue Feather officers.'

'I will delay them,' Felix said, growing up to elbow height. 'Go now, quickly. Time is short. Jemima, find somewhere safe to wait.'

'I will not!'

'You must.'

'No!'

'Jemima,' Taggie said in exasperation. 'This is Felix's job. I can't look after you as well as find Lord Colgath. Don't be difficult, not now, there's no time! Please.'

'All right,' Jemima said sullenly. 'I'll go and hide like a baby then.'

'Thank you,' Taggie said. She sat astride the olobike's saddle, next to Lantic. 'What do I do?'

'Just ride,' he said.

Taggie watched him start pedalling. It looked ridiculous: he was heading straight for the base of the tower and going far too fast. She started after him, pedalling harder, trying to catch up. From the corner of her eye she saw Sophie shrug out of her fleece, and slide her crossbow round so it was across her chest. Then the skymaid took off. It had been a good distraction, because Taggie was now almost at the tower. *About to crash into the tower*, her instincts told her. She caught up with Lantic, surely going fast enough to break the glass. But the olobike's front wheel hit the big dark pane at pavement level, and began to roll upwards. Her perspective abruptly shifted. The sheer wall of glass became the ground, and behind her the road had flipped round to the vertical.

'Oh yes!' she laughed in elation. 'This is how it's done.'

Beside her, Lantic gave her a fierce grin. 'Absolutely. Let's go and give Lord Colgath the surprise of his life.'

When Taggie looked down at her feet she saw an Ethanu

pressed up against the window she was cycling over. Its narrow mouth was visible, open wide in amazement. She chuckled wildly.

Somewhere behind – below! – Jemima was shouting frantically.

'Oh just do as you're told for once,' Taggie muttered to herself. Trust Jemima to spoil the exhilaration of this amazing ride.

A harsh mechanical droning sound started to rise, swiftly getting louder.

'What is that noise?' Lantic shouted.

Taggie tried to make out what she was hearing. 'Helicopter, I think. Maybe two by the sound of it. There are loads of them flying across London all the time. Especially around here.'

'Ah. Very well. Taggie . . . what is a helicopter?'

'Outer Realm flying machine. Not steam powered,' she added hastily. 'They have different engines. Turbines I think . . .' though it was becoming hard to talk as the helicopters were so loud now. Puffing from the effort of pedalling, she glanced back over her shoulder to see Sophie keeping level with the two olobikes. The skymaid was peering round uneasily as she flew.

'What is that?' Sophie shouted above the din.

Taggie rolled her eyes. *Here we go again* . . . 'Helicopter. That's an Outer Rea—'

The dark silhouettes of two helicopters zoomed into view above Canada Square, their navigation strobes flashing bright as they cut across the illuminated skyscrapers beyond. They were squat shapes with small stubby wings that carried long pods: military helicopters.

The helicopters swung about, adjusting their positions so their noses lined up on the two cyclists. Flame leaped out from the pods of the lead helicopter, and the glass behind Taggie erupted into a million shards as machine-gun bullets slammed into the tower.

26

LORD COLGATH HAS VISITORS

Standing at the base of the tower, Jemima watched in horror as the helicopters opened fire on Taggie and Lantic. Then she sprinted for Canada Square just as a cascade of lethal glass daggers rained down on the pavement where she'd been standing a few seconds earlier. Cowering, with her arms over her head, she raced over the road junction to the corner of the square where the trees lined the side of the grass. Wind plucked at her black denim jacket, sending the loose fabric flapping.

'Jemima?' Felix was yelling above the roar of the helicopter guns. 'Are you all right?'

She looked round to see him standing ten feet away, one forepaw gripping his glowing green sword, the other holding a dormant firestar. 'Yes.' She nodded.

Up above, the helicopter stopped firing. Taggie and Lantic pedalled furiously round the corner of the tower. The helicopters rushed forward to follow them.

'Oh no,' Jemima gasped.

Behind her, the glass wall of the tower's lobby suddenly shattered. The Ethanu stepped out on to the pavement. Six of them raised their arms, long black fingernails pointing at Jemima. She squealed. Sparkling, icy-blue wizard light streamed across the road to hit Jemima full on the chest. Her jacket and baggy combat trousers ignited, engulfing her in a maelstrom of fierce flames that soared high into the air. Blackened embers of cloth snowed on to the tarmac as the flames died away.

As one, the Ethanu stopped and stared at what should have been her charred corpse. Jemima was standing there, hands on her hips, and a huge sneer on her face. Her *athrodene* armour gleamed as if it was reflecting moonlight. She stuck her tongue out at them, and blew a raspberry.

'Jemima!' Felix yelled in exasperation. 'Don't provoke them!' He flung a firestar, which chopped savagely into the closest Ethanu. The figure in the leather coat crumpled.

Arms began to rise again, black fingernails lining up.

Felix's paw gripped Jemima's hand, tugging urgently. 'Run!' he shouted.

Captain Feandez led the squad of his fellow Blue Feather officers into Canada Square as the sound of helicopter gunfire ended. The whole place seemed deserted except for the little Blossom Princess on the other side of the grass. She was running fast, wearing an astonishing suit of shining *athrodene* armour – you could buy entire Second Realm estates with that much of the fabulous substance. Captain Feandez was just recovering from the shock of seeing that, when a blast of deadly magical light struck her back, and she staggered forward. But the *athrodene* protected her easily, of course. That was when she saw him.

They stared at each other for a long moment, both of them uncertain. 'Get back,' she called out. 'The Ethanu will . . .'

Her voice was lost in the mechanical howl from above. Captain Feandez instinctively looked up as Sophie flashed overhead, her red contrail sparkling against the night sky. One of the helicopters chased after her. When he looked back down he saw eleven Ethanu walking their slow deliberate walk across the road, closing on the shining princess. The squirrel was slashing at one with a luminous green sword, while the Ethanu fought back with a slim orange blade.

Captain Feandez knew his orders were to apprehend the Queen of Dreams and her friends, but as a soldier his duty was clear. His purpose in life was to defend people from the forces of Darkness, no matter what.

'With me,' he called to his fellows as he drew his sword. All the Blue Feather regiment officers drew theirs.

'No, no,' Jemima shouted. 'Get back. I'll deal with them.'

Captain Feandez smiled at the badly misplaced bravery and pride of the little princess, and raced forward on to the park.

Jemima turned and hugged the tree closest to her. Its small dozing spirit was delighted at the uplifting touch of the Blossom Princess herself. 'Help me,' she implored.

A hundred thousand leaves rattled in a chorus of anger as every tree around the square awoke, anxious to shelter their precious Blossom Princess. Deep below the grass, roots burst into life, burrowing fast through the soil, wrapping round the cables and pipes that lay there. They tugged and tore at the electricity cables, ripping them apart. The Ethanu following her hesitated as they sensed the surge of hostility directed towards them.

All the lights in Canada Square and the surrounding skyscrapers went out. Somewhere behind the tower, the other helicopter started firing its machine gun again.

Jemima could see Felix's green blade dancing through the darkness, clashing with the orange blade of his Ethanu opponent, both moving with remarkable speed. Another orange blade appeared behind Felix.

'You leave him alone,' Jemima snarled. She asked the trees to reach for the Ethanu. Thick, wiry roots began to surge towards the surface, precisely where booted feet could be felt treading down on the grass.

Taggie twisted the olobike handlebars sharply as the bullets ripped through the glass behind her. Her enchantment shield hardened as the bullets came ever closer. Then she and Lantic surged round the curving corner of the building. The machine gun fell silent.

'I'll do what I can,' Sophie shouted, and soared away into the burly gusts of wind blowing between the skyscrapers.

'What do we do?' Taggie yelled.

'Keep pedalling. We have to stay out of its sight,' Lantic shouted back.

They'd almost reached the other side of the wall when a lone helicopter came charging into view, turning sharply over North Dock station so its weapon pods lined up on them. The machine gun opened fire again, chewing up the skyscraper wall in a wave of disintegrating glass.

Taggie screamed as they shot round the next corner. The bullets were coming terrifyingly close. A small swarm of glass shards had smacked against her enchantment shield, creating a patchwork of purple fizzes. She heard Lantic cry out in alarm.

'What happened?' she shouted in panic. 'Are you all right?'

'My wheel,' he yelled back as the firing stopped. 'It's been hit.'

Taggie looked over at him. His olobike was badly damaged, wobbling along as the mangled rear wheel quivered from side to side. She turned to see where the helicopter was. They were cycling directly over the low section of the building that held the entrance. Next door was another massive glass office block. But the distance between the two skyscrapers was too narrow for the helicopter to follow them. Instead it was wavering about over North Dock, trying to get a good line of fire.

'What do we do?' she cried.

'Keep going,' he called back. 'You have to get to Colgath. Leave this one to me.'

As he said it, he turned the handlebars, angling away from her, heading towards the roof of the entrance building. It was going well until his front wheel hit a broad band of metal vents in the skyscraper wall. The olobike began to judder violently as it crossed them. Then the helicopter opened fire again. Lantic flinched, ducking down over the handlebars. With the olobike rocking unpredictably, he lost his balance and fell flat against the skyscraper wall.

It probably saved his life. The machine gun ripped a line of destruction that overshot him as the olobike skidded unexpectedly down the wall.

Lantic yelled as his chaotic slide picked up speed. Gravity began to reclaim the damaged olobike, and he fell the last ten feet, to land with a painful thud on the flat roof of the entrance building.

As he lay there groaning, Taggie vanished round the corner of the skyscraper to the front wall. The machine gun stopped firing. Lantic had lost his glasses when he hit the roof, so he squinted at the helicopter as it swung from side to side like a lost insect before shooting upward over the top of the building next door.

He scrambled round in his satchel amid the blurred

shapes, and pulled out the illuminious bird. The instructions he incanted were fast and direct. It fluttered away into the night. Next he grabbed a spider. It quickly spun a gossamer thread around the end of a metal support, and with one hand clutching tightly at its body he rolled over the edge of the roof.

At the moment the lights of Canada Square went out, Captain Feandez cast the spell to animate his beautiful scarlet-and-black tunic. The threads of its cloth flipped over and hardened. Within a few seconds he was clad in a dark suit of armour, rich with shield enchantments. One of his fellow officers threw a firestar at an Ethanu, who chopped the flaming circle in half with a glimmering orange sword.

Despite himself, Captain Feandez was impressed with the Ethanu. Then the sword vanished, engulfed by the darkness.

'Altras? Homenz?' he called softly.

'Here, Captain,' they replied.

'Protect the Blossom Princess. The rest of you, we will take the Ethanu. Go swiftly.'

'Aye, Captain.'

More Ethanu were drawing their swords, whose blades glowed with orange runes, casting a weak luminescence at angles that made little sense. They continued their methodical advance across the grass towards the Blue Feather officers. The shining princess had vanished.

Captain Feandez ran across the grass towards the dark creatures, hoping the princess had not already been struck down. '*Falavor*,' he chanted. His illumination spell sent a flare of brilliant white light arching over the square.

In his heart, Captain Feandez knew that the Hell Realm was just a story, a tale that parents employed to scare children with, to make them clean their teeth properly and eat their vegetables. But if it did exist, he knew, it would undoubtedly look something like this. The ground of Canada Square was splitting open as cracks multiplied across the grass. Long sinuous roots clad in dripping mud were reaching up from the depths of the earth like blind vindictive serpents. Three of the Ethanu had already been caught, with roots coiling round them, lifting them off the ground like puppets. They flailed round, trying to hack at the dirty wood with swords. Being upside down didn't help; their coats flapped about, impeding every movement they made.

He had to duck fast as roots came sliding up to grab him. Then jumped as a fissure split open beside him. Slashed with his sword at a root that lashed through the air like a whip.

Finally he was clear and stumbling on to the road which was covered in broken glass. The illumination spell was fading, allowing shadows to swell out and engulf Canada Square once more. His headlong flight from the angry trees sent him crashing into an Ethanu. Long black fingernails raked down his armour. To Captain Feandez's horror they gouged deep grooves into his breastplate. The armour was supposed to be enchanted against any weapon. So he battered the Ethanu away with his fist and brought his sword round. Five of his Blue Feather comrades were standing with him on the road now. All of them holding their enchanted swords ready to fend off the line of Ethanu who were walking steadily towards them.

As the two helicopters appeared and opened fire with their machine guns on her friends riding their olobikes up the glass tower, Sophie yelled, 'I'll do what I can,' before shooting up as fast as she could. She curved in a fast loop above their whirling rotor blades, and tugged her crossbow off its strap as she headed down again. When she was below the blades she could see the machine clearly, and started. A Karrak Lord was sitting in the cockpit. She fired a bolt at him.

The armoured glass cracked when the bad magic tip hit it, but didn't quite break. The Karrak Lord turned to look at her, then tilted the helicopter's joystick. The helicopter swung round in response. Sophie didn't wait; she took off fast over Canada Square, streaking round towards the West India Docks. The helicopter came roaring after her.

She caught sight of a large black eagle flying in from the middle of the city. It glided silently over the line of Ethanu battling the Blue Feather officers, then soared round to the Upper Bank Street side of the tower and slipped easily into the huge ragged gap in the glass which the machine guns had just torn open.

Sophie frowned as she flew on; there was nothing she could do about the odd intruder now. She waited until the helicopter followed her out over the water of the colossal West India Dock, then banked sharply, curving back under and round. She fired her crossbow again. The bolt struck one of the engine casings, and penetrated two-thirds of its length. The engine pitch changed slightly. She streaked away again, pushing hard into the turbulent wind blowing across the water. What she wanted was to keep the helicopter chasing her, keeping it away from Taggie.

Given its bulk, the helicopter was surprisingly fast, and considerably more agile than she'd anticipated. Bullets sprayed through the air around her as she zipped about like a dragonfly, changing direction, diving, soaring high, dropping. The Karrak Lord was a good pilot, and he kept up with her.

It wasn't long until they were out over the Thames itself. A big white dome was perched on the opposite bank. Sophie had no idea what it could be, but tall yellow pylons stuck up out of it at an odd angle. As she zoomed towards it through the swirling wind she could hear the thumping music Taggie and Jemima liked to listen to. Coloured lights were playing around the dome. There was some kind of concert inside. There would be a lot of people attending. And the Karrak Lord wouldn't care about that, wouldn't care where the bullets struck the ground. Sophie desperately altered course again as the machine gun fired once more, curving round the yellow pylons and heading up so the vile gun would be aimed into the air. Up ahead was an even larger white pylon on the side of the river. An identical one rose up from the opposite bank, with a slightly smaller third pylon beyond that. Sophie grinned fiercely and hurtled forward.

The spider lowered Lantic to the ground in front of the tower's three revolving doors. It was very dark in the square; he could just make out the shadowy figures of the Blue Feather officers fighting the Ethanu along the side of the park. Glowing sapphire-blue swords struck against swords that simmered like amber flames, spraying out rainbow sparks as their enchantments struggled against each other. He squinted up to see Taggie's dark silhouette on the front wall of the tower, still not quite yet halfway up.

The helicopter came charging over the neighbouring building, and turned sharply. Somewhere in the air close to it, the little illuminious bird that Lantic had released earlier poured out all of its stored light in one gigantic flash, directing it at the front of the helicopter. In its cockpit, the Karrak Lord screamed, and twisted his head aside as his smoke cloak seethed in reaction to the terrible penetrating light. The helicopter bucked in mid-air as he thrashed about, veering away back over the square, narrowly missing the skyscraper on the other side.

'Go on, Taggie,' Lantic bellowed. 'Go for the top.'

He wasn't sure, but she seemed to be pedalling even harder. The helicopter was flailing, but the Karrak pilot would recover soon enough, he knew. So Lantic, Prince of the Second Realm, flung his arms wide and cast the cleverest and most powerful enchantments he could conceive.

The woeful little skymaid had led Lord Quinadox a merry dance over the river, always flitting about just outside the target sight of the helicopter's machine gun. He really liked the destructive power of the bulky Outer Realm machine, but the clever people who had designed its efficient killing systems had never anticipated it would be chasing a nimble flying girl.

He fired off burst after burst of gunfire at the skymaid with her red looping contrail. But every time, she annoyingly managed to elude the gun's flaming muzzle. She was making him very cross. Killing her would be a pleasure.

Now finally he was closing on her as they both curved away from the white dome on the south bank of the river. She must be tiring after such a demanding flight; she was certainly slowing down.

At last, right above the wide dark river, she stopped and hung motionless in mid-air as the wind surged round her. The helicopter hovered as its targeting lasers and heat sensors locked on to her. Lord Quinadox's long bone fingers flicked the red safety cover off the missile control button. Then he laughed in scorn as she aimed her pathetic crossbow at him. He even caught a glimpse of the violet glow shining from the bolt's tip as it flew ridiculously off target, soaring high over the helicopter.

'Missed,' he sneered.

Sophie watched the bolt flash above the helicopter, perfectly on target. The glimmering magic tip cut effortlessly through the cable stretched over the Thames between the twin white pylons. A cable thick and tough enough to carry large cable cars back and forth across the water. Quinadox hadn't seen it because the cars weren't running in the high wind.

The severed cable fell directly on to the helicopter hovering below it. Long powerful rotor blades were instantly tangled and shredded. The fuselage spun helplessly as the writhing cable chopped into it. Ammunition and fuel detonated in a violent explosion.

Sophie streaked upward as fast as she had ever gone, teeth gritted with effort, fists together to punch through the air, keeping ahead of the debris hurled out by the awesome fireball. Behind her, the flaming wreckage plunged down into the black water of the Thames.

In the midst of his ferocious swordfight, Captain Feandez saw two of the Ethanu turn and walk towards a figure that had appeared from nowhere in front of the tower's entrance. He blinked, recognizing the slim young man he so disapproved of back in Shatha'hal. 'Prince Lantic,' he called in warning. An orange blade came slashing for his neck, which he just parried amid a burst of scarlet sparks. Black fingernails scratched down his leg, and bit into the armour's knee joint. Captain Feandez wailed at the hot pain stabbing into his flesh at the back of his leg, and chopped down with all his might. His sword sliced through the Ethanu's arm, and the pain dulled a little. The Ethanu fell to the ground, emitting a high-pitched shriek.

Captain Feandez turned to see magical light streaming out of the prince's fingertips, creating long waving lightning threads that played over the two bronze lion statues. The prince was oblivious to the two Ethanu closing on him.

'No!' Captain Feandez cried. He hobbled towards the prince as fast as he could on his damaged, agonizing knee. All he could see was Queen Danise's face as she entrusted him with bringing her last son home alive. Now the stupid, wretched ana-nerd prince was lost in some crazy enchantment while Blue Feather officers were fighting and dying to protect him.

The Ethanu closing on the prince raised their arms.

'Look out!' Captain Feandez shouted, knowing it was all hopeless. He brought his sword up, ready to fling it at one of the Ethanu – the ultimate futile gesture. How could he ever face his Queen again?

Something slammed into his side, sending him tumbling to the ground, his sword skittering away. He twisted round in time to see the prince finish whatever enchantment had obsessed him. Then the glimmering orange blade of an Ethanu's sword appeared above him, poised to stab down. Captain Feandez snarled his defiance at the dark creature, then gasped in shock.

Two paces behind the Ethanu, the bronze lion on the plinth that guarded the entrance to the tower slowly stood up and shook out its mane. The Ethanu, still with his sword poised above Captain Feandez, turned his head at the most peculiar motion.

The lion roared so loudly that Captain Feandez could hear nothing at all. Then it swiped a hefty metal paw at the Ethanu, smashing him clean across the road, claws ripping through coat and flesh alike.

The two Ethanu closing on the prince turned as fast as they could. Not that speed was ever going to save them. The lion sprang at them. Huge jaws opened.

Captain Feandez started laughing hysterically. Animating a statue was utterly impossible, a myth beyond the greatest anamage houses. But somehow the prince had done it. He watched in newfound humility as Lantic thrust a victorious arm into the sky, rigid finger pointing up the tower. 'Kill!' the prince cried.

Taggie was pedalling as hard as she could, heading right for the top of the tower, which was only a few floors away now. She heard the helicopter coming back, and tried to move her legs even faster. The olobike wasn't built for speed. She was so close. 'Come on,' she moaned. '*Please.*'

The helicopter flew directly overhead, turning neatly above the tower. One of the spheres on its nose swivelled round. A scarlet targeting laser stabbed out, sweeping round as it sought her out.

Then Taggie heard the oddest noise from somewhere behind her. Glass was crunching, as if someone was hitting it with hammers. Repeatedly.

A huge bronze lion sprinted past her, running straight up the side of the tower, ignoring gravity as easily as her olobike. Taggie gave it an astonished gasp, hardly believing what she saw.

The lion reached the top of the tower, and jumped. It crashed into the helicopter above, paws clawing savagely at the fuselage. They tore through as if it was made of cardboard. The helicopter whirled round and round as the pilot lost all control. Taggie saw it vanish behind the tower. Then there were some huge banging sounds. The engine noise cut out. Several seconds later she heard an awful crunch as it landed on the side of North Dock Station, followed by the painful crump of an explosion as the fuel tanks erupted in a furious fireball.

Completely out of breath, Taggie pedalled up the last few metres to the top floor of the tower. Her destruction spell blew out a wide pane of glass. Yet more crystalline shards tumbled down on to the road far below. A curtain fluttered out of the gap Taggie had made. She eased herself triumphantly round it.

CHOICES

Breathing hard and sweating badly, Taggie pushed past the fluttering curtain and looked round. The top floor was a huge single room with the concrete lift shaft in the centre. Red-and-yellow-striped OUT OF USE tape criss-crossed the metal doors. Gauzy black curtains covered all the windows. Half of the floor was empty and undecorated. The other half was somebody's lounge: an enormous flatscreen television was stuck on the lift shaft wall, showing a live European Cup football match; big expensive speakers made the crowd's chanting and cheers sound very lifelike. A black globe chair was perched in the middle on the thick carpet.

Taggie gave the chair a disapproving look.

'Is this really much better than Red Loch Castle?' she asked.

The football match vanished and the chanting faded away. The globe chair slowly rotated so its open side faced her. Lord Colgath was sitting inside it. There were no sunglasses on his shockingly white face; instead, his eyes were patches of perfect silver. Scarlet and green ripples wiggled across his smoke cloak, as if it was a phosphorescent sea. 'The food is certainly much improved,' he said smoothly. 'As is the entertainment.'

'And is that how you measure your life now? Volpas kebabs and the number of subscription channels you can stream? You're the brother of the Grand Lord.'

'I was wrong, Queen of Dreams,' he said, as his cloak's colourful ripples sped up, swirling and clashing like a miniature storm. 'You don't live up to your reputation, you exceed it – by a long way.'

'Thank you.' She gave him a jaunty grin. 'So, how did you escape?'

'Some of my old supporters managed to smuggle a file up with a meal. It took years, but I eventually cut through one of the window grilles. My rathwai flew me away.'

'Ah. That was Lantic's guess.'

'An astute young man, despite what everyone says about him. And how about you, Queen of Dreams, how did you escape?'

Taggie tried to sound nonchalant. 'Blew up the toilet and slid down the sewer.'

Lord Colgath's laugh was like the chimes of a particularly resonant bell. 'You survived the sea serpents' nesting cavern? Well done.'

She sighed and took a few steps into the big empty room. 'I need your help, Lord Colgath. We have to stop the war.'

'Are you giving me a choice?'

'Actually, yes, a small one. But it is yours to make. I'm

not going to force you to come with me, but if you do you'll be safe in the First Realm.' She gestured at the flimsy curtains fluttering in the wind that came in through the missing window. 'Unless you have somewhere else you can hide away in fear? I'm guessing your brother sent the helicopters.'

Lord Colgath stood up, his smoke cloak churning round him. Eyes that were perfect mirrors focused on Taggie. 'He would have done, yes. My estranged brother is rather well connected with Outer Realm weapons manufacturers.'

'I suspected as much. So, your choice?'

Lord Colgath strode past her to the broken window, his opalescent smoke cloak swirling behind him. He looked out across the shimmering haze of London's artificial light that stained the night sky. The vast grid of sodium streetlights was reflected in his eyes. 'So many people live in the Outer Realm. So many lives, innocent and otherwise. I grew to hate the killing. It never solved anything. Not for us. Not really. We will always be foreigners in this universe. So what is your plan?'

'Find Mirlyn's Gate, and open it so you can go home.'

'Oh, youth's foolish optimism! Do you know where Mirlyn's Gate is?'

'No. Not yet. But I'll find it,' she said with more confidence than she had any entitlement to. She went over to stand by Lord Colgath's side. 'Many of your people died in the First Realm when I took back the throne last year. I've been to the Fourth Realm and seen what you've done to it.

Yet here we are talking instead of fighting. I know it's a small thing, but isn't it a start? Trust has to begin somewhere. Only that can banish the fear.'

Lord Colgath turned to her, and said, 'I spoke out when I grew weary of the eternal conflict my brethren wage against this universe. For that I was accused of heresy and condemned. I did not fight them, I surrendered to their judgement. Now I do not live any more, I skulk in the shadows, forever fearful. That is not how the son of a Grand Lord should live. Perhaps I should be searching for my courage again.'

Taggie nearly laughed at that. 'I've come to learn that courage is a dangerous companion.'

The lift doors *dinged* softly.

'I enchanted that lift myself,' Lord Colgath said in surprise, turning around to look at it. 'Only I can use it.'

Taggie instinctively strengthened her enchantment shield as the lift doors slid open.

Katrabeth stood inside, wearing an elegant red silk

dress, posing as if she was a model at a fashion show.

'Hello, cousin,' Katrabeth said pleasantly. 'Fancy seeing you here.'

'Cousin . . . ?' Lord Colgath asked in confusion.

Katrabeth clicked her fingers. The blue-white lightning of a death spell smashed across the room. Taggie was ready for it, bracing herself. It struck Lord Colgath instead. His enchantment shielding protected him, but the impact of the spell sent him stumbling back; wisps of colour escaped from his boiling smoke cloak, stretching out in his wake. The flimsy fluttering curtains were the only thing behind him. He tore through them, and screamed as he fell through the open window.

Katrabeth raised a finger to her lips. 'Ooops,' she mocked. 'Was that all of your hopes and dreams that just went out of the window?'

Taggie didn't say anything. Didn't fling her own spell in retaliation at the diabolical girl. Instead, she simply turned and dived out after the Karrak Lord.

Taggie fell headfirst with the air blasting at her face, and actually smiled as she stretched her arms out wide. She was at peace with herself as she hurtled towards the ground, because this was what she knew she had to do. Her mind was clear, and resolute. '*Adrap*.'

The shapeshift spell bloomed around her in a seething layer of magic, transforming arms to wings, skin to feathers, feet to talons. All of it white. This time she had pictured the beautiful snow eagle she'd seen in the Fourth Realm, graceful and dignified, enduring all the heartache which had befallen its world. It was adorable. Perfect. This was her choice, what she believed in, not the predatory black eagle that was Katrabeth's form.

Taggie twisted her wings, beating them in short powerful bursts to accelerate her fall. She was halfway to the ground now, which was rushing up to strike her very quickly. There, almost directly below her, was Lord Colgath, still screaming as he scrabbled manically at thin air. She altered the direction of her fall with a simple flick of her tail feathers – how simple and delightful flying was!

She reached out with her talons and grabbed the terrified Karrak Lord round his shoulders. Taggie flung her wings wide, and felt a huge pressure pummelling against her as they curved out of the fatal plunge. They swooped over the glass-littered road, slowing to land. She let go of Lord Colgath as his feet touched the pavement. He crumpled to the ground, his gaudy smoke cloak churning wildly.

Taggie alighted elegantly, and dismissed the shapeshift spell. Her body reverted to human form as the exotic magic fumed around her.

'Taggieeee!' Jemima squealed. One of the trees along the side of the park had wrapped its branches around its trunk as if they were furled sails. They unwound to reveal Jemima and Felix sitting on a branch twenty feet up. Jemima's *athrodene* armour was shining, surrounding her in a starlight halo.

'I saw that,' Jemima yelled as she scrambled down. 'You

did it! You shapeshifted, Taggie. You really did.'

'Yes. I did. Didn't I? Amazing how you can focus when you really have to.' She laughed.

Lantic came running over to her, followed by the second bronze lion. 'Are you all right?' he asked desperately.

'Yes, are you?'

'Yes.'

They looked at each other for a long moment, then hugged.

'You were amazing up there.'

'You too.'

'I love the lions you animated.'

'You became a snow eagle!'

'Yes,' Taggie said, suddenly realizing what she was doing, the way she was pressed up against him.

Lantic realized at the same time. They broke apart, looking anywhere but at each other.

'Well done.' Lantic cleared his throat.

Taggie squeezed her hands together, examining them intently. 'Thank you.'

Sophie sank down out of the night sky. She looked round Canada Square in bemusement. The once-neat park now resembled a ploughed field. Several Ethanu were lying on the ground, three of them looking weirdly broken. Four more were bound up in spider gossamer, with a bronze lion and five surviving Blue Feather officers standing guard over them. Captain Feandez was sitting with his back to an empty plinth, with a bandage round his knee. And a

Karrak Lord in an oddly colourful smoke cloak swayed about as he regained his feet. 'Everyone OK?' she enquired.

'I think so,' Taggie said. She turned to Lord Colgath. 'How about you, my lord?'

The Karrak Lord bowed to her. 'I am in your debt forever, my Queen of Dreams.'

'See, trust isn't so hard, after all,' she told him.

'So it would seem,' he acknowledged. 'And the lesson is one I am unlikely to forget quickly.'

Together they looked upward. Taggie could just make out the empty window on the top floor. Katrabeth was nowhere to be seen. But she refused to worry about that right now. *I've finally mastered shapeshifting!* A Karrak Lord had joined their quest. And best of all, her friends had come through their ordeal without harm.

Somewhere in the distance she could hear sirens approaching. 'We'd better go,' she told everyone.

The remaining lion climbed back on his plinth and settled down.

'Oh, can't we take it with us?' Jemima asked plaintively.

'Not really,' Lantic said. He looked sheepishly round the ruins of Canada Square and the tower. 'It belongs here. And I think we've caused enough mayhem for one night.'

'I'm glad I don't have to explain all this,' Sophie muttered.

Taggie pulled her mobile out, and called Prince Harry. 'Fortunately,' she said, 'I know someone who can.'

28

TAKING STOCK

The big black eagle flew down out of London's night sky and perched on the corner of a large pale stone building on the junction of Southampton Row and Theobald's Road. Pigeons who'd been sheltering on the roof hurriedly took flight to escape the strange bird. It ignored them, casting a wardveil before settling down to watch the junction below.

After twenty minutes it cocked its head to one side in interest as four large executive cars with blacked-out windows eased their way out of London's busy traffic to pull up outside the disused Kingsway tram tunnel that occupied the middle of the junction. The cars braked next to the railings which blocked off the end of the ramp. Front doors opened smoothly and several Knights of the Black Garter stepped out, looking round alertly. Their suits were darker than a midnight sky, and their slim ornate caps were woven with a silver filigree that seemed to capture the orange streetlight that fell on them.

The eagle watched with unblinking eyes as one of the Knights went over to the gate in the railings and opened it with a tiny flash of purple magic. The rear doors of the executive cars slid back.

Taggie stepped out, followed by her friends. The Knights clustered round Lord Colgath in a formation which shielded him from anyone at ground level. The eagle craned its neck forward when Captain Feandez and several Blue Feather officers climbed out of the last of the big cars.

'Thank you,' the eagle heard Taggie say to the senior Knight of their escort as she reached the top of the ramp.

'Ma'am.' He saluted, and waited until Taggie reached the first of the brick alcoves set in the wall at the side of the ramp. At her quiet command, the bricks at the back of the alcove hinged back, revealing a set of iron spiral stairs leading down. One by one the odd group followed her in. The bricks hinged forward again, sealing the alcove. The little convoy of MI1 vehicles slipped back out into London's eternal traffic.

After a while, the eagle spread its wings and flew away.

Taggie thought it was probably the strangest scene the huge banqueting hall in the First Realm's palace had ever seen. Lord Colgath sat on one side of the huge ash table. Ten fully armoured Holvans from the palace guard stood behind him, holding not-so ceremonial swords, shields and fireangs lightly, ready for any sign of trouble or treachery. Dad had insisted on that, and Taggie didn't have the heart to object. When she and Jem stepped out of the Great Gateway Taslaf into the treehouse in the palace gardens he'd been so relieved to see them, he hadn't stopped hugging and holding them for the first hour. Then there'd been the equally lengthy scolding to endure as Taggie sheepishly told him what they'd done.

'Wait till your mother hears about this,' he'd told her in dismay at the end.

But even he had agreed they deserved a decent meal and a bit of a party before sending word to the Second Realm where Mum was still taking part in the Gathering. Taggie had ordered the curtains to be drawn across the hall's big circular windows, reducing the light so Colgath would be more comfortable. Lightstones in the candelabras hanging from the vaulted ceiling glowed with a rich gold hue, which brought its own warmth to the table.

Taggie sat opposite Lord Colgath, staring at the twin images of herself reflected in his silver eyes. Lantic was sitting on her left, with Captain Feandez next to him. His leg had been wrapped in clean bandages after Jemima had healed the worst of the Ethanu wound. The remaining Blue Feather officers sat, somewhat ill-at-ease, along the table. Dad sat on her right, with Felix, Jemima and Sophie occupying the seats next to him.

Taggie took a long time to tell Captain Feandez everything that had happened since Katrabeth's first failed attack, missing nothing out. When she finished, the captain looked deeply troubled.

'Is this true?' Captain Feandez asked Lantic.

'Yes,' Lantic said solemnly. 'All of it. I have been to the Fourth Realm.'

Captain Feandez stared at the Karrak Lord on the other

side of the table. 'And your brother has been hunting the princes of our Realms to deliberately provoke a war?'

'A war to overthrow all the Realms has been his goal since the day of Rothgarnal,' Lord Colgath replied.

Taggie put the one remaining bullet on the table and slid it towards Captain Feandez. 'Whether you believe all of my story or not, this evidence must be shown to the War Emperor. It is our belief that the Grand Lord has somehow gathered a regiment of soldier gols, who are armed with machine guns. You saw the power of such weapons yourself in the Outer Realm.'

The captain gave a tight-lipped nod as he picked up the brass tube, taking care not to touch its glowing lead tip. 'Yes, Majesty. The War Emperor must be told. There can be no invasion of the Fourth Realm.'

Taggie resisted the impulse to shout 'Yes!' at the top of her voice. She had to show the captain that she was the Queen of Dreams, and fully in control. 'The knowledge and the bullet must be taken to the Gathering.'

'Majesty,' Captain Feandez said. 'It would be my honour and privilege to be the one who presents this to the War Emperor. I was charged with escorting you back to the Gathering, but I see now my true duty as an officer of the Blue Feather regiment.'

'Thank you, Captain Feandez. I know how difficult this must be for you.'

Captain Feandez stood and bowed to the Queen of Dreams. 'The right path is never difficult to take.'

'There is a ship waiting for you, it will take you directly to Shatha'hal.'

'Then we will go at once.'

'May the Heavens smile upon you, Captain,' Taggie said as the Blue Feather officers departed.

While her friends finished the excellent food and gave the musicians requests for favourite tunes, Taggie and Lord Colgath sat together at the other end of the table.

'The bullet and your story will buy you time,' Lord Colgath said. 'But the War Emperor will still want his vengeance for Prince Rogreth just as the King in Exile wants to reclaim his Realm.'

'It's time we can use to our advantage,' Taggie said. 'A solution has to be found. One that will end this conflict permanently. That's what we have to do now.' She looked down the table to where Jemima was giggling wildly with Felix, and Sophie was teasing Lantic about something – the poor prince was blushing scarlet. How she ached to join them.

'So now we have to find Mirlyn's Gate,' Lord Colgath said. 'No small task – it has eluded everybody for centuries. I fear it may prove impossible.'

'We have to try. But I also have to know the effort is worthwhile.' Taggie looked unflinchingly at the Dark Lord. 'My Lord, if it were to be found and unbound, would your brethren go back through it?'

'Such a question has not been asked since the days of Rothgarnal. But I believe that if you offered them the opportunity, many would. Yes. Contrary to your belief, we do not exist simply to oppose you. We are victims of circumstance, as are all the folk from this universe who travelled the other way when the cursed gate was first opened.'

Taggie had never thought about it, but she supposed there might be humans and other folk trapped on the other side, suffering as the Karrak Lords suffered here. 'I told Lady Dirikal I would find Mirlyn's Gate because it was the only way I know to end this conflict,' she said. 'I will keep that promise. I will search for the gate no matter how long it takes. Will you join me, Lord Colgath?'

The Karrak Lord slowly stood up. The light reflected by his eyes seemed to grow brighter. 'I owe you my life, Queen of Dreams. And I know you would never ask that debt to be paid, for you have true honour. Nonetheless, I will join you. We will search for the impossible answer.'

Taggie stood, and held her hand out to the Karrak Lord. It was something she never thought she would find herself doing. At the other end of the table her friends had fallen silent to watch intently.

The Queen of Dreams and the brother of the Grand Lord shook hands in agreement. 'Together,' they said.

THE END . . .

. . . of *The Hunting of the Princes*. The final part of Taggie's quest to stop the war will be told in *A Voyage Through Air*.

Read an exclusive extract from

A Voyage Through Air

Book three in Peter F. Hamilton's

The Queen of Dreams trilogy

Coming in summer 2017

1

SECRETS NEW AND OLD

Lorothain, the capital city of the First Realm, was on the edge of an approaching nightshadow. As the vast border of shade drew closer, tiny sparks of bluish lightstone illumination began to prickle the windows of the exuberant domes and elevated towers of the grander mansions, while the neat streets of terraced houses glowed a rich sapphire from the wakening streetlights.

In the private wing of the capital's royal palace, Jemima Paganuzzi, the Blossom Princess of the First Realm, was getting ready for bed. 'I'm so tired,' she said to Taggie, her older sister, and the First Realm's Queen of Dreams. 'Do you think Dad will mind if I don't do my teeth?'

'I'm sure he won't mind you missing one night,' Taggie replied. 'Hang on, I'll shut the curtains.'

As the Blossom Princess, Jemima was entitled to her own suite of rooms in the palace. They were rather sumptuous for a twelve-year-old, with ornate furniture, marbled floors and gilt-edged paintings.

'I'll do them twice tomorrow,' Jemima promised unconvincingly as she climbed into her huge bed and pulled up the duvet.

Taggie grinned as she walked over to the tall window. 'There's probably a spell for teeth cleaning,' she said as she pulled shut the long velvet curtains.

She smiled to herself. It had been an incredible day for the two of them, ending in a thrilling and at times utterly terrifying showdown with the Grand Lord's forces in London's Docklands. Their ordeal had proved worthwhile, for they'd found Lord Colgath, the one Karrak Lord who might be able to help them prevent the coming war between the Grand Lord and the War Emperor.

Outside, the moonclouds were expanding across the entire First Realm. Taggie nodded in satisfaction. As Queen, her magic controlled the First Realm's nature, of which the moonclouds were an important part. Normally only half of the First Realm was in darkness at any one time, but these weren't normal times.

'If that's a real spell, Mum will know it,' Jemima said drowsily. Their mother was a Third Realm sorceress, who seemed to know just about every sort of magic.

'When she gets back, we'll ask her,' Taggie said.

'Do you think she'll be back soon?'

'With any luck she'll be able to leave the Gathering as soon as Captain Feandez hands over the bullet to the War Emperor.'

'I hope so. I really miss her, Taggie.'

'Night, Jem,' Taggie said, and leaned over the bed to kiss her sister.

Jemima's eyes were already closed. 'Are you going to dream tonight?'

'Of course I am,' Taggie said. 'I'm the Queen of Dreams; it's what I do. And tonight I'm going to reassure everyone about the war.' Whenever she slept in the First Realm, Taggie would drift into the dreams of everyone else, soothing away their troubles and offering all the comfort only a truly kind heart could.

'Oh, good.'

Jemima dreamed, as did everybody in the First Realm that strange all-encompassing night. In her dream she walked through the halls and corridors of the palace she'd grown familiar with in the year since she and Taggie had overthrown the Karrak Lords and Ladies who had tried to usurp the First Realm.

But in this dream, on this unusual night, other people were walking through the palace with Jemima: Holvans with their four arms, giants with their green hair, ordinary men and women and children, the folk who were almost spherical, a few centaurs, some hearty trolls. Much to Jemima's delight there were even elves sharing her dream, tall and ebony-skinned with long plumes of hair reaching all the way down their backs.

Thousands upon thousands of people streamed into the throne room, which in her dream was much bigger than it was in real life. Yet Jemima, along with everyone else, was standing close to the dais which held the shell throne. Taggie sat on the purple and scarlet silk cushions of the throne, watching serenely as every dreamer appeared before her. When Jemima waved excitedly, she didn't notice.

Taggie stood up and looked round the dream throne room with its weirdly insubstantial walls. 'I cast this night across the First Realm because I have something to tell everybody who lives here.' Her voice carried clearly across the room. 'A War Emperor has been anointed once more. He has summoned together all the armies of the Realms so that he may lead them into battle against the Grand Lord. Well I will not be ordering any soldier of the First Realm to fight in this war. We have fought the Karraks in a conflict that has lasted for generations. This has to end. Too many have died already. There has to be another way. I intend to devote myself to finding a peaceful answer to the conflict between our kinds once and for all.' She inclined her head at the massive audience. 'Thank you for attending. May the Heavens guide us all safely.'

Jemima saw many smiles of gratitude and relief among the crowd. As she started to walk out of the throne room she caught sight of a dark, motionless figure. It was an old woman in a black dress made of some stiff fabric. A veil covered her face, which instantly made Jemima curious to know what she looked like.

Everyone else was flittering away from the dream like ghostly moths, but the old woman remained still and solid.

'Hello,' Jemima said.

'Dear Blossom Princess,' the old woman replied in a

thin voice. 'How nice to finally meet you.'

'Who are you?'

'A messenger. Your mother asked me to seek you out.'

Jemima looked around frantically for Taggie, but her sister was nowhere to be seen. 'You know Mum?'

A chuckle emerged from behind the veil. 'A very long time ago I was her nurse. Now I'm just a simple seer, helping out where I can in these troubled times.'

'Gosh, really?'

'Your mother wants to know if you are all right.'

'Yes, tell her we're fine. Tell her we're going to stop the war.'

'I will. She'll be so proud of you. And she asked me to say she thinks she may have found a cure for Felix's curse.'

'*What?*' Jemima squeaked. 'I thought only the Karraks could lift that curse.'

'The sorceresses of the Third Realm have studied Karrak wizardry ever since the dark lords and ladies first emerged through Mirlyn's Gate. It is not easy, but some sorceress mistresses now believe they can cure their evil curses. It is one of these academy mistresses that your mother has sent for. '

'Really? Mum can do that?'

'You are very fond of Felix, are you not?' the old woman said in a sympathetic voice. 'I heard that he single-handedly saved you from the gols in Shatha'hal's docks.'

'Well, yes, he did. What did Mum say? It would be so fantastic if we could cure him. I can't imagine what it must be like to live like that every day. I so want to help him,' Jemima said eagerly.

'The sorceress mistress is on her way to your mother and should arrive quite soon. Will you be here? These sendings are difficult for me, especially if you're moving round.'

'Er, Taggie said we might be travelling again soon.'

'Oh, perhaps you could let me know where you are,' the woman said smoothly.

'Well, it's kind of a secret.'

'I understand. I'm sure Felix can wait until you get back.'

'No, wait!' Jemima said, desperate for the chance to help Felix. It was just that she didn't want to do anything that might cause a problem for Taggie's quest. She tried to think of a way round it. 'I can cast a wardveil that will let you sight me,' she said slowly. 'But you must promise not to tell anyone where we are.'

'Your mother will want to know. She's desperate for news.'

'Well of course you can tell Mum,' Jemima said, slightly indignant.

'All right then.'

'And you'll give us the cure as soon as you get it?'

'Absolutely,' the stooped old woman bobbed about anxiously. 'It is not my place to tell royalty what to do, but if I can give you one word of advice, Blossom Princess—'

'What?'

6

'Don't tell Felix that your mother is trying to find the cure. If it doesn't work —and by all the stars in the Heavens let us hope it does — he will be so bitterly disappointed.'

Jemima could well imagine that. Poor Felix. She couldn't stand to raise his hopes only for them to be broken. 'I understand,' she said earnestly. 'This'll be just between you and me.'

The woman bowed slightly, her black dress rustling. 'You are so honourable, Blossom Princess. I consider myself fortunate to have met you. Goodbye, my dear.'

'Goodbye.'